RAVEN'S WATCH

RAVEN'S CLIFF
BOOK ONE

ELLE JAMES
KRIS NORRIS

TWISTED PAGE INC

ISBN EBOOK: 978-1-62695-659-9

ISBN PRINT: 978-1-62695-660-5

To Kris…
You're an incredible author, friend
and a complete badass.
I'm honored to work with you
on this exciting project.

To Elle…
This has been an amazing adventure.
Here's to Hawaii and more great ideas.

To Jen…
You're so much more than a friend.
You're a soul sister.

AUTHORS' NOTE

Elle James is a *New York Times* and *USA Today* bestselling author known for her heart-pounding romantic suspense and thrilling adventure novels. **Kris Norris** is an acclaimed storyteller with a passion for weaving intense action and gripping emotion into every story. Together, these talented authors have combined their creative forces to launch the exciting new *Raven's Cliff* series.

The idea for the series was born during a writers' retreat in Hawaii, where inspiration flowed as easily as the ocean breeze. Set against the rugged coastline and resilient communities of the Pacific Northwest, *Raven's Cliff* delivers high-stakes danger, thrilling rescues, and unforgettable romance. With their combined talents, Elle James and Kris Norris invite readers to dive into a world where every moment counts and heroes are made when lives are on the line.

RAVEN'S WATCH

RAVEN'S CLIFF BOOK #1

New York Times & USA Today
Bestselling Author

ELLE JAMES
&
KRIS NORRIS

PROLOGUE

JSOC mission… Undisclosed location

"Beckett."

Major Foster Beckett nodded at his copilot, Sean Hansen, before banking the Pave Hawk over as the next burst of machine gun fire whizzed past the chopper, lighting up the darkness behind them. "I know, buddy. This guy just won't give up."

He tipped the machine farther forward, picking up speed as he skimmed across the top of a ridge then dropped the bird down the other side. Barely missing a crumbling wall as it materialized out of the night.

One of his four teammates groaned in the rear cabin. Whether it was from the way Foster tossed the helicopter around or because they were on the verge of bleeding out, he wasn't sure. But if he didn't lose the bogey on his tail, it wouldn't matter.

They'd all be dead.

Sean made a wet, gurgling sound, and Foster nearly plowed the machine into the ground as he snapped his attention toward his buddy, wondering how it had all gone sideways so fast.

The damn spooks.

Once again, the CIA had screwed them over. Because Foster bet his ass the agency knew two of their agents were dirty. That they'd set up Foster and his crew as bait when their supposed rescue mission had turned into a shootout minutes into the return flight. Calm, cool extraction one moment, an all-out attack the next with Agent Stein and Agent Adams leading the charge. The one scenario his teammates hadn't counted on. Not when they'd been working with the bastards for the past six months. Men they thought could be trusted. Would have their backs. Discovering they were the ones selling intel...

Foster should have recognized the signs over the past few weeks. The beads of sweat along their brows. The slight twitch in their hands. Their increasing reluctance to look Foster or his buddies in the eyes.

And now, his brothers were paying the price.

He banked again, narrowly avoiding the next round of gunfire. "Hang in there, Sean. Once I lose this asshole, we'll be back on course."

Sean panted, lifting his arm and jabbing his finger at the only nav screen still working — leaving a bloody smear across the surface. "Here."

Foster frowned, dodging up and over another ridge before following the hill around to the right. Hugging the surface to the point dirt and stones kicked out behind him in twin eddies. "I realize we're desperate but even I think that's crazy."

Not that it stopped him from altering his course. Heading for that speck on the map glaring at him from beneath the smear of blood. Rain splattered across the bubble, flashes of lightning giving him fleeting glimpses of the landscape. A bulging rock face on his right. A lone tower on his left. What might be his saving grace when damn near every other navigational aid was dead. Even his night vision had gotten damaged, leaving him with nothing more than that one flickering nav screen and twenty years' worth of experience.

Foster hit the winding gulley leading to the narrow opening going as fast as the aircraft could handle. More than it could handle based on the how the controls vibrated in his grasp, the odd alarm chirping to life. He divided his attention between the screen and the walls quickly closing in on him, mentally counting down the distance.

He was about twenty feet back when he banked the chopper hard to the right, holding it steady as the sluggish controls fought to respond — definitely a hydraulic leak hampering the inputs.

The gap appeared in front of him like an abyss spiraling into the rock. The utter darkness drawing them in. He hit the tunnel going some insane speed, the controls still shaking as the engine whined from the strain. Any hint of light cut out. Even the nav blinked off for a few moments before he shot out the other side, a welcomed flash of lightning saving him from flying the machine into the side of the cliff as it curved around in front of them.

He cranked the helicopter over, trying to get more distance between them and the opening when the chopper surged forward as the sky lit up behind him, the force of the explosion spinning the aircraft.

Flames erupted from the fissure, parts of the other chopper whizzing through the air. Something hit the back end, pitching them sideways as a shrill whine echoed through the cabin. It took a few moments to get the bird stabilized, the controls like lead weights in his hands, with the last impact claiming what little hydraulics he'd had left.

Sean coughed, splattering blood across the window as he met Foster's gaze. "Hooyah."

"I got lucky. Nothing more."

Sean shook his head, his mouth pursing tight as he tapped his chest pocket. "My letter…"

Foster grunted, wishing he could move his arm enough to punch Sean in his thigh. "No. No talking about that damn death letter we've all written. You're going to be fine. You just have to push through."

"Beck…"

"I mean it Sean. Don't you dare give up…" He cursed under his breath, giving Sean a nod when his friend managed to reach out and leave a bloody handprint on his arm. "I'll get it to Cheryl. I promise."

Sean nodded, closing his eyes as a shudder raced down him, blood seeping through the bandages around his neck and ribs. He'd taken the brunt of the attack when Stein had opened fire, lunging over to cover Foster after Foster had gotten hit twice in the shoulder. Their pararescue medic and Foster's best friend, Chase Remington, had done what he could to minimize the bleeding once he and his other buddies had dealt with Adams and Stein, but it was obvious it wasn't working.

Foster huffed. "Stay with me, brother. I've got this baby turned around. I'll have you on the ground and into a surgical room within fifteen. Ten, if I can get more speed out of her."

Sean chuckled, the raspy sound fading into that eerie gurgling noise as his head lolled back and he slumped against the window.

"Sean! Damn it, Chase, I think he's coding."

Chase popped into view, his hands covered in blood. "I need a minute, Foster."

"Sean doesn't have a minute."

"Neither do Zain or Kash. I can only spread myself so thin."

"We're not dead yet, dumbass." Zain Everett — their SAR specialist, sniper and all 'round badass. Though it sounded as if he was even worse than Chase had hinted at. "Take care of Sean."

Chase pursed his lips, fisting his hands for a

moment before vanishing then reappearing with an armful of supplies. He checked Sean's neck, looking back at Foster before applying more bandages and giving the guy a shot of something.

Chase turned to face him, mouth pinched tight. Eyes shadowed. Blood oozed from a gash on his forehead, more soaking the hem of his shirt. What looked like multiple hits to his vest.

Chase had been with Foster from the start. Had been the one constant throughout his career — until they'd met Sean, Rhett, Zain and Kash a dozen years ago. The six of them had fallen into sync on their very first mission, and they'd fought hard to stay together since.

Chase tugged on the tape holding Foster's shoulder together, muttering obscenities under his breath. "Your damn shoulder's a mess. I'm not sure how you're even moving that arm. Everything's shattered."

Foster would have shoved him off if he'd had the strength. Instead, he merely nodded toward Sean. "How is he?"

Chase glanced away, making it look as if he was getting more supplies out of his bag. "He's lost at least two liters of blood, and I'm out of saline and plasma."

"But if I get him back…"

"You just focus on staying conscious as long as possible. Try to get us as close as you can to the base. Okay?"

"Chase…"

"I'm just a medic, buddy. I can't raise the dead."

Foster looked over at Sean. He hadn't moved in the past few minutes, his skin so damn white he swore it was see-through. "No. It can't end like this. You have to do something. That should have been me. My blood. My sacrifice. He's got a wife. Kids. I have to…"

To what? Save him? Because Foster knew if Chase couldn't save Sean, no one could.

Chase packed more gauze around Foster's wounds, adding another layer of tape. "Let me check on the others, then I'll be back. Do what I can to help keep you awake."

"You worry about Zain, Kash and Rhett. I'll be okay."

"No, you won't." Chase cut him off. "You're bleeding through the clotting powder. Your face is nearly as white as Sean's and your good hand is shaking so bad, I'm surprised the damn chopper isn't vibrating through the air."

"My hand's shaking because I've lost hydraulics. Go. I'll shout if I'm gonna pass out."

"Right, because self-preservation has always been first on your list. Just, don't fucking die on me."

"Says the man who's bleeding worse than me. And yeah, I noticed. How bad are you hit?"

"Enough I'm extremely pissed."

Chase disappeared, Zain's groan sounding above the engines a moment later. The fact Foster hadn't heard their flight engineer, Rhett Oliver, utter so much as a sigh since his team had finally overpowered Stein and Adams meant the guy was either dead or unconscious. Just like their dog handler, Kash Sinclair.

The engine chugged, dropping the bird several feet before it stabilized. They couldn't afford to land. Not while they were fifty miles from safety with Foster's entire team struggling to hold on.

Which meant, milking every ounce of speed out of the aircraft. Taking it as close to the edge as possible without actually blowing the engines or killing the transmission. That fine line between all-out and too far. One he'd skirted on more occasions than he should be proud of. But the mission and his team always came first.

Not team. Family. That's what they were to him. Brothers. Men he'd kill for. Or die to protect. The only reason he'd made it through twenty years without losing his sanity.

His soul.

To think it would go down like this — betrayed by their own people. Lost on the wrong side of a volatile border. A fate he could alter if he rose to the challenge. Pushed past his limits.

Rain pummeled the bubble, the lone wiper barely keeping up. Not that he could see much with streaks of black cutting across his vision. But he kept that bird pointed north. Kept the machine on the verge of crapping out as he raced across the landscape, the wind and thunder following in his wake. Like Apollo chasing them with his chariot.

Was it getting colder? Darker? Or was Foster simply running out of time.

Chase's hand closed over his good shoulder, jerking him back from that numbing haze. "If you have to put her down..."

Foster shook his head, pounding the heel of his other hand against his temple in an effort to clear his vision. "Not... an option."

"Foster. Brother, you're barely holding on."

He shook his head again. Or maybe he'd only thought it. He couldn't tell. Could barely feel his fingers he was so cold. "How..."

Shit. One word. That's all he managed before his tongue got too heavy to form more.

"Don't worry about anyone else. That's my job. You focus on flying and not hitting the ground."

"Can't..."

Another one-word reply. And it cost him. Had more than just his good hand shaking. He wet his lips, forcing his eyelids open. Glancing over at Sean whenever he wanted to pack it in. Give up. Because if there was even a glimmer of hope he could still be saved...

Bile crested his throat, his eyes burning as he stared at the raging storm beyond the glass. The lightning hardly making a difference in his visibility, anymore. It was too late. He knew it. Felt it. From the way Chase kept shifting his weight, unable or unwilling to even place his hip on the edge of Sean's seat, to the utter silence from the other side of the cockpit, Foster knew Sean was dead. But Foster kept going. Clinging to the false hope that if he could stay awake — make it one more minute, one more mile — it wouldn't be in vain.

That he hadn't failed his brothers when they'd needed him the most.

That maybe one day, he'd be able to look at his own reflection and not see Sean's ghost staring back.

* * *

"I'm not sure what I was expecting, Foster, but damn. You look like shit. Though, the bandages do kinda go with the long hair."

Foster twisted toward the door, shaking his head at the man leaning against the frame. Hands shoved in his pockets, looking almost as haggard as Foster felt. Keaton Cole, Foster's cousin and the only family Foster had left, other than the men gathered in his room. His teammates.

His brothers.

Foster arched a brow, brushing his hair out of his eyes. A leftover from his time in Flight Concepts, when he was encouraged to look like anything but typical military. He gave Keaton a once-over, waving the length of him. "And yet, still a thousand times better than you, buddy."

"Oh, someone didn't get their pain meds, today."

Keaton sauntered in, grinning at Chase, Kash and Zain. "You're obviously taking fashion cues from my cuz, Remington, because you look just as bad, with Sinclair and Everett only slightly better."

Chase flipped Keaton off as he leaned back in the chair. "At least we have a reason, Cole. What's your excuse?"

Keaton chuckled. "Civilian life. Who knew it was crazier than the Navy." He crossed his arms over his chest, waiting until Zain and Kash had wheeled their chairs over to Foster's bed. "So, rumor has it you four might be considering your options."

Zain grunted, absently rubbing his knee. Or more accurately, the new hardware hidden beneath the bandages and stitches. Foster wasn't sure if Zain even realized he was doing it, but the pain and frustration bled through his usual facade. Testament to how much their last mission had cost them.

Foster knew his buddy was in agony. He'd heard the muffled shouts and hushed curses as Zain dragged his ass up and down the hallways several times a day. The price of reclaiming even a hint of his former mobility. Though, Foster knew Zain would push until he was only a slightly broken version of his former self.

Zain shrugged. "It's come up."

Keaton nodded, walking over and resting his hip against Foster's bed. "I feel that. Been where you all are, myself."

Which was an understatement. Keaton had been

through hell. Had suffered a similar loss on his last mission, when their covert op had gone off the rails and one his best friends had been killed. While Foster didn't know the specific details, he knew Keaton. And based on the hollow look in his eyes — the tremor in his voice that was only now starting to ease — he'd experienced something truly horrific. Not that it had been the first time.

Keaton's fiancée had died in a plane crash a dozen years ago, shortly after he'd joined the SEALs. Foster had come close to losing the man back then, despite all Foster had done to try and help Keaton cope with the loss. But words and a shoulder were rarely enough compensation for the kind of scars that took more than time to heal.

Though, Keaton had more than paid Foster back when Foster's parents had been killed in a car accident a month ago. Foster and his team had been running those traitorous CIA assholes all over hell's backyard on one covert mission after another and he hadn't been able to extract himself long enough to head home. But Keaton had dropped everything and stepped up.

Foster would never forget that.

Foster shuffled back a bit, giving Keaton a thorough once-over. "I can't believe I'm saying this, but Florida looks good on you. You sound better."

Keaton sighed. "Getting there. Which reminds me... You should all come down for a visit. See the town. Get a feel for what we do. There's always room for guys like you."

Kash chuckled. "Are you suggesting we consider retiring to Florida?"

Keaton grinned. "Sunshine. Beaches."

"Gators. Mosquitos."

Zain swatted Kash across the chest. "And don't forget the pythons. I hear those fuckers grow really big."

Keaton rolled his eyes. "You've all been hanging around Foster for too long. The Everglades are fine."

"Sure, if you're looking to disappear." Chase pointed a finger at Keaton. "Permanently."

"Just, keep it in mind. Though, I suppose my dumbass cousin is trying to talk you all in to heading to Oregon, where there's nothing but gray clouds and rain."

"I'm not trying to talk them into anything." Foster shifted on the bed, not that it helped eliminate the pain throbbing through his shoulder. "But my parents did leave me that turn-of-the-century manor house they'd been renovating. Sounds like a good place to start."

Keaton laughed, nearly falling off the bed before he straightened. "You're going to fix up that old dusty inn? Are you all nuts?"

"Beats swimming with gators."

"You keep telling yourself that. Besides, Raven's Cliff is so small, you have to run to the next town to change your mind."

"And Calusa Cove is your idea of big time? I hate to break it to you, cuz, but it's just as small." Foster smiled. "And there're gators."

Keaton shook his head. "Still as stubborn as a damn mule. Though, I guess some things never change. Like us. Whether you're ready to face it or not, sooner or later you'll have to admit that we're all just hardwired differently. No way you'll be able to stay out of the fray for long."

Foster pursed his lips, Sean's gurgling rasp sounding in his head. Foster glanced over at the windows, hating the eerie apparition standing in the graying light. Blood still dripping from its neck and ribs as the ghostly image tapped its chest pocket.

It wasn't real. He understood that much. Just a by-product of the pain and anger and loss. Too bad that knowledge didn't make it disappear.

Keaton sighed at Foster's silence, looking over at the window then focusing on him, again. "Hey, didn't you mention something about an old JSOC commander of yours starting up a search and rescue organization there?"

Foster snorted. "Colonel Atticus Parker. Bastard's already called me twice. Wants to know when we're all signing up."

"And?"

"I told him I wasn't interested, but *no* isn't in the old man's vocabulary."

"Is this where we start a pool on how long it'll be before you've all been recruited?"

"About as long as it would for me to move down to the Everglades." Foster shifted again, but it only shot pain down through his ribs. "I don't suppose you'd do us a solid?"

Keaton laughed. "I already ordered a few pizzas. Just thought I'd stop in and visit while they were being made. I'll go grab them. Keep my seat warm."

His cousin headed for the door, pausing at the threshold. "Whatever you jerks decide, do yourselves a favor — stick together. Civilians really are crazy and knowing I still have my team watching my six is the only reason I've stayed sane." He made a finger gun at Foster. "That, and you, cuz."

"Just grab the pizzas before we all start puking."

"Your wish." Keaton headed out, leaving a strange void in the air. As if he'd taken most of the oxygen with him. Left nothing but uncertainty behind.

Foster cleared his throat, looking each of his buddies in the eyes. "I know we talked about calling it quits. Going to Oregon and seeing if a change in venue somehow fixes the broken parts the doctors can't splint. And there'll always be a place waiting there for you jackasses to hang your hat. But there's no pressure. Given some time and enough rehab, you all might—"

"Might what, Beck?" Kash shuffled in his seat. "Get the urge to jump back in the saddle? Put our lives in the hands of some traitorous agents, again? Because I don't know about Zain and Chase, but there's not a chance in hell I could go down that road, again."

Some of the color drained from Kash's face and Foster suspected he wasn't the only one reliving that night. Though, Kash had nearly lost his four-legged partner, Nyx, on the gauntlet run back to the chopper. Realizing she'd almost died in order to protect two traitors who'd then killed Sean and put Rhett in what might be a permanent coma had obviously affected Kash on a whole other level.

Kash sighed. "I'm not saying that staying on the sidelines is in the cards. But I'm ready to try something new. While I'm still alive enough to enjoy it."

Zain gave Kash's arm a pat. "What he said. We're all up for re-enlistment over the next two months. Seems almost poetic in the timing, if you ask me."

"Which is why we didn't." Chase dodged Zain's slap. "And you're not pressuring us, Foster. After everything that went down…" He swallowed, looking as if he might puke. "I think we could use a fresh start. Don't much care where that is, other than Florida. That's just wrong."

Foster nodded, a bit of the tension in his chest easing. "Then, it's settled. I'll contact the lawyer — get him to send over the papers he's been keeping for me. Just remember. I warned you all ahead of time that nothing exciting happens in Raven's Cliff. So, make peace with that. Things are about to get really boring."

CHAPTER ONE

Raven's Cliff, four months later…

"I told you we never should have let Kash pick up the food."

Foster stopped painting as he glanced over at Chase, laughing at the furrow along Chase's brow. His buddy paced in front of the window, pausing to stare up the long driveway before grunting then moving, again.

They'd been in Raven's Cliff for six weeks, and it was obvious his best friend was starting to climb the walls. Not that Foster was surprised. Kash and Zain had already broken ranks and joined Atticus Parker's organization, Raven's Watch. And Foster knew Atticus had been equally pressuring Chase, trying to get the man to jump on board. Not in a bad way, because Foster bet his ass that Atticus was all too familiar with the restlessness that accompanied retirement. What had likely been the man's main purpose for starting up the non-profit search and rescue unit. But it was obvious Atticus wasn't backing down until they'd all signed on.

Foster put down the roller and walked over to the cooler in the middle of the room. Not that the kitchen wasn't already fully functional. In fact, his parents had done most of the heavy lifting. But Foster and his buddies had done their best to limit tracking dirt and debris around the finished areas of the house. Which meant improvising.

He grabbed a couple beers and stood in Chase's path until his buddy all but bumped into him, then held out the drink. "Someone's hangry. See if this takes the edge off."

Chase accepted the bottle, popped off the cap then tossed it into the trash. He took a long pull, exhaled a slow breath and shook his. "I'm not hangry."

"Something's bugging you because you've been antsy for the past couple days."

"Of course, I'm antsy. I just chatted with Rhett's doctor, and he doesn't have any more answers than he did before we retired. All he keeps saying is that Rhett's still in a coma and only time will tell if he ever wakes up."

"Which we knew from the start." Foster held up his hands when Chase crossed his arms. "I'm not saying it isn't cruel and unfair. That I don't want to run into the forest and just scream after visiting him and seeing what those bastards did. But you're generally better at boxing all this up, which suggests this is more than fate kicking us in the ass, again. Or maybe, still." Foster arched a brow. "Something else you need to share with me, brother?"

Chase stared at him then sighed, taking a few heavy steps away. "Actually, there *is* something I've been meaning to talk to you about."

Foster leaned against the wall. He had a feeling he knew exactly what Chase wanted to chat about, but he needed his best friend to say it, first.

"I'm listening."

Chase pursed his lips, fisting one hand at his side. A clear sign Foster had nailed it, and his buddy was trying to find a way to break the news to him — confess he'd sided with the enemy. "It's about..."

"Wow, what a storm."

Kash barreled through the door, drowning Chase out as thunder crashed overhead, a flicker of lightning flashing in the distance. Nyx trotted behind him with Zain bringing up the rear, carrying another case of beer. They continued through, placing the boxes on the kitchen counter before turning and staring at Foster and Chase.

Foster chuckled. While he loved Kash like a brother, the man had a habit of being oblivious to social cues, rarely reading the room correctly. Though, Foster had a feeling it stemmed from how in tune Kash was to his four-legged partner. In fact, Foster had never met a handler that had the kind of rapport Kash did with Nyx — as if they read each other's mind.

Kash frowned. "Why are you both staring at us like that?"

Chase shook his head. "Maybe because you've been gone so long, we thought we'd have to send search and rescue out to look for you."

"Shut up. We weren't that long. Besides, I doubt anyone's flying in this. It's raining so hard, the guys in the marina are building an arc. And the foghorn from the lighthouse is echoing all through town." Kash walked over and handed Chase a plate with a couple slices of pizza on it. "I dare say even Foster might not fly in this crap."

Foster grabbed slice, planting his butt on one of the kitchen stools. "Hate to break it to you, Kash, but we flew in weather far worse than this."

"You just have to crush my little safety bubble, don't ya? Though, that reminds me. Isn't it about time for Atticus to make his weekly visit?"

"The guy's a day late, actually. Which I hope means he's finally given up on trying to entice us over to the dark side." Foster pointed at Kash and Zain. "Especially when you both caved so quickly."

"We didn't cave, we simply realized what Keaton said was true. We're not wired to stay on the sidelines, which is why Atticus won't give up. He knows it's only a matter of time before you finally say yes."

"Cold day, buddy." Foster tipped his beer at

Chase, knowing this would force the man into owning up. "Here's to solidarity, brother."

Zain coughed, spitting some of his beer across the counter. "Shit. You didn't tell him, yet?"

Chase groaned, giving Foster a cautious side eye. "What do you think, dumbass? I was waiting for the right moment. Which you two jerks interrupted when you barged in here, bringing all the rain with you. But thanks to you, now, I don't have to."

Foster placed his palm over his heart. "*Et tu, Brute?*"

"I told you I'd have to get back into the paramedic field eventually." Chase thumbed at Zain. "Especially if Zain keeps helping out with the renovations. Who knew our master SAR specialist was such a shit handyman."

Zain gave Chase a playful shove. "Hey, I'm not that bad."

"You shot yourself with the nail gun."

"It was only a flesh wound, and that thing was faulty."

"I guess that drill was faulty, too. And let's not forget about the Super Glue incident." Chase grinned at Zain when his buddy flipped him off. "Which all boils down to me needing to stay current and search and rescue offers me the most robust opportunities."

Foster held up his hand, cutting Chase off. "Don't even bother giving me the speech. I've heard it twice before." He shook his head. "It's like rats leaving a sinking ship."

"Which is your cue to jump back on the horse." Kash shuffled in beside him. "While I know Atticus is happy we're all on board, it's you he really needs. Who he really wants."

Foster waved it off. "There are plenty of pilots who could do the job."

"But none he trusts. And after everything that went down with his son last year..."

Foster scrubbed a hand down his face, warring between wanting to smack Kash up the side of his head and knowing his buddy was merely trying to emphasize the old man's position. But the last thing Foster needed was more guilt. He already had a lifetime's worth of it weighing him down, so heavy it threatened to crush him into the ground some days.

But Kash had a point. Foster was all too aware of what Atticus had been through. How his son, Josh, had been killed when a rescue mission had turned into a shootout with Josh's own crew gunning him down. Daniel Shaw and Brad Newport. Two former military men and guys who should have been rock solid. The authorities suspected Josh was on the wrong side of a drug smuggling deal and got caught in the crossfire. And the eerie similarities between that incident and Foster's last mission hadn't been lost on him.

Kash muttered something under his breath, giving Foster's arm a pat. "Hey, I didn't mean—"

"It's fine. And you're right. I understand how hard it must be for Atticus to trust someone he can't personally vouch for. Though, I thought you said he'd just hired a new pilot?"

"I think they arrived last night. He was pretty hush hush about it. But that'll only cover half the shifts."

"Half? What about that Henry guy you've been working with?"

"Bastard quit. Got offered some cushy job for a private air ambulance firm down south. Which leaves this new guy to cover it all."

Foster nodded, knowing there wasn't really anything else to do or say. It wasn't that he didn't miss flying. He'd gotten his pilot's license at sixteen and had never looked back. With his dad having served as an Army Ranger for twenty years, opting for the Air Force had always been Foster's end goal. And it wasn't as if he hadn't experienced his share of loss during his career. But losing Sean that way...

It had changed him in ways he couldn't describe. Knowing it was his fault. That if he'd reacted quicker — all but barrel rolled that chopper before he'd gotten clipped twice in the shoulder — his team might have subdued Stein and Adams before anyone had gotten hurt. Before Sean had sacrificed himself to shield Foster because his friend firmly believed Foster was the only one who'd had the skills to get the rest of the team out alive. Who could fly them through the storm while countering the attack chopper that had appeared out of nowhere.

What Foster believed was part of Stein's agenda.

The last piece in his and Adams' escape plan and what had been their signal that it was time to launch their attack.

It didn't matter if Foster hadn't agreed. Sean had taken the choice out of Foster's hands and now...

Now he was left battling a ghost.

Kash gave him another pat, looking as if he was going to apologize — or worse, sympathize — when a horn cut through the thunder and rain, the loud noise shaking the glass in the old wooden windows. Footsteps sounded on the gravel path before the door crashed open, Atticus Parker's formidable silhouette filling the doorway.

He swiped his hood off his head as rain ran down his jacket, pooling beneath his muddy boots. He pointed at Foster's team, his weathered face twisted into a snarl. "Don't just sit there chugging beer, grab your damn gear and run your asses out to your trucks. I've got a van full of tourists hanging by some rocks and roots on the bypass up here. And if we don't get them out in the next five minutes, the whole rig's gonna career down the embankment."

Kash and Zain were on their feet and heading for Zain's truck before Atticus' voice had even faded, Nyx racing behind them. Chase paused just long enough to zip up his med kit and sling it over his shoulder, nearly colliding with Atticus as he followed the others out. He tossed his bag into the rear cab then jumped behind the wheel of his truck.

Both vehicles were already moving by the time

Foster snagged his coat, meeting Atticus at the door. "Guess this means I'm riding with you."

Atticus grunted, then turned, making his way to the driver's side. He didn't talk, just waited until Foster hopped in beside him before spinning the truck around — driving down the muddy road. Water ran in braided trails through the rocky dirt, spraying across the doors with every bounce. Atticus got to the main road then turned left toward town, still sitting in utter silence beside Foster.

Foster lasted two minutes before he glanced over at the man. While he wouldn't call Atticus a friend, he'd worked under the former colonel several times throughout his career while with different Joint Special Operation Commands. And Atticus and Foster's dad, John Beckett, had been Army Rangers together for a dozen years. Which was likely the reason Atticus had picked Raven's Cliff to start up his new venture. There was safety in numbers and Spec Op guys tended to stick together.

Of course, Foster hadn't been around when they'd chummed it up. Had barely been home over the past few years, on what had seemed like one deployment after another. But he'd always thought he'd have more time. That his dad would live forever.

Just another source of guilt to add to his ever-growing collection.

Foster huffed, giving Atticus a quick side eye. "So, are you going to tell me anything about this situation or is my team winging it?"

Atticus returned a quick glance, holding the wheel steady when the truck hydroplaned on a section of standing water, sliding a few feet onto the soft shoulder before the older man wrangled it back onto the lane. "Already told you what you need to know. The rest you'll have to evaluate at the scene." He poked a slightly crooked finger at Foster. "You *are* going to help, right? I assume ground support isn't included as part of your current boycott?"

Foster bit back the retort on his tongue, reminding himself all the reasons he shouldn't push back. "So, this is how it's going to be? You're going to be an ass until I agree to fly for you?"

"Pretty much." Atticus grunted when Foster simply stared at him. "I need a pilot."

"Rumor has it you just hired one."

"One. I need two. Hell, I'd prefer to have four so everyone gets to have an actual life — so I can expand and get a second chopper — but beggars and all that."

"I'm sure there're other pilots who'd measure up if you gave them a chance to prove themselves."

"This isn't just about skill, Beckett, and you know it." Atticus twisted to fully face him for a second, his weary brown gaze boring into Foster's before he focused on the road, again. "I need pilots I can trust. Who I know can't be bought or broken."

Foster sighed and turned to stare out the window, looking anywhere but at Atticus. "And therein lies the rub." He pointed to the next bend where a set of tracks led off the side of the cliff. A section of the inadequate metal fence hung over the side. "Is that it?"

"No, it's some other place with muddy skid marks and half the rail missing. Of course, that's the spot."

"Glad to see retirement has softened that gruff exterior. How far out are the cops?"

"We'll be lucky if an ambulance gets here before we're done. They're dealing with a multi-car pileup due to some local flooding and their resources are spread extremely thin."

"And your chopper?"

"My pilot's already pulled a double shift. I can't ask Mac to come out in this. It would be reckless." Atticus pulled over and shoved the truck into park. "Which means you and your team are on your own."

Foster merely nodded, doing his best to push aside the fact that this spot was nearly identical to the corner where his parents had gone off the edge and died. Except they hadn't been given a fighting chance.

That deathtrap was farther down the road, where the ridge turned unforgiving and any vehicle sliding over the side plunged mercilessly onto the rocky shoreline. But that didn't stop his brain from picturing them, here. Seeing a ghostly version of his dad's truck barrel off this ledge.

Atticus grabbed his arm when he went to leave. "What you said before. Is that your way of suggesting you can be bought? Because I have a hard time believing that."

Foster slipped out, looking at the man across the hood as thunder roared overhead, a thick fog curling in off the ocean. He glanced at his buddies as they parked behind him, already grabbing supplies out of their trucks. "Nope."

"Then what *are* you saying, Beckett?"

"That you're too late because I'm already broken."

He headed for the front of the truck, grabbing the winch cable. He doubted Atticus' truck could hold the van if the ledge really let go, but they'd need a way to bring up the injured since descending onto the rocks in the midst of a raging storm wasn't an option.

His buddies didn't waste any time, slipping on their harnesses and setting up their ropes. Kash took a few minutes to walk the area — give Nyx a chance to search for anyone who might have gotten ejected before the vehicle had gone over the edge. But after several sweeps, he returned, putting Nyx back in the truck then donning his own harness.

Foster handed Kash the spinal board Zain kept on the roof of his Chevy. "Chase performed a preliminary triage. He's got at least two patients who'll need to be carried out. Zain's doing his best to shore up the area beneath the van in the hopes it might hold together long enough to get everyone up. I'll suit up and we'll take turns assisting those who can move up the cliff while Atticus works the winch."

Kash nodded. "How long has it been since you've done any ground rescue work?"

"Longer than either of us would like."

"But here you are. Face it... you're just like us, Beck."

Foster didn't correct his buddy. Not because he knew Kash wouldn't listen to reason, especially once he'd made up his mind. But because the lie wouldn't form on Foster's tongue.

Kash simply smirked, the bastard, as if he knew exactly what Foster was thinking, then he was over the edge and racing down the cliff. Maybe four leaps and he was at the van — was halfway inside. Foster checked his equipment, made a mental note not to get himself killed, then moved to the edge, wishing he'd spent more time training with his teammates. Sure, he could fly a chopper through the eye of a needle, but this...

It was way outside his comfort zone. And everyone knew it.

Not that it stopped him from pushing off — allowing the rope to slide through his gloved hands for a few moments before he landed against the dirt. He took a breath then went again, continuing until he reached the vehicle. Kash already had their first passenger hooked up — was talking them through the procedure.

Foster shuffled over, giving Atticus a twirl of his finger. Nothing happened for a few moments then the line pulled taut and the person started moving. Foster followed along, maintaining contact while he worked his ascender, keeping the victim correctly positioned until they reached the top. It took a few moments of pushing and shoving before they were up and over the edge, all but falling onto the ground.

Atticus had his flatbed open with what looked like a few blankets and towels spread across the back — the full canopy saving everything from getting trashed. He helped Foster remove the harness, reactivating the winch as Foster turned and retraced his path down the cliff.

Kash took the next survivor, climbing up the side like freaking Spider-Man — making Foster feel as awkward as he'd probably looked earlier.

He definitely should have done more training.

He shook out his right hand, hating how all the metal plates and screws holding his entire right side together ached from the searing cold. The numbness that crept into his fingers when he pushed his shoulder past some arbitrary limit. Or maybe it was like Sean's ghost — a manifestation inside Foster's head that appeared whenever he started questioning his own worth.

When it was more than just his life on the line.

He shoved away the thoughts, taking up the next passenger once Kash returned with the harness. This trip was much trickier than the last with mud and rocks sloughing off as they tried to climb the embankment. There were a few moments of uncertainty — the guy in the harness panicking when his feet slipped off and he was dragged across the gravelly surface as the winch kept turning — but Foster managed to get the man's feet underneath him. Prevent him from getting a bad case of road rash as he crested the top.

Kash didn't seem to have any issues finding traction on the slick mud, walking up the side of the embankment as if he was taking a stroll along the boardwalk. Though, even he looked haggard by the time he descended again.

The wind kicked up, twirling small eddies across the cliff. The hollow echo of the coastal foghorn sounded in the distance. Foster couldn't see the rotating light, but there was no mistaking the occasional glow through the fog way off on the horizon. And if he hadn't been hooked up to a rope on the side of a cliff, he would have found the storm invigorating. The sheer power of the waves as they crashed against the jagged rocks, shooting water twenty feet into the air, nothing short of breath-taking.

Until all that rain had the dirt beneath them slipping away, dropping that van a few more inches as the entire slope shifted. Kash grabbed the next person, barely getting them secured before he was racing up that hill. Helping the line along.

Foster stuck his head into the van. Chase was working on one of the last two passengers, sticking something in his chest as he muttered to himself. He glanced over his shoulder, cursing when the van shifted again, nearly knocking him on his ass.

Foster was at Chase's side a second later, grabbing the man's upper body as he motioned for Chase to take his legs. His buddy scowled but moved, helping Foster carry the man out as the vehicle grated along the rocks, the screeching noise sounding around them like some kind of evil premonition.

They cleared the van as it shimmied sideways, glass breaking on the far side. Kash grabbed the edge of the spinal board, clipping the hook around it as Chase set the guy down then dove back inside, emerging a few moments later with the last victim slung over his shoulders.

Kash reached for him, locking his fist around Chase's harness as the vehicle rocked toward them, looking as if it might fully tip. Foster released the tension on his rope enough to drop another twenty feet and grab Zain by the back of his harness. He yanked them both to the left, kicking his feet clear of the van a moment before the entire slope collapsed, hurtling the vehicle down the rocky cliff and onto the rocks. Glass and metal shot into the air with the incoming breaker, crashing back into the water and disappearing beneath the next monster wave.

Zain relaxed against Foster's chest, shaking his head as he looked up at him. "I'm never going to hear the end of this, am I?"

Foster grinned. "Not a chance. You good?"

"Still breathing, thanks to you. But I didn't want

to stop trying to keep it steady until I knew Chase was out."

"You two are freaking nuts, you know that?"

"Says the pilot hanging on the end of a rope."

"Don't remind me."

He eased Zain over, then made his way back up. Chase was perched on the edge, his damn pride somehow keeping him and his patient glued to the side of the cliff as the wind and rain tried to blow them off. Foster shouldered up beside him on the right as Zain moved in on the left, the two of them taking turns helping Chase climb as the other kept the tension taut on his rope. It took twice as long to crest the cliff, but they made it.

Atticus had Zain and Chase's trucks repositioned, the other patient already in Zain's cab. "I just talked to emergency dispatch. If we can get everyone to the clinic, they'll arrange for transport once they've got an available unit. They've got doctors en route, so they'll be in good hands."

The men nodded, ushering everyone over to the trucks.

Foster stepped back as the last person scrambled in, waving to his buddies. "You guys go. I'll catch a ride with Atticus."

Zain glanced at the older man then back to Foster. "Are you sure that's in your best interest? He doesn't look like your biggest fan right now."

"The guy's as ornery as a mule, but it's all good.

And don't eat all the pizza if you bastards get back before me."

"No promises."

Foster flipped them off, nodding at Chase when he mouthed that he'd wait for Foster at the clinic. The trucks swerved onto the road, spraying out mud and rocks as they fishtailed on the slick surface, then headed for town.

Foster darted over to Atticus' truck, shaking out his hand in an effort to ease the ache. Though, he had a feeling nothing short of a couple beers and a hot shower would work. "Are we good to go or have you found someone else who needs to be rescued?"

Atticus snorted. "Don't tempt me, son."

Foster pursed his lips. While he knew Atticus was more bark than bite, it didn't stop him from wanting to smack the old coot. "Just get in the damn truck."

He opened the passenger door when a low whop echoed through the fog. He paused, staring toward the ocean when a chopper materialized out of the fog and rain, screaming toward them. Fifty feet off the deck with twin vortices trailing behind it. It banked hard to the right, making a tight turn before coming into a high hover over the cliff.

Atticus palmed his CB radio, clicking the mic as he all but growled into the phone. "What the hell are you doing, Mac? You're timed out, and it's pissing like the apocalypse out here."

There was a blast of static, then a scratchy voice.

"Did you seriously think I'd just sit it out? When you had multiple victims?"

"Yes, I did because that was a direct order. Besides, we're done. Everyone's en route—"

"Not done. There's someone near the bottom of the cliff about fifty feet to your starboard. Probably just out of sight from where you are. I can't tell if they're alive or not, but they won't be unless we get to them. Now."

Foster cursed then took off, scanning the rocks as he made his way along the edge. He was just about to question the pilot's sanity when he spotted a flash of yellow amidst the frothy spray.

He darted back to the truck, shaking his head as he looked at Atticus. "I've got our vic. But the winch cable isn't going to reach that far."

The voice snorted, the sound higher than he'd expected. Softer. "Then, it's a good thing I came along. I've got Charlie with me but he's only qualified to work the hoist. Which means I need someone to harness up and get our vic into the basket I send down."

Foster froze. Actually froze because… he was their only option. And that meant facing the real possibility that he'd end up inside the helicopter.

CHAPTER TWO

"Dad? Do you still copy?"

Mackenzie "Mac" Parker stared down at the guy standing beside her father's truck, wondering what the hell was going on. If maybe the storm had crapped out their radios because there was nothing but an eerie silence over the comms.

A few more moments of absolute silence, then her dad's gruff voice. "Send down the basket. Just do me a favor and land both back on the road if possible."

Mac glanced at Charlie, wondering if she'd imagined her father saying to land everyone back on the road instead of hoisting them up and heading straight to the clinic, but the man merely shrugged. "Say, again?"

"You heard me. Drop them back off if it's safe."

"Roger."

She wasn't sure what that was about — if there

was some form of danger she was unaware of — but she'd do her best. "Okay, Charlie. Mission's a go."

The gusting wind buffeted the chopper as she moved into position, holding it steady as Charlie opened the doors then lowered the basket. Rain blew in through the open space, chilling the cabin as the temperature dropped. She clenched her jaw, adjusting the controls as the guy hooked himself up to the harness then gave her a twirl of his finger.

She moved, lifting him several feet above ground level before easing the helicopter sideways. Battling the fierce drafts cutting across the embankment until she was over the person lying motionless on the rocks.

The basket swung, the mixture of the rotors' downwash and the wind spinning it dangerously close to the shoreline. She countered, moving with it until the whole unit finally settled, staying just right of their patient.

The guy glanced up then reached for the cliff side, grabbing ahold when she shuffled over enough for him to wrap his hands around a large rock. The weight beneath her shifted, then eased as he put some slack in the line, climbing along the slippery surface before going to his knees.

She kept the bird steady, working her hands and feet in an effort not to yank him over or drag him across the shoreline. Rain pummeled the bubble, a flash of lightning rattling the cabin as it shot across the sky, far too close for her liking. She looked down, mentally willing the guy to move his ass when Charlie's voice sounded in her helmet.

"Um, Mac. Please tell me that's not what I think it is?"

She frowned, focusing out the left window. A twisting funnel of frothy white water zigzagged across the surface, gaining speed and volume as it headed their way. "Crap."

Mac keyed up her mic. "Hey, buddy."

An exasperated huff rasped over the comms. "Kinda busy here."

"Yeah, well, you might want to speed things along. We've got a bit of a situation forming and time isn't on our side."

The comms went dead followed by a harsh curse. "You've got to be kidding me."

The line pulled tight for a moment, the weight shuffling from side to side as the funnel drew closer, spraying water across the ocean as it intensified, quickly doubling in size.

She held firm, aware she had no other option but to hope he gave her the green light before it reached them when her comms clicked.

His voice rasped over the static, followed by a harsh, "Go."

She moved, quickly gaining altitude as she banked away from the cliff. What she hoped would prevent the basket from crashing into the rocks if the wind caught it before she got them clear.

The line pulled tight, tugging against the chopper as the top few feet of the funnel snared the basket, spinning if for a few horrifying seconds, water shooting out in all directions. She stopped short, maintaining just enough tension on the line it wouldn't slingshot the guy sideways when they finally broke free. Pressure built through the controls, some of the gauges edging toward the red, when the spout passed, crashing into the cliff in a stunning display of wind and rain. The line went slack as the basket dropped a few feet, finally settling beneath the chopper, again.

She shoved the cyclic forward, getting them clear of the cliff before banking it over and paralleling the shoreline. Any hope of dropping them off beside her father's truck fading into the thick fog curling up the base and across that road.

Charlie nodded when she gave him the thumbs up, activating the hoist and reeling in the line. The chopper rocked with the shifting center of gravity until the constant whining of the hoist stopped followed by the clatter of the basket skidding across the rear cabin.

Her comms chirped then her dad's voice sounded over the radio. "You all okay?"

She clicked the button. "Fine, dad. But we'll have to head for the hanger. Can you call dispatch and get an ambulance headed our way? I'll never make it over the hills to Providence in this weather."

"Already done. They'll pick up your patient then

head on to the clinic. I'll see you later. And Mac, we're not done talking about this."

She chuckled. If only her father knew some of the missions she'd flown while in the Coast Guard. Though, he probably did but was choosing to selectively forget anything that didn't jive with his line of thinking. That she was still his little girl.

Boots scuffed the floor off to her right, and she chanced a quick glance behind her. The guy was splayed across the floor, water pooling beneath him as he fumbled with the carabiner. Charlie shuffled over and released the clip, thanking the guy before focusing on the other person bundled in the basket.

The man scanned the chopper, eyes wide. His mouth pinched tight. He met her gaze, his nostrils flaring as he seemed to take short, choppy breaths.

She sighed, talking loud enough he'd hear her over the wind still howling through the open doors. "Sorry, but between the spout and the fog, I couldn't access the road, again."

He frowned but nodded, still looking around as if he expected the entire machine to either crumble around him or swallow him whole.

She motioned to the vacant spot beside her. "There's a seat up here, if you'd like."

He glanced at the empty chair, shuddered, then stood, making his way between the bulkhead before stopping. Looking as if he might pass out.

Mac frowned, staring into the darkness. At least the lighthouse was working, each flash of light guiding her back to base. Not that she couldn't distinguish the shoreline but between the pouring rain and the encroaching fog, it was getting sketchy, even for her.

A minute passed before she looked up, motioning to the spot, again. "Either sit there or grab a seat in the back. Just do something before some turbulence tosses your ass across the cabin."

He muttered something under his breath then shuffled over, leaning his hip against the chair. Not standing but definitely not fully sitting. More of a modified squat. As if he planned on diving across the cockpit at a moment's notice.

She shook her head, secretly wondering how her father always seemed to find the crazy ones, when he picked up the spare headset and slipped it on.

He clicked on the mic, looking over at her. "In all the rush, I didn't get your name."

The fact he hadn't introduced himself first, seemed a bit odd. But then she'd just been commenting on the fact she already thought he was nuts.

She smiled, absently noting how stunning his eyes were. Some enchanting combination of blue and green, that sparkled with every pass of the lighthouse beacon. "Mackenzie. But everyone just calls me Mac."

Those gorgeous eyes widened, and he mumbled something resembling, *fucking Atticus*, before he huffed. "Mackenzie. As in Parker. Atticus' daughter."

"You know my dad?"

The guy chuckled. "You could say that. I flew missions under him in a number of JSOC operations. Nothing long term, but you get to know the people commanding you pretty quick."

"You flew…"

Well, damn. She gave him a more thorough once-over. The guy was tall, well over six feet and had the kind of physique that came from hours in the gym. His hair was long — more of a *Winter Soldier* vibe than the clean-cut *Steve Rogers* look she'd imagined — and he had a few days' worth of growth on his jaw. Not a full beard but well past a five o'clock shadow.

He was handsome, she supposed, if she pushed aside all her preconceived notions about the guy.

She dodged the chopper around a pocket of thicker fog, noting the way his breathing kicked up as he fisted his hand. "You're *Beckett*."

Foster Beckett. Major. Retired. And part of the reason she'd finally decided to give up the Coast Guard to help her father.

Though, to hear him talk about the man, Beckett was more legend than mortal. Had received a shoebox full of metals for various acts of bravery while under fire. She'd come to refer to him as *the ghost*. Always there but never seen. Her dad had been trying to get the guy to join Raven's Watch for the past six weeks, but all he'd gotten was the same three words. That Beckett wasn't interested.

Beckett's mouth twitched. "I see you share your father's current opinion of me."

She snorted, angling the machine toward the shore in the hope of beating the advancing fog bank. "All I know is that my dad finds something wrong with every pilot I send his way because in the end, none of them are you. Which means, I'm now stuck working double duty while my father tries to woo you."

Beckett stared at her, his eyes narrowed as he constantly shook out his right hand. As if it had gone numb and still hadn't come back to life. "Woo me?"

"Something wrong with my choice of words, Major?"

"Only in the sense that Atticus Parker doesn't *woo* anyone. Threaten? Sure. Bully? Definitely. Hell, he might even resort to asking somewhat nicely if the stars are in alignment. But he'd never *woo*."

"Maybe you don't know him as well as you think?"

"Or maybe you're projecting your own feelings into the matter."

"My feelings? I don't even know you."

"But something tells me you believe you know my type. That maybe I think I'm too good to work for your dad? Or too lazy?" He arched a brow. "I'm close, aren't I."

He hadn't phrased it as a question, and she merely shrugged. "You do you. Just do me a favor and send some fellow Air Force jackass his way so I can get more than a few hours of sleep. This time of year is the most dangerous, weather wise. And people out here seem to lack any form of common sense when it comes to self-preservation."

"I'm aware. I grew up here. And I've offered to send guys his way, but he blows me off before I can give him any names."

"I told you. They're not you. Which raises the question of why you keep saying no?"

Beckett stared at her, snapping his head to the back of the cabin when their other passenger made some weird gurgling noise before taking a few loud, gasping breaths. He swallowed, coughed, then looked back at her, shaking out his right hand, again. As if simply hearing that odd sound had affected him.

He rolled that same right shoulder, wincing as it rotated. "Other than three plates and a few dozen screws?"

"You managed that rescue like a pro. Flying doesn't require nearly that much mobility."

"I'm retired."

"Right."

He furrowed his brow. "What's that supposed to mean?"

"Nothing, it's just..." She blew out a rough breath. "Guys like you, like my dad, never really retire. I mean, I know my dad tried. Lasted all of a month before he decided he needed to start up this search and rescue business. Though, I suspect he'd planned it that way from the start so he could argue that he'd given retirement the ol' college try. Just like your buddies."

"Maybe I'm not like them."

Mac spared him a quick side eye as she lined the chopper up with the big H on the tarmac. "Or maybe this has nothing to do with retirement or plates and screws and everything to do with why you chose now to leave the Air Force. The reason you wanted me to drop you off at the truck instead of bringing you on board."

She made full eye contact this time. "Why you can't bring yourself to actually sit in that seat."

Beckett inhaled, clenching his jaw so tight she thought it might crack before he looked away. That right hand still fisting and releasing. She gave herself a mental slap, realizing a bit too late exactly what she'd said. She'd definitely crossed a line. Especially considering he'd just jumped into the fray to help people he didn't know. Had put his own life at risk when he could have walked away.

He didn't owe her or her father any explanation.

She berated herself under her breath, fighting the gusting winds and punishing rain as she landed the chopper on the tarmac, quickly spooling down the engines. She hadn't even had the chance to look over at him before he was up and moving, helping Charlie carry the basket out of the chopper and into the hanger.

Red and white lights reflected off the fog beyond the building, the ambulance obviously waiting for them.

Mac shut down the aircraft, grabbed the tow hook

and lined it up. Five minutes flat, and she had the machine bouncing along behind her as she rolled it into the hanger then shut the doors, shaking her head at how the rain pelted the metal side, each hollow ping reverberating through the large space. Charlie appeared a moment later, the collapsible basket tucked under one arm as he made a beeline for the chopper.

She stopped him just shy of the doors, nodding at the main entrance. "Is Beckett already gone?"

Charlie nodded. "That new medic your dad just hired, Remington, I think. He was waiting in a truck outside, and your buddy Beckett jumped in as if his ass was on fire." Charlie chuckled. "Not that I'm surprised. You were a bit..."

"Honest?"

"Sure, let's go with that."

"Charlie..."

Charlie propped the basket against the chopper, looking at the door then back to her. "I realize it was probably the fatigue and anger talking. I mean, you did give up a lot in the name of family. And I know working for your dad isn't all rainbows and puppies. He's gruff, stubborn and tends to yell first, consider apologizing later. But you might have been a bit... harsh with Beckett. Especially if you were trying to give him a reason to join."

Mac sighed, resting her ass against the chopper door. "Don't hold back, Charlie. Tell me what you really think."

"You know I love you and your dad like family. Adopted family that I often want to disown, but family, nonetheless. But you both tend to go straight for the jugular when you're passionate about a subject. And sometimes, that comes back to bite you in the ass."

"I wasn't wrong."

"I never said you were."

"But you're saying I went all pit bull on him instead of being a snuggly golden retriever."

"Sorry to break it to you, honey, but you'll never be a golden retriever. A husky, maybe."

"Oh, so I'm the dramatic type?"

"God, you're so much like Atticus and Josh it's downright scary." Charlie paused as her brother's name slipped out before he sighed. "Like I said, you're family. Why else would I stick around when I could make double the money working somewhere sunny and warm. With babes in bikinis."

"You're perfectly primeval."

"Get some sleep. And maybe consider buying that guy some whiskey. You know that old saying, sugar catches more flies…"

"I doubt a bottle of Glenfiddich is going to sway him."

"Maybe not. But it wouldn't hurt. And seeing as the rest of his former team work here, it might be nice if you two didn't shoot daggers at each other every time you ended up in the same room." Charlie shrugged. "Just a thought. I know all too well you'll do what you want, and nothing and no one will change that."

"Wow, you're on fire tonight."

"I'm tired, too. And cold. Now go. And remember you're only on call tomorrow, so don't show your face in here unless I page you."

She saluted him then struck off, stopping at the doorway when he called her name.

Charlie held up a wallet as he darted across the hanger, placing it in her hand. "This must have fallen out of Beckett's pocket when he got knocked over by the basket. Be a doll and see he gets it back."

"Be a doll?"

"Are you seriously going to bust my ass every time I use an old phrase?"

"Only when they're sexist or just plain wrong."

"Goodnight, Mackenzie."

She flipped him off, shaking her head as she made her way out to her Wrangler. She jumped inside, tossing Beckett's wallet on the passenger seat as she started her Jeep, letting it idle until the heated seats had taken away the worst of the chill. She glanced at the worn leather, debating whether she should drop it off tonight or just give it to one of his buddies when she inevitably saw them at work.

Her earlier words echoed inside her head, his pale skin and hollow eyes wavering in her rearview. Charlie was right. She *had* been harsh. But more than that, she'd been judgmental. And she knew, firsthand, never to judge someone before she'd gotten to know them. Had a chance to see beyond the curtain because as sure as she'd be eating crow giving back his wallet, there was a much deeper reason Foster Beckett didn't want to get behind the controls. And she had a bad feeling she'd manifested that demon tonight.

CHAPTER THREE

Foster sat in Chase's truck as they drove through town then took the long winding road out to the property. His buddy hadn't said a word since Foster had jumped into the passenger side as if tangos were hot on his ass, mumbling a harsh, "Go," as he'd closed the door and leaned back in the seat.

Chase had glanced at the hanger then hit the gas, occasionally looking in the rearview as if he expected a black SUV to jump out behind them, machine guns firing. An obvious threat to explain Foster's odd behavior.

Mackenzie Parker.

He hadn't seen that coming. Not when Atticus had mentioned — repeatedly — how she'd joined the Coast Guard. That she'd serve until the organization either forced her to retire or she died in the process. Though, after what had happened to Josh, it all made sense.

Which only added to the guilt slowly suffocating the cab. How she'd likely given up her career because her dad needed someone he trusted. That Atticus' own sanity was hanging by a thread. Foster hadn't really looked at it from that perspective before — hadn't considered why Atticus kept pushing for him to join.

They aren't you…

That's what she'd said. Twice. Which explained the harsh tone, the scathing way she'd glanced at him. Her father had put Foster on some kind of impossible pedestal and he'd more than fallen off it tonight.

He'd crushed it. Broken it into dust, which had blown away with the wind and the rain.

He wasn't sure if she thought her dad would have insisted she remained in the Coast Guard if Foster had signed up. Or if she'd gotten a less than warm welcome home. Either way, his name was at the top of her shit list. And she hadn't held back.

Chase sighed beside him, finally taking a moment to look him in the eyes. "That bad, huh?"

Foster chuckled. "That's what I love about you, buddy. No small talk or brotherly encouragement. You just jump right in with both feet. Straight to the heart of the issue."

"First of all, you hate small talk. Second, you'd deck me if I tried to coddle you. And third, we both know it must have been pretty fucking awful for you to jump into the truck and just yell at me to go."

Chase pointed a finger at Foster. "And yeah. You yelled."

Foster scrubbed a hand down his face, wishing he'd taken Zain's offer and hopped into the man's Chevy. Instead, he was left scrambling for some form of damage control. "Fine. It sucked. You happy?"

"Do I look happy?"

Foster eyed his best friend. "You look like crap."

"Thanks for noticing. Nothing like stabbing a guy in the chest to relieve a tension pneumothorax while stuck in a van, teetering on a crumbling cliff, to get me back in the game. Talk about being baptized by fire."

"You didn't even blink."

"Are you high? My damn hands were shaking." He pinned Foster with an intense gaze. "My hands never shake."

"Of course, they were shaking. You were halfway frozen. We all were. And you saved his life. That's the takeaway here." Foster inhaled, cringing a bit as he turned to face Chase. "You *did* save his life, right?"

"You'd be feeling pretty damn bad if I hadn't. And yeah, I did, but the point is... You're not the only one trying to find their way here. We're all struggling."

Foster huffed. "Zain and Kash are *not* struggling."

"They were. They just found their rhythm quicker than most." Chase checked his mirrors then turned onto the pitted dirt road. "Besides, they don't remember that night the way we do. A blessing I guess."

"Nothing about that night was a blessing. And I have a feeling they recall far more than they've let on." Foster sighed. "Probably because they're afraid I'll go off the deep end or something."

"Are they wrong?"

He glanced out the side window, watching the trees bend as the wind howled beyond the glass. "I made it back without killing anyone, didn't I?"

"Did you? Because I was somewhat worried you'd cracked and left a bunch of carnage behind when you'd told me to *go*. Like you'd robbed a bank or something."

Foster laughed. "Nope. Just trying to save a hint of my pride. Do you know who this new pilot is?"

Chance frowned, shoving his truck into park after he pulled into his spot off to the left of the main building. "No idea. Kash wasn't lying. Atticus hasn't said shit about it."

"That's because it's Mackenzie."

Chase stared at him, obviously waiting for him to continue before he shook his head. "And that's supposed to mean something to me?"

"Mackenzie. As in his daughter. Ex-Coast Guard, and the woman who likely has a hit out on me."

Chase's jaw dropped open before he burst out laughing, wiping at imaginary tears a few moments later. "Let me get this straight. Your first time even sitting in a chopper in five months, and you lose your cool in front of Atticus Parker's daughter. Oh man, that's rich. Wait until I tell the guys."

"This isn't funny, jackass. I practically hyperventilated in there. But what's worse, she knew exactly who I was. Apparently good old Atticus has been singing my praises only it's this version of me that showed up and she's struggling to see even a hint of the man her father painted me to be."

"Was it the hair?" Chase grinned. "It's usually the hair."

He groaned as he shook his head, letting it fall back against the seat. "What's that saying? You can never go home?"

Chase schooled his features, pushing out a long slow breath before he punched Foster in the arm. "Well, I'll be damned. You like her."

Foster jerked his head around, torn between wanting to smack Chase and wondering if he'd suffered some kind of head injury during the rescue. "Where the hell did that come from?"

"Please. You're never this worked up unless there's a whole lot of emotion involved."

"Yeah, the angry kind mixed with a healthy dose of self-loathing. Maybe a splash of embarrassment."

Chase merely raised a brow. "How long have we been friends?"

"Is that what this is? Because I'm feeling very attacked right now."

"Twenty years. And when have I ever been wrong about something?"

"Will a numerical list do, or..."

"You're not crazy, and you're not broken." Chase

rolled his eyes when Foster stared at him. "Okay, maybe a little broken. But not beyond fixing. Whether that involves you getting back behind a set of controls or moving on to something new, this is all part of the process. And if Mackenzie is anything like her old man, she's just frustrated that her life has taken a turn, too. I'm sure she's still dealing with losing her brother. Changing careers."

Chase slapped Foster's arm. "Though, I would have paid good money to be a fly on the wall in that chopper. How are her hands?"

Foster laughed. "Only you would ask that instead of if she was smart or pretty."

"And?"

"She's got some mad skills."

"I bet she does. And is she smart and pretty?"

"More sarcastic with a side of blood lust."

"Sounds like the woman of your dreams, buddy."

"Not a chance. Now are we going in or just staying out here because Kash is staring out the window like some anxious mother hen waiting for her chicks to come back to roost, and I'm betting Zain has eaten all of the good stuff."

"Definitely going inside. Just wait until I tell them you've got the hots for the boss' daughter."

"Chase, I swear…"

But the man was already out and hoofing it to the door. Kash met him in the foyer, bending over laughing when Chase said something as he pointed at Foster. The two men stopped, met Foster's glare then started up again, disappearing into the main house as lightning danced across the sky.

Foster opened the door and stepped out, darting over to the house as the rain got impossibly harder. He instinctively reached for his keys, mumbling under his breath when he realized he hadn't driven. Discovering his wallet wasn't in his back pocket sent a shiver down his spine. What was shaping up to be one hell of a mishap because it had either fallen out during the rescue, which meant it was lost. Or it was on the floor of Atticus' truck. Maybe in the chopper. Either way, it meant he'd have to man up and face both Atticus and Mackenzie again.

* * *

This was crazy.

She was crazy.

Mackenzie stared at the turn-of-the-century mansion as she sat in her Jeep, wondering how she'd even gotten there. The last thing she recalled was listing all the points why confronting Foster now — while her harsh words still echoed in her head — was courting disaster. Yet, her damn Wrangler had just turned onto the long winding gravel driveway before she'd even realized it. And now, she was sitting there, gathering the courage to face the man.

The fact there were three other trucks parked off to one side set off warning bells. That he likely wasn't alone. She wasn't sure if the rest of his team lived nearby or if they simply made a habit of hanging out most nights together. Because with the rain still coming down in sheets and the wind threatening to blow away anything not tied down, it seemed unlikely that they'd simply stopped by for a chat.

Though, maybe that was her saving grace. What would allow her to simply hand him his wallet then slink off. Avoid touching on what had conspired between them in the chopper. How she'd done exactly what Charlie had said and let her fatigue and anger color her words.

She groaned. Who was she kidding? She'd been pissed at Foster Beckett long before tonight. Ever since her brother had been killed and her father had started combing the earth for someone to take his place. His determination to only hire men he'd worked with. Once Atticus had learned Beckett and his team were retiring to Raven's Cliff...

He'd been obsessed with having the man join Raven's Watch. When Foster had turned her dad down...

She'd realized Atticus would never truly be satisfied unless she took her brother's spot. Gave him an anchor when she knew he was drifting. She was drifting, too and that had definitely shown in how she'd reacted tonight.

Mac rolled her shoulders as she grabbed Beckett's wallet and opened the door, giving herself a quick pep talk. "Just... walk on up and knock on the door. Give him his wallet and walk away. Piece of cake."

Except where her stomach wasn't sure if it wanted to launch up into her throat or drop down into her shoes as she ran up the muddy path then onto the porch. A warm light brightened the entrance, muffled laughter drifting from beyond the door.

Great. He was definitely not alone.

Mac took a deep breath then held her head high as she slammed the ornate door knocker against the tarnished brass plate. The loud bang echoed through the air, cutting off the voices. Footsteps sounded a moment later before the door creaked open and Foster's imposing form filled the doorway.

He inhaled, eyes rounding before he smiled and leaned against the frame. Those brilliant blue-green orbs staring at her. "Are you here for round two? Because I'll just concede now and save you the trouble."

She smiled despite the uneasy fluttering in her stomach. "A military man surrendering that easily? I find that hard to believe."

"I'm retired, remember?"

"It's hard to forget." She held out his wallet. "And I just came by to give you this. Charlie found it in the back of the helicopter. It must have fallen out when you first boarded, and that stupid basket knocked you over."

He grinned, the simple motion taking him from somewhat handsome to stunning. As if he'd removed her blinders and she was getting her first real look at him. "I wondered where I'd lost it. I thought for sure it was in your dad's truck."

"Oh, wouldn't that have been awkward."

His smile widened and it took her breath away. All full red lips with a hint of white. What looked like the beginnings of dimples in his cheeks. "More than you know. Which has me wondering why you decided to return it instead of watching me suffer?"

"I would have given it to you immediately if you hadn't buggered off like a frat boy avoiding the cops."

Foster sighed, still leaning against the frame. "I think we both know why I left in a hurry."

"Do we? Because it was either something I said…" She inched closer. "Or something I didn't say."

"Both, I suppose."

He looked over his shoulder when one of his buddies yelled at him to get his ass back to the poker table so they could make more easy money.

Mac held up her hand as she took a step back. "Sounds like I interrupted you and your team. I just wanted to return that."

"Sorry to take you out of your way."

"It really wasn't."

He straightened, glanced over his shoulder again, then blew out a rough breath. "You want a beer?"

Was her mouth hanging open? Maybe some drool trickling down the side of her face? Because it sounded as if he'd just invited her in for a drink. "What?"

He chuckled and damn, it made her stomach feel as if a thousand butterflies had suddenly taken flight. "I said, would you like a beer?"

She furrowed her brow, wondering if she'd fallen asleep in her Jeep and this was all a dream.

He frowned. "If you'd rather not..."

"You got any worth drinking?"

That made his eyes sparkle like back in the chopper. "Zain brought Corona, and Kash has some German brand."

"And you?"

"Smithwicks."

"Now, you're talking."

Foster backed up, waving her inside. "It's still a work in progress so watch your step. And forgive the mess. It's way better in the finished areas."

"How much more do you have to renovate?"

"Not much. My parents did most of the work. Just a few rooms left but one of them is the first one you see, so that doesn't instill confidence."

She thanked him when he took her coat, hanging it on an old-fashioned rack before waving her through the construction zone and into the room beyond. His buddies were seated at a massive mahogany table, beers and pizza stacked beside them. Cards and chips tossed in for good measure. They glanced her way, nodded, then snapped their heads back. As if they'd just realized Foster wasn't alone.

Foster motioned to an empty seat as he disappeared through another doorway only to appear a few moments later carrying a beer bottle. He popped the cap off with some fancy bottle opener, waiting until she'd taken her seat before placing it in front of her. "Hungry? Because I'm betting you haven't eaten much if your dad's had you working a double."

"I'd love a slice."

He nodded, stopping as he groaned and shook his head. "I swear, my mother would smack me up the backside of the head. Guys, this is Mackenzie. Atticus' daughter, and your new pilot. Mac, starting on your right that's Chase, Kash and Zain. Oh, and the mutt is Nyx."

Mutt?

A cold, wet nose nudged her wrist a moment later, and she jumped as she stared into a set of soulful brown eyes. She gave the shepherd a scratch, laughing when the dog licked her hand before turning and disappearing under the table again.

"Who's the handler?"

Kash grinned. "Guilty. And she's far better than any of these other jackasses."

"You included." Zain offered his hand. "So, you're Atticus' secret weapon. Interesting."

"Secret weapon?"

Zain shrugged, leaning back in his chair. "That's what you father said. That he was bringing in a *secret weapon* he knew would change the scope of the unit."

"He's still referring to everyone as a unit? That man."

"Old habits." Chase glanced at Foster when he returned with a few different types of pizza on a plate. "Foster says you've got mad skills."

Foster coughed, looking as if he wanted to sucker punch Chase in the jaw as he placed the plate in front of her. "Unlike these jerks who lack any form of tact."

"Mad skills, huh?" Mac raised the bottle and took a tentative swig. The cool ale tasted sweet and fresh, and it eased any remaining tension straining her muscles. Dispelled the worry that accepting the invite was going to be an epic mistake. "That's far kinder than what you could have said."

Beckett paused short of taking his seat, glancing at Chase then back to her. "You didn't say anything I didn't already know."

Kash cleared his throat. "Beck? It sounds like you have something you didn't share with the class."

"And it's going to stay that way." Foster took a long pull of his beer. "So, ex-Coast Guard. You get a chance to work in any of their TACLET units?"

Work. That was a conversation she could embrace.

"Just finished my sixth rotation with them before I came here." Mac tilted her head. "Talk about a wild ride. But then, you'd know all about that. Flight Concepts. The 563rd. That's an impressive resumé."

Foster's smile faded a bit as he glanced at his buddies. "Atticus has way too much time on his hands if he's talking about that."

"It slipped out here and there. But I'm an excellent listener."

He leaned forward, resting his massive forearms on the table. "Why does that sound scarier than Atticus chatting about my CV?"

"Because you're paranoid. All you ex-Spec Op boys are. But I suppose it's part of your charm." She shifted in her seat, suddenly aware the rest of his team were sitting there, watching them. Amused smiles curving their lips.

She switched gears, motioning to the house. "So, when do you think this place will be open for business? You *are* planning on turning it into an inn or something, aren't you?"

Foster eased back, taking another long drink. "That's what my parents wanted. I'm just focusing on finishing to start. See what feels right later."

She nodded, admiring the old-world craftsmanship and how the new renovations blended perfectly with the antique charm. "It looks fantastic. It seems you gents have more than one skill. Do you all live nearby?"

Chase chuckled. "We actually live on the property. It was the first thing Foster did once we arrived. He handed us each a deed from his lawyer where he'd had the estate subdivided, giving everyone a couple of acres." Chase tipped his beer bottle toward Foster. "Way more than we ever expected, and we're extremely thankful."

"Luckily, there were already structures on each

section." Zain nodded at Chase. "A guest house on Chase's lot. A giant ass workshop turned into another home on mine and Kash got the old barn that had been partially renovated. We finished it up, first, before turning our sights on Foster's mansion."

Foster snorted. "It's not a mansion. It's just got a few more rooms."

"Would you prefer manor house? Stately residence maybe?"

"You're such an ass."

Zain batted his eyelids at Foster as he blew him a kiss. "I know."

Foster rolled his eyes, drawing his attention back to her and it made the room feel suddenly hot. All that blue-green gaze focused on her. As if everyone else had disappeared. "Are you staying at your dad's for a while?"

She snorted, nearly spitting some of her beer across the table. "God, no. I love my father, but he's impossible to live with. I'm renting one of those refurbished cabins farther up the road. They aren't as nice as this but they're clean."

"And about as far away from Atticus as you can get."

"There's that, too. I'm hoping it will dissuade him from dropping by."

Kash laughed. "I wouldn't count on it. He's been making weekly trips out here in the hopes of browbeating Foster..."

Kash's voice trailed into a grunt before he glared

at Chase. His buddy frowned, nodding at Foster and her. Kash rolled his head to the side then gave her a small smile as he sprang to his feet. "Anyone else need another beer?"

Foster chuckled. "Forgive, Kash. He does better with four-legged company."

"I heard that, you bastard."

"See?"

Kash returned, pointing at his cards as he flopped in the chair. "Did Foster mess with my stuff while I was in the kitchen?"

Foster groaned. "Why would I mess with your crap?"

"For the same reason you've been moving our shit around then denying it."

"Hand to god, Kash, I didn't touch your freaking mug that day."

"Right. Just like you didn't rub bacon on my jeans last week so Nyx wouldn't stop sniffing my ass."

Foster chuckled, shrugging at her as they fell into a comfortable conversation, recounting a few harrowing tales as they teased each other. More like a group of brothers than friends. Foster moved them into the other room, offering her a cozy winged-back chair as the rest of them spread out, nursing their beers as they joked. Chase was talking about some insane rescue when a hand closed over her arm, jerking her awake. Mac blinked a few times, groaning when she realized she'd fallen asleep.

Foster removed his hand, looking as if he wasn't

sure if it was him or the fact he'd touched her that had made her jump. "You're exhausted."

She shifted forward, bracing her elbows on her knees as she speared her fingers through her hair. "How long was I out?"

"About fifteen minutes. I would have let you sleep but there's no way you could spend the night in that chair and actually move tomorrow." He curled his fingers at her. "Come on. You can stay here tonight."

She could stay there? With him?

Mac stumbled to her feet, emitting an embarrassing high-pitched screech when her foot caught on the area rug and she reeled backwards. Foster lunged forward, catching her around the waist and drawing her against his chest before she fell on her ass. Or worse... Cracked her head on the coffee table off to her right.

Mackenzie closed her eyes, willing the floor to open up and swallow her as his buddies darted across the room, their footsteps echoing through the house. She gathered what was left of her pride then eased back, smiling like a fool as he let his arms fall to his sides. "And that's definitely my cue to leave. Before I completely embarrass myself."

Kash chuckled. "Trust me. You haven't seen Zain try to work a nail gun. Talk about embarrassing."

Zain slapped his buddy on the chest. "That's it. Keep laughing when you know I can put a bullet in your ass from two miles away."

Kash batted his eyelashes. "Oh, I love it when you talk dirty to me."

Mac laughed. She really liked these guys. "Thanks, but..." She yawned, nearly tripping again when the room tilted a bit.

Foster cupped her elbow, waiting until she looked him in the eyes. "Sorry, but you're in no shape to drive. And yeah, we've all been there. So, you can either stay in one of the spare rooms or one of us can take you home. Your choice."

She bit at her bottom lip, feeling strangely on display as everyone stood there, waiting, when the entire house shook as a boom of thunder crashed overhead. She jumped, cursing again when she ended up leaning against Foster's chest. Her pulse racing. Every nerve ending on edge.

"Mackenzie..."

Had his voice always sounded that low? That sexy? With a slight rasp that gave it a dark edge. Like aged bourbon. And the way he said her full name...

A sure sign she really wasn't fit to drive.

Mac sighed. "I'm not going to make any of you drive an extra thirty minutes in this deluge. So, if you've got a room to spare..."

"I've got a dozen. But the one next to mine is the nicest. And I promise I don't snore."

Chase moved in, slapping Foster on the arm before heading for the door. "Don't make promises you can't keep, big guy."

Foster rolled his eyes. "He's an ass."

"So, you've said." She eased back, hating that she missed his warmth. "And I just need a few hours."

"You can stay as long as you need."

Foster headed for the stairs, flipping off his friends when they all yelled for him to behave, before motioning for her to follow him. He made his way up the stairs, turning right and heading down the hallway until he reached the last door on the right. "Mine's on the left. You've got your own bathroom. There're towels and other toiletries in case you want to take a shower. Just do me a favor and shoot me a text if you leave before morning. So, I know it's you setting off the door alarm and not some random perp trying to get inside."

Mac arched a brow. "We're kinda in the middle of nowhere…"

"You can't be too careful."

She nodded. "Will I set off any motion alarms if I wander around?"

He grinned. "If you want to check the place out, be my guest. I only have exterior alarms. Which Zain reminds me, daily, aren't enough. But I don't really want to mess with the charm of this place. Or feel like my every move is being monitored. Though, I suppose I'll have to reevaluate once all the renovations are finished. And like you said, we're in the middle of nowhere."

"Noted. Now, I just need your number."

He motioned for her to give him her cell, opening her contacts and adding his name and number. He held onto the edge when she went to take it back. "Guard that number with your life. I rarely give it out."

"With great power, I suppose…"

"Exactly." He opened the door and waved her in. "I know you won't need anything, but if you do…"

"You're right next door."

"Goodnight, Mac."

"Night, Foster."

He paused for a moment, then continued into his room — left her standing there, wondering, again, if he'd turned up the heat. Or if maybe she was having some kind of stroke.

She shook it off then walked inside, closing the door before bracing her weight against it. If she didn't know better, she would have thought something had sparked between them.

Which seemed highly unlikely. Especially after what she'd said in the helicopter. While he hadn't called her on it other than his remark when he'd answered the door, it was obvious she'd struck a nerve earlier. And she had a feeling it wasn't one that was easily soothed.

CHAPTER FOUR

He was tired. Exhausted, really. The events from earlier stressing his physical and mental well-being. Straining him to the point he should have passed out as soon as he'd climbed into bed.

So why he was staring at the ceiling a few hours later was a mystery.

Foster groaned, glancing at the clock for the hundredth time. Three o'clock. Exactly twenty minutes later than the last time he'd checked. And an hour since the time before that.

He rolled onto his side, staring at the far wall. The one that separated his room from Mackenzie's. Sure, there were bathrooms and closets between them, but she was essentially on the other side of that partition. Sleeping.

At least, he assumed she was sleeping and not wandering aimlessly around the house. He hadn't heard so much as a cough or a scuff from that side of the house since he'd said goodnight three hours ago. And he hated that he'd been actively listening.

He pushed onto his elbows then swung his feet over the edge of the bed. He didn't like feeling this disjointed. As if he'd walked into a movie halfway through and was left trying to figure out the plot. But that's essentially what she'd done.

After her comments in the helicopter, he'd expected any future meetings to be civil but tense. Like two adversaries dancing around a shaky ceasefire. But then she'd stood on his porch, looking so damn beautiful with her long chestnut-colored hair tousled about her head, the ends curling from the rain, and her deep blue eyes staring warily at him, that all his previous tensions had vanished. He still wasn't sure why he'd invited her in, the words slipping free of their own accord. But he had to admit, he'd thoroughly enjoyed her company.

She was smart and witty, with a voice that prickled his skin, sending shivers along his nerves. And when she laughed... It was almost hypnotic in nature.

None of which was generally something he noticed. Not that he hadn't had relationships before. But he didn't *do* serious ones. Had never met anyone who'd had such an instant and intense effect on him. As if she'd woken a part of him he hadn't realized had been dormant.

Foster carded his fingers through his hair. The stress of being in the chopper had obviously messed with his head because this was so out of character, he was sure one of his buddies must have drugged him. Or used some kind of hypnosis on him while he'd been unconscious at the hospital. Something to explain why he'd rather sit there, staring at the wall, imagining her sleeping than close his eyes and actually sleep.

Chase. He was the reason Foster was tied in knots. Ever since his buddy had claimed Foster had feelings for Mac, he'd been stumbling. That hint of an idea bouncing around inside his brain until it had found a way to manifest itself.

Not that he was going to act on his feelings. Especially when he was convinced she still saw him as the guy who'd let her father down. Who was obviously fighting against demons and losing. Who was so close to the edge, it was a crap shoot which way he'd fall.

Foster stood, rolling his right shoulder in an effort to ease his muscles — stem the near-constant ache of all those plates and screws from the rescue. He took a step when his phone pinged, a message showing on the front. He grabbed it, sighing when he realized it was from her.

Hey, Beckett. Just letting you know I'm heading out. Thanks for letting me crash, so I didn't crash. Mac

Was that disappointment souring his gut? Making the room feel as if it was tilting? Or was the lack of sleep finally getting to him? Messing with his head the way the chopper ride had.

He glanced at the door when hers creaked, her hushed footfalls moving down the hall. They paused, as if she'd stopped to glance back — what he hoped was her having second thoughts — before continuing down the stairs. Each step echoing in his head until he thought he'd lose his mind.

Who was he kidding? He'd already lost his mind that fateful night. Buried the sane part of him with Sean's remains, leaving the ugly parts behind.

Foster lowered his butt onto the edge of the mattress as he closed his eyes and focused on breathing. On stilling his mind and reminding himself of all the reasons he was better off alone. How he'd never have to bare his soul — make peace with that night — if he stayed his course. Indulged in the odd one-night stand when the voices got a bit too loud.

And he was halfway to fooling himself into believing it when she screamed, her voice springing him into action. He was on his feet with his Sig in his hand and his cell shoved under the waistband of his pajama pants before the sound had faded — was clearing the hallway then racing down the stairs two seconds after that. Muscles primed. His head on a swivel.

Mackenzie had her back to the wall in the sitting room, staring at the window as her chest heaved, each frantic breath echoing through the room.

He hit the landing moving a bit faster than he should, clearing each direction before heading her way. The door was open, wind and rain blowing inside as more lightning flashed in the distance. She gasped when he shuffled in beside her, looking as if she was about to dump him on his ass before her head fell back against the wall, her fists dropping to her sides.

She swallowed, coughed, then drew herself up, pointing toward the window. "There was a silhouette standing in the doorway. I thought it was you, but then the guy turned and..." A shiver raced through her. "I realize now he was wearing night vision goggles but damn, seeing his head like that before it registered."

Mac wet her lips, pointing to the entrance. "He ran down the driveway but not before I saw someone else standing outside your window."

Foster nodded, shifting so he was between her and the door. Not that he thought they were still at risk, but he wasn't taking any chances. He palmed his phone, sending off a nine-one-one to his buddies. The word tangos highlighted in all caps.

Then he had her snugged at his back as he motioned to the kitchen. Mac fell in behind him, shadowing his every move as he cleared the sitting room, then continued on. He stayed in the main areas, heading for the kitchen when Chase barreled in the side door, his Sig leading the way. Zain swooped in like a wraith from the front a moment later, searching every shadow for a possible target.

He side-stepped over to them, signaling for them

to head for the counter as Chase joined Zain in the hallway. A few more hand signals, and they were gone, slinking down the hall then into the dark. Vanishing like shadows, an eerie silence taking their place.

Foster held his ground, wanting to help clear the house but aware he was better positioned there. Where anyone gunning for him or Mackenzie would have to show themselves, first. Though, why anyone would be hunting them, he wasn't sure. Only that whoever Mac had interrupted had scared her to the bone. And she didn't strike him as someone who frightened easily. Not if she'd completed six tours with the Coast Guard's Tactical Law Enforcement Teams, likely chasing drug dealers and weapons traffickers. The kind of assholes who shot first and worried if they'd killed the wrong people later.

A clock ticked in the background, the house falling into silence when Kash appeared out of the shadows, Nyx leashed to his waist. She was completely focused on Kash, practically twitching as she mirrored his every move, stopping when he stepped in beside Foster.

He scanned the room, his rifle notched at his shoulder. "Chase and Zain?"

Foster nodded toward the corridor. "Hallway and back rooms."

"I've cleared the perimeter. I'll check upstairs."

Then Kash was off, keeping his back snugged to

the wall as he climbed the stairs, disappearing down the hallway a moment later.

Mac gave Foster a slight shove. "Despite my initial reaction, I don't need a babysitter."

Foster snorted, not budging an inch. "Good because I'd prefer a partner. And we're staying here in case someone was looking for one of us. And yeah, I know that sounds crazy but..."

But he'd lived crazy for twenty years. And he wasn't about to ignore all his training now.

Mac stiffened behind him, her breath feathering across his back and shoulders as she inched a bit closer, her small hands landing on his waist. He smiled and eased back just enough to increase the pressure — calm the pounding in his chest.

While he wasn't as skilled as his buddies in ground combat or hand to hand, he could more than hold his own. Had faced off against a variety of threats when missions hadn't gone as planned. Or he'd had to break ranks in order to rescue a fellow soldier. But this was different. Knowing some dickhead might have been targeting Mackenzie — had followed her here in the hope of catching her once she'd left. Just thinking how she would have been exhausted and alone, possibly missing the fact she was being tailed...

Foster gave himself a mental shake. They didn't have any proof she was being targeted. In fact, it made more sense that if this wasn't some kind of sophisticated crime ring, the men had come gunning for him or one of his buddies. But he'd plan for every contingency until they'd put them all to rest.

Rain pattered against the window and roof as they stood there, waiting, until Chase and Zain reappeared, their guns no longer at the ready. They headed for the counter just as Kash came trotting down the stairs, Nyx still alert at his side.

His buddies converged on Foster's location, scanning the room one last time before relaxing slightly. Not enough they wouldn't respond to any sudden threat, but a few notches down from their DEFCON 1 state when they'd entered.

Zain arched a brow. "Everyone okay?"

Foster glanced back at Mackenzie. "Why don't you tell them what you saw."

She pursed her lips then repeated the story — a man with NVGs standing in the doorway. At least one more outside the window.

Zain frowned. "So, what are we thinking? Tech savvy burglars or something more sinister?"

Foster shrugged. "Hard to say, though the fact they were wearing NVGs is a bit… concerning. And with all this rain, any footprints or other evidence will be long gone by morning."

Zain nodded, still scanning the shadows. "Okay. Time to cut through the bullshit. We've all mentioned how we've come home a few times over the past six weeks and felt as if objects had been moved slightly. Nothing taken and nothing overt but…" Zain motioned to Kash. "Kash's mug incident with the handle facing the wrong way or my photo that was turned to name a couple. And we keep blaming each other for pulling a prank but the buck stops here. Beckett? You're our prime suspect and let's face it. It's the kind of crap you like to pull, so, have you been jerking us around or..."

Foster palmed his face, shaking his head. "I told you it wasn't me."

"You also said you weren't the one who'd wired all our headsets to blast *Baby Shark* every day for a week in Kandahar."

"And you claimed it wasn't you who put those Whip snakes in our sleeping bags in Serbia." Chase crossed his arms. "You know I hate snakes."

"Let's not forget about when we came back from the mess hall, and someone had nailed everything inside our tent to the floor." Kash arched a brow. "We know for sure it wasn't Zain, now."

Zain groaned. "I'm really not that bad with tools. And we also haven't missed how it all abruptly stopped as soon as we called you on it. Until now."

Foster sighed. "Fine. I'll admit. The headsets and the creative use of nails was me, but Sean put the snakes in everyone's sleeping bags, including his. Bastard excluded me because he knew you'd jump to conclusions. But I get your point. Except where I'm telling you I haven't been messing with you, and I haven't been moving stuff around."

Zain muttered under his breath. "Well, crap. You know I hate getting caught with my junk hanging out and I feel like I'm giving everyone a real good show right now. Though, it doesn't really make any sense. Who breaks in and only moves a mug or a photo around?"

Foster sighed. "I don't know but we definitely need to find out."

Mac moved out from behind him, giving him a guarded smile as she blew out a rough breath. "I should have noticed the guy sooner. Maybe I could have gotten a photo of him or watched to see if he jumped into a car — written down the license plate."

She coughed. "And while I'm not proud of how I reacted, for a split second, I honestly thought it was a monster. Or maybe a ghost. Something other than a creep wearing goggles."

Foster gave her shoulder a nudge. "We've all been caught by surprise and it's definitely not something you'd expect to see. Besides, you should hear Zain during a horror movie. It's tragic."

Zain rolled his eyes. "Shut up. I don't scream that much."

Chase gave Zain a slight shove. "Brother, you sound like Kash does when he sees a spider."

Kash gave Chase a much firmer shove, shaking his head in mock frustration. "I won't apologize for that. Spiders are just wrong."

Zain shrugged as he leaned against the counter. "Well, whoever it was is gone. But, we'll take turns patrolling, just to be safe. And I'm definitely upgrading your security."

He held up his hand, cutting Foster off before he could interrupt. "I know. I can't mess with the *charm* of the place, but they obviously bypassed the exterior alarms, so if nothing else, they need to be replaced."

Foster snorted. "You'll do it whether I approve or not so..." He cupped Mac's elbow. "Not that we have any proof these creeps were targeting you or me, I think it would be wise if you stayed until morning. Just to be safe. Besides, Atticus would have my ass if you got hurt on my watch."

Mackenzie cocked her head to the side. "I didn't realize staying here implied it was your watch?"

"We're ex-military. Anyone under our roof is part of our watch."

She eyed the door, releasing a weary breath as some of the tension eased from her shoulders. "I suppose it's the least I can do considering I started all of this."

"More like you saved me from getting caught with my pants down. If you hadn't been on your way out..." He didn't want to think what could have happened if the men had been looking for more than a quick score.

Kash pointed to the door. "Nyx and I will take first watch. She's way too hyped to settle for a while. I'll tag Zain in once I've worked off some of her energy."

Zain nodded. "I'll be ready, brother."

Mac cleared her throat, meeting each of their gazes. "I was thinking. I happen to know one of the deputies in town — Greer Hudson. She was an FBI agent for several years before moving out here. I could call her. Maybe have her meet us at the Lighthouse Café later in the week. I could ask her to do some discreet digging to see if there have been any other reports like this. Maybe see if Foster's parents had any run-ins?"

Chase arched a brow. "She'd do that? Off the books? Because I'm not sure we want to publicize it just yet. Give away any chance at sourcing this out without everyone in town knowing. No offence, but people spread rumors faster than wildfire around here."

"I'm pretty sure she'd keep it on the down low. If I ask nicely. The current sheriff's a bit of a tool. Hates anyone looking into closed cases or stuff he thinks isn't worthy of his time. But Greer's good people. And it wouldn't hurt to at least put it on her radar. In case this is some sort of ring, and they start targeting other homes."

Zain nodded, again. "Sounds like a plan. That should give us time to do a thorough walk through of all our places. See if anything's actually gone missing, now that we know it hasn't been Foster being his usual charming self."

"Then, it's a date. I'll call her first thing, and we'll say Friday after everyone's off shift?"

"I'll make sure Foster writes it down." Chase twirled his finger near the side of his head. "He's a bit nuts."

"Jackass." Foster gave them a once over. "And it's good to see you haven't lost your edge yet."

"Says the guy wearing only pajama pants. Do you seriously sleep in those?"

Foster walked his buddies to the door, nodding his thanks as they headed out. Kash took off with Nyx, oblivious to the rain still pouring down. Foster shut the door, checking the locks, twice, before looking at Mackenzie. Wondering how he'd missed that way her hair tumbled over her shoulders, the thick mass swaying with every subtle movement. Hints of gold gleaming with every flash of lightning. "You sure you're okay?"

She sighed, toeing one foot against the old wood floors. "Other than being completely embarrassed for a second time? Great."

"You've got nothing to be embarrassed about."

"Right because I didn't freeze and scream like a four-year old instead of tackling that asshole to the ground and ripping off those goggles like I've been trained to do."

"Nobody's perfect. And it doesn't make you any less of a badass because you didn't immediately go for the kill shot. But god forbid you come across as human."

"The Coast Guard didn't train me to be anything less than lethal."

"Point noted. And I'll be sure to stand back and let you take lead, next time." He smiled. "Besides, it gave me a chance to be a bit less of an asshole."

"I never thought you were an asshole, Beckett."

Foster leaned in, getting his mouth even with hers. She inhaled as she dropped her gaze to his lips then back to his eyes. "You know it's rude to lie to my face this early in our relationship, right?"

God, had he really just used the R word without even hesitating?

Mackenzie didn't flinch, inching impossibly closer. "I'll keep that in mind. Now, how do you feel about putting on a movie and falling asleep on the couch? Because there's no way I'm going to get any rest lying in some bed, wondering if every creak and groan is because the house is a hundred years old or because that jerk decided to come back."

"I think I can manage that. But behave yourself. I have a reputation to consider."

She laughed, the easy sound just as mesmerizing as before, then plopped down on the couch, smiling over at him when he sat next to her. She didn't talk, just snuggled under the blanket he gave her, falling asleep before he'd done more than flip on the television and dial in some cheesy romantic comedy.

Foster eased back, listening to her snuffle in her sleep, every breath whispering through the air. He had a bad feeling he'd gotten in way over his head, and it had nothing to do with the men who'd infiltrated his home.

CHAPTER FIVE

There must be something in the water in Raven's Cliff. A drug or maybe a parasite. A scientific reason that explained that how in less than a week, Mackenzie had gone from wanting to punch Foster Beckett in the mouth, to wanting to kiss him.

That, or she'd simply lost her mind.

Mac leaned back in the chair, sipping on her coffee when the door to the Lighthouse Café opened, and Beckett breezed in wearing jeans, a black hoodie and a puffer vest. His dark brown hair was windblown from the next incoming storm, and he stabbed his fingers through it as he scanned the crowd, his gaze clashing with hers.

He smiled, and her heart did a weird flutter. She wasn't sure if it stopped or sped up, but it took her breath away as he wove his way over, giving Chase a slap on the back when his best friend stood up.

Chase shook his head, motioning to the empty

seat beside Mac, and she couldn't help but wonder if they'd planned it so Foster would have to sit beside her. "How is it you always manage to be late?"

Foster shrugged. "Because you're closer than I am. You were supposed to text me *before* you left, remember? I was in the middle of finishing the woodwork on the sitting room wall. It took a hot minute to get the last piece in right before I could leave."

He looked at her, thumbing toward his buddies. "How do you work with them and not want to kill them?"

She laughed. "Who said I didn't?"

"Now we're talking."

He slid into the seat, a subtle mixture of pine and cottonwood drifting over to her. Was he wearing cologne? Or was that just his natural scent? Either way, it had her heart fluttering again as she smiled for no apparent reason.

Mac gave herself a mental slap. She needed to get a grip before she started giggling like a freaking teenager. Sure, the guy was handsome. She'd acknowledged that from the start. And she'd definitely seen a different side of him the other night. He'd been charming and intelligent, with a quick wit that had put her at ease. And when he'd appeared out of the dark, dressed in only those sexy pajama pants, all the muscles in his arms and torso flexing as he'd swept the room with his Sig — his long hair tousled around his face — she'd gotten a good look at the man her father had painted. The warrior part of him that wasn't suffering from some kind of trauma like in the helicopter.

And that had been the start of her descent into madness. One she was obviously continuing as she sat there, trying to focus on anything other than how good he smelled. It didn't help that he'd dropped by the hanger a few times during the week, bringing coffee for the crew. He'd even braved a couple conversations with her father, staying remarkably calm as he'd handed the man a cup.

Her dad had frowned, glanced at her, then smirked. After that, Atticus had stayed eerily quiet whenever Foster had stopped by. As if he knew something they didn't.

Obviously, Atticus had taken Foster's less confrontational approach as him starting to bend to her dad's way of thinking. And maybe Beckett was. Though, a part of her hoped he'd braved the visits because of her. Because he was just as confused as she was at whatever was transpiring between them. That moment she'd thought they'd shared the other night.

Before the men had broken into his house.

She shivered, goosebumps racing along her skin as she recalled the instant the guy had turned and all she'd registered were those monstrous eyes. She *never* screamed. Not during a scary movie and certainly not when faced with a threat. Yet, for a split second, she'd truly believed she'd come face-to-face with a monster.

Which was ridiculous. Sure, there were more than a few legends and ghost stories circulating through town. A couple directed specifically at that old manor house. But she'd never given them much credence. Had never shied away from a fight.

Fingers brushed along her arm, and she jumped, cursing inwardly when Foster frowned, glancing at his hand then up to her. "You back with us?"

She cringed when she realized his team was staring at her, eyes wide. Slight furrows in the brows. She smiled, doing her best to shake it off. "Never left. Why?"

"Either you were daydreaming or you're seriously reconsidering there should be a round two between us because I asked how the flight was and you just stared into space."

"I..." She scoffed, leaning back in her chair. "I guess I'm still on edge from screaming like a banshee the other night. I swear I will *never* live that down."

Foster scrunched up his face as if he thought she was nuts. Which, she probably was. "Forget it. Besides, the guys said you tackled some creep to the ground when he came raging into the hanger this morning. Sounds like your mojo's just fine."

"I think they exaggerated the incident a bit."

Kash snorted. "If anything, we underplayed it so Foster didn't get all protective. He has this thing about anyone threatening or disrespecting his team."

She glanced at Foster, smiling at how he looked as if he wanted to throttle Kash. "I'm not part of his team."

The three men chuckled, nodding at each other before answering, "Right," in unison.

Foster leaned in as he draped his left arm over the back of her chair. "As usual, ignore them. They share a brain when they're not working."

He'd said something about a brain. She knew that much. But everything else had gotten lost into the warmth of his arm against her back. How that tempting aroma surrounded her.

She blinked, praying he hadn't noticed how she'd all but sniffed him like a dog, only to groan inwardly when that sexy, traitorous mouth of his kicked up into a smirk. "Are you sure it's just the three of them and not all four of you?"

"Ouch." He removed his arm as he placed his hand on his chest. "Someone's showing their claws."

"Not quite." She nodded toward the entrance. "But we'll have to save that discussion for later because that's Greer."

The men turned as Deputy Hudson walked through the doorway, her long auburn hair twisted up into a messy bun. She wasn't wearing her usual uniform, opting for jeans, a sweater and a wool jacket. She waved to Mac, weaving her way through the crowd before stopping at the table. All four men stood, and Chase held out the chair to his right for her.

Greer arched a brow but accepted his offer, looking straight at Mac. "And they say chivalry's dead."

Chase cleared his throat as he reclaimed his seat. "It's a show of respect. Nothing more."

Greer smiled. "Easy there, flyboy. I'm just yanking on your chain."

Chase thumbed toward Foster. "He's the flyboy. I'm the medic."

"Ah, that means you're Chase Remington, right? And he's *Beckett*."

Foster coughed. "Why does everyone say my last name like that?"

Greer shrugged. "Like what?"

"Like it's the town's new curse word."

"Atticus might have used it like that for the past couple months. I guess it's caught on."

"I'll have to remember to properly thank him."

Greer nodded at the server when she held up a coffee pot. "Which means you must be Kash Sinclair and Zain Everett."

Zain frowned. "I'm not sure if we should be impressed or concerned you already know all our names. I'm pretty sure we haven't actually met."

"Nope, but I make it a point to learn a bit about everyone in town. Though, you boys made it easy. Ex-military with impressive records. I didn't even need to venture past page two."

Kash coughed, rubbing his chest when his coffee

must have gone down funny. "You have multiple pages on us?"

"Can't be too careful after what went down last year." She gave Mac a slight nod. "That's a black mark on my record, and I won't let anything like that happen again on my watch."

Foster eyed Greer, and Mac felt an odd pang in her chest. Surely, she wasn't jealous of Greer because Beckett had smiled at the other woman. Though it wasn't the same way he smiled at her, was it?

Beckett must have felt Mac staring at him because he shifted his gaze, and damn — the way his face lit up. As if he'd won the lottery. Or maybe it was just wishful thinking on Mac's part, and he beamed at everyone like that.

Greer accepted the coffee mug, taking a cautious sip as she relaxed in the chair. "So, Beckett. Mackenzie said you had some unwanted visitors the other night."

Foster nodded. "Two, according to Mac. And we're fairly certain either that crew or another one has been inside before. What my buddies had brushed off as me pranking them but wasn't. Though, it's strange. They don't appear to be taking anything, just the odd object not put back correctly."

Greer nodded, scribbling some notes on a pad she'd removed from her pocket. "There're four buildings on the property, right?"

"And from what we can tell, they've been in each one."

She reached into her inner pocket, removing a stack of folded papers. She slid them across to Foster, waiting until he'd opened them. "So, I did as Mac asked and looked into the recent history of that house you inherited. Seems your father reported a series of suspicious incidents starting shortly after they purchased it a year, ago. But based on the rather flimsy files, it was all just brushed off as kids or vagrants looking for a place to stay. As you know, the house was vacant for nearly twenty years before it finally came on the market."

Foster drew his finger along one of the sheets, then passed it to his buddies. "There's barely anything in here? Did Sheriff Thompson even drag his ass out there?"

"Hard to tell. I'd only been here about six months, and I'd been relegated to all the remote jobs. For that first year, I hardly spent any actual time in town, always driving out to check on bogus poaching reports. Or seemingly non-existent petty crime. But I had the same reaction you did, so I dug a bit deeper. Have any of you heard of a man named Dr. Elias Carrington?"

Chase nodded. "Isn't he the sketchy doctor who engineered that drug the military was hoping would be a game changer for PTSD patients? Vexarin I think?"

Greer grinned. "Yahtzee. It underwent a series of trials, but according to the FDA, prolonged use resulted in a number of severe side-effects including paranoia, hallucinations, and aggressive behavior. They refused to approve the drug, and it seemingly vanished shortly after."

"I encountered some soldiers who were taking it. To say their behavior was unpredictable was an understatement. But what does that have to do with Foster's place, Raven's Manor?"

Greer nodded at the next page in Foster's hand. "Seems Dr. Carrington also tried to buy the property, but the will stipulated that a local had to take possession. Carry on the legacy I suppose."

Foster tapped the top sheet. "And you think, what? That Carrington's suddenly donning night vision goggles and lurking around my house in an effort to scare me off so I'll sell?"

"I don't know but if you look at the very first report your dad made when he first started the renovations, he found some old invoices and script sheets from Carrington's company, GeneTide. The only reason it's even in the record is because an ex-deputy, Bodie Page, took that initial call your father made of suspicious people trespassing on the property. Recorded it separately. After that, Thompson was the only officer to deal with the incidents. And it was never mentioned again."

Foster frowned, glancing at Mac before shaking his head. "I realize the lawyer implemented some peripheral security, but the property was essentially vacant for three months. If someone didn't want me here, they could have torched it or something equally damning. Persuaded me not to come, at all."

"Except where your dad had already hired that private security company. I only know that because that ex-deputy I mentioned — Page — owns it. He told me John Beckett signed a contract for twenty-four-hour overwatch with them staying in one of the finished outbuildings shortly after that first call when Bodie decided to go private. And Page said they maintained that round-the-clock vigil until you moved in."

"My dad was an ex-Army Ranger. He wasn't the kind of man to outsource security. Why the hell would he hire people to watch the house and not tell me what he thought was going on that he needed that level of protection?"

"That, I don't know." Greer leaned back in her chair, taking a healthy gulp of her coffee. "This could all be nothing more than a new brand of burglar or some kind of hazing for local frats. That place does have a bit of a ghostly history. And I'm sure there's a logical reason as to why there might have been some old papers in the house. It's not like it had any kind of robust security before they bought it. Just a caretaker, I think. But I'd be lying if I said something didn't feel off. Though, I'd have to call in a few favors if I wanted to look deeper into Carrington and GeneTide and see if there were other incidents at the house that are buried in old records. Especially if you want me to keep it on the down low. Which I'll do, but I wanted to see what you thought. Let you know it could take a week or two to get the intel."

Foster looked around at his buddies, and Mac swore something passed between them. As if they'd had a conversation without saying a word. "And you'd do that?"

Greer smiled. "For you? Undecided. But for Mac? She's already promised to lend a hand if I ever need a chopper. And Atticus would have my badge if I disrespected his *golden boy*."

Foster coughed, pounding on his chest a few times as he swallowed. "Golden boy?"

"Hey, don't hate the messenger. Though I find it ironic that he alternates between cussing you out and singing your praises. Guess we're all waiting to see which side of the coin you finally land on."

"Good to know I have options."

"Do you? Because..." Her voice trailed off as she focused on the front of the café.

Mac turned, scanning the crowd when their server palmed the counter, clearing it in a single leap before grabbing some hulking biker guy by the arm. She ducked the swing he aimed at her head, landing two hits to his neck and chest before spinning and smashing his head into a nearby table. Pinning his arm behind him as she kicked his feet apart.

Another guy lunged at her, but she downed him with a boot to the knee followed by another to his jaw when he tried to stagger to his feet.

Foster and his team were charging over a second

later, beating her and Greer to the table by a couple steps. Chase and Zain grabbed the guy splayed out on the floor, yanking him to his feet as Foster and Kash stopped next to the guy still face-down on the table. Blood pooling beneath his nose.

The woman leaned over, lifting his arm higher until he cried out. "Next time, don't pick on someone you think is weak, or I'll get serious."

She released him when Kash nodded at her, bending to retrieve a tattered purse off the floor. She returned to the counter, handing it to an elderly lady who looked as if a strong wind could blow her over. "Sorry for the inconvenience, Shirley. I'll cover your tab."

Shirley shook her head, eyes wide. Her hand visibly shaking. "How did you do that?"

The woman shrugged, glancing around at the room full of people staring at her. As if just now realizing she was the center of attention. "Self-defense classes at the Y."

"Those must have been some classes. And you don't have to pay—"

"My pleasure. And get a can of that pepper spray I talked to you about. Creeps like that tend to take advantage of sweet ladies like yourself."

Shirley nodded, shuffling around the scene then out the door.

Greer walked over, shouldering up beside the woman. "That was impressive. Jordan, right?"

Jordan nodded. "Sorry about the scene. But I saw

him grab her purse, and I just kind of reacted." She walked over and grabbed a cloth. "I don't like bullies."

"So, I noticed."

Jordan wiped down the table once Kash had moved the guy over to one of the stools at the counter, giving him what Mac could only describe as one of his death glares. "I also saw a white Tacoma drive past." She paused to make eye contact with Greer. "Three times. Which is odd when there are parking spots right out front. The driver was a white dude with a military-style crew cut. I tried to get the license number, but it was caked with mud. I did confirm that it had California plates. Might be worth checking out, in case it's some kind of gang."

Greer looked at Mac then back to Jordan. "You noticed a truck driving past? With the café practically overflowing?"

"It was pretty obvious."

"Right." Greer handcuffed the two men, thanking Zain and Chase when they volunteered to drag them out to her car. "You ever consider police work? Something tells me you'd be damn good it."

Jordan chuckled. "Not really my thing. But thanks."

"Let me know if you change your mind." Greer walked over to Foster. "So, Beckett? You want me to do that deep dive?"

"If you're willing." He smiled and motioned to Mac. "And it won't cost Mackenzie her soul."

"Her, never. You, on the other hand." She slapped him with her notebook, nodding at Mac. "I'll be in touch."

Kash cozied up across from Jordan when she moved back behind the counter. "The Y, huh?"

Jordan glanced up, paused as she studied Kash for several moments, then looked away. "Every woman should know how to defend herself."

"No argument there. Though, that looked a bit more than simple defensive training."

"Did it?" She continued to clean the same spot. "You guys cashing out or..."

Mac waved. "I'm starving..."

Her pager went off a moment before Kash, Chase and Zain's joined in as the other two men walked back inside, the telltale tone killing any hopes of calling it an early night. Maybe seeing if Foster was up to watching a movie. Not that she'd ask him, but she'd been secretly hoping they'd suggest a game of poker at his place or something equally benign, and she'd have an excuse to hang out.

Foster handed Jordan a few bills, waving it off when she arched a brow before placing his hand on the small of Mac's back and ushering her toward the door. Heat seared across her skin, the simple touch nearly dropping her to her knees.

She managed to make it outside without face-planting on the floor, waving to his team when they headed for their trucks. "Thanks for the coffee."

"Not quite what I'd had in mind but..."

She bit her tongue before she could ask him what he'd been hoping for, unsure if she was prepared to hear the answer. "Guess this means you can get back to your woodwork."

"I'm living the dream. Which reminds me, I have something for you."

Foster darted over to his truck, rummaging around in the rear before closing the door and jogging back over. He handed her a box, crossing his arms once she'd taken it. "Open it."

She held up her hand when one of his buddies honked their horn. "And here I didn't get you anything."

Foster huffed. "Relax. It's not a ring or anything."

She tore open the cardboard, staring at the advanced nav unit. "You got me a new Forward Looking Infrared screen?"

"The camera mount on your rig is actually pretty decent, but the screen in your chopper's a piece of crap. I don't know how Atticus expects you to actually see anyone who isn't standing out in the open waving their arms with what he's got connected."

"How do you even know what's there?"

"I realize I was on my ass in the back for part of the ride, but I noticed." He shrugged. "It's no big deal."

"No big deal?" She turned it over in her hands, praying her mouth wasn't hanging open as she read the specs. "These things are more elusive than Bigfoot. How did you even get your hands on one?"

"I have connections."

She balked. "You had one of your Air Force buddies acquire this for you?"

Foster smiled, and it was just like back in the café with his face lighting up as his eyes burned into a deep turquoise. "I'd tell you, but…"

"Right." She groaned when Chase pulled his truck up as close as possible. "I'll be right there."

Chase scoffed. "Just freaking kiss already. We've got a call."

Foster closed his eyes as he tipped his head back. Looking as if he was searching for some form of Zen before focusing on her. "Chase was obviously dropped on his head as an infant."

She tiptoed up and gave him a peck on his cheek. "Thanks. This was really…"

"Just go. And get Charlie to hook that up so your father doesn't think you're reckless."

"He'd never call me reckless."

"Sorry to break it to you, sweetheart, but he already did, that first night."

Sweetheart?

Foster inhaled as soon as the words sounded around them, staring at her until Chase honked, again. "Be safe. And make smart choices."

"Pretty sure you're the risk taker."

She held up the box then rounded Chase's truck, jumping inside. Chase made a face at Beckett then drove off, leaving her staring out the back as Foster slowly faded from sight.

She turned the navigational unit over in her hands, again, an unfamiliar warmth spreading through her core. While she'd had her share of boyfriends, they'd never really embraced her job, which was part of the reason nothing had ever gotten serious. Not that Foster was her boyfriend. In fact, she wasn't sure what he was, other than a source of frustration. An unrelenting ache slowly building in her gut.

Mackenzie pushed the thought away as Chase pulled into the hanger parking lot, already jumping out and heading for the main doors. She pressed the box against her chest as she followed suit. She'd take it slow. Maybe find a way to drop by without *looking* as if she was dropping by. And if she was lucky, fate might intervene.

CHAPTER SIX

"Damn it."

Foster shook out his hand, rubbing his thumb as he tried to ease the stinging ache shooting through his palm. This was the third time he'd jammed his finger trying to get the shelving to slide through the groove, and he was about ready to toss the entire bookcase across the room.

Fatigue strained his shoulders, and he rolled them, acutely aware of how the right one clunked, the plates and screws shifting a bit with every rotation.

The wind howled outside, rattling the windows in what was shaping up to be another biblical-like storm raging across the coast. After spending so much time overseas, he'd forgotten how intense the Pacific Northwest was during the fall and winter. While the thunderstorm they'd experienced a few weeks ago was a rare occurrence, fierce storms with punishing rain and damaging winds swept through often. Though, it was also one of the reasons he loved this part of the country. It always seemed so alive.

Foster tossed the mallet onto the pile of wood then, made his way over to the window. Fog curled through the trees as they lashed against each other, rain already running in rivulets down the driveway. The setting sun cast the entire area in an odd gray glow, the last remnants of daylight fading into the growing dusk.

He speared his fingers through his hair, unsure if it was the weather or his thoughts that had him on edge. He and his buddies had patrolled the property ever since Mac had interrupted those men that night two weeks ago but hadn't found any concrete evidence. Nyx had picked up on some kind of scent more than a few times, but Kash had always come up empty. Just the odd footprint to suggest they weren't imagining the incidents. Though nothing they could trace back to Carrington or GeneTide.

Hell, to anyone.

And the fact there hadn't been any form of unwanted intrusions since that night seemed to suggest Foster and his team were making far more out of this than needed. That it was likely as benign as they'd guessed. More tech-savvy burglar ring and less mercenary out to cap one of them.

Foster hadn't allowed the lack of activity to stop

him from searching through his father's stuff. All the boxes he'd shoved in his dad's office because he'd either been unable or unwilling to go through it. Even now, almost five months later, simply looking at it gutted him. Knowing he'd wasted those last few years. More than a few if he were being honest. Not that his parents had ever complained. They'd lived the life long before he was born, and Foster knew they were proud he'd chosen to dedicate his life to the service.

Continue his father's legacy.

He swallowed. Maybe if he'd found something to connect their unexplained experiences with his current ones, he wouldn't have this hollowness in the pit of his stomach. An emptiness that had only grown with Sean's death and what threatened to eventually pull him under.

Except when he was with Mackenzie.

For some unknown reason she scattered all the guilt and hurt, filling that void with a sense of excitement he hadn't felt outside of flying. All the times he'd avoided a bogey or taken a crazy risk only to have it save his ass. He'd only known her for a few weeks, and already she'd become a habit he wasn't sure he could break.

Foster tipped back his head. He was losing it. Slipping off the deep end because he wasn't even sure if she liked him. Sure, she'd found excuses to drop by most nights — just like he'd manufactured reasons to show up at the hanger. Hell, he'd purchased more avionics and imaging equipment than she could probably fit in her helicopter, just so he could see her without looking as if he was trying to see her. But there was something intoxicating about watching her face light up. Knowing she was a thousand times safer than when he'd first flown with her.

He glanced at his watch, wondering how it seemed so dark when it was only five thirty. Chase had texted him thirty minutes ago to say that with the intensity of the incoming system, they'd called it a day and that he and Zain were heading over to the sheriff's station to meet up with Greer. She'd hinted she might have some intel. Which meant Mackenzie would have been bouncing along the gravel driveway by now if she was going to show up.

There was no mistaking the instant punch of disappointment at the empty road.

He wandered into the kitchen and grabbed a pop, all that restless energy making his muscles twitch. This was why he sucked at relationships. He'd never figured out how to successfully navigate the airspace between friends and lovers without eventually crashing and burning. How far to push that envelope until he'd inadvertently busted right through, usually with him getting the boot. Not that he'd ever really been thoroughly invested, but this time felt distinctly different. And he couldn't help but wonder if he'd waited too long. Left that part of him lonely and buried to the point it was beyond resurrecting.

If there wasn't enough of his heart left to save.

He bounced the thoughts around, ambling back toward the sitting room when someone banged on the door. He placed his drink on a coaster then picked his way over to the entrance, yanking the slab open.

Mackenzie stood on the porch, hair dripping, a case of beer in one hand. She tilted her head to the side, her gaze traveling the length of him and back as she bit at her bottom lip, looking incredibly sexy in her obvious indecision.

Foster swung the door aside, leaning against the frame as he nodded at the six pack. "Do you plan on sharing that?"

Her mouth curved into a stunning smile, and he had to fist his hand against the wood to stop from grabbing her jacket and dragging her against him. Finally claiming those full lips with his. "It seemed like an appropriate offering in order to quell my curiosity."

"Curiosity?"

"I needed to see for myself if you had a helicopter stashed in one of the rooms and were bringing it to the hanger one piece at a time."

"Just the instrument panel." He waved her in, shutting out the wind and rain before leaning against the door and wondering how the room felt suddenly full just by having her walk inside.

Mackenzie turned, brushing some of her wet hair off her face as she set the beer on the floor. She shook out her jacket, hanging it on one of the ornate hooks before turning to look at him, a hint of pink slowly coloring her cheeks.

She shifted on her feet, finally blowing out a rough breath when he just stood there, staring. "Have I got something on my face?"

He opened his mouth to utter a witty comeback but all that made it past the lump in his throat was a harsh rasp.

Her smile faded and she took a step closer. "Beckett?"

He moved. Covered the three steps separating them before snagging her around the waist and pulling her close. She inhaled as he spun, backing her up until he'd effectively changed their places, her body pressed against the door. Foster braced one arm above her head, palming his other hand beside her waist as he forced air in then blew it out. Anything to try and regain some control.

Mackenzie blinked, as if she was still trying to get her bearings before she relaxed against the door, looking up at him with that brilliant blue gaze. He leaned closer, getting his face even with hers when she lifted one hand and touched his cheek, her cold damp fingers sending shivers down his spine.

She waited, her gaze locked on his before she sighed and inched closer. "Foster."

The way she said his first name... It pooled heat in his groin — had him picturing all the ways he wanted to touch her. Feel all that creamy skin pass beneath his hands.

He sucked in a shaky breath, muttering the first thing that formed on his tongue. "God, you're beautiful."

Her fingers curled against his jaw, the tips catching on the thick layer of stubble. "Have I gotten this all wrong or has there been something brewing between us since that first night in the chopper?"

"You haven't gotten it wrong. It's just..." He huffed, trying to find the right words. "I'm crap at this."

She arched her brows. "At foreplay? Because that's not the way I'd describe you."

The corner of his mouth twitched. Just thinking she was on the same page as him messed with his head. Had him considering utterly foreign thoughts. "Then, let's put that theory to the test."

He brushed his mouth over hers, keeping the contact light. Drinking in her gasp of anticipation as she held her breath, the hand on his cheek shaking slightly before she closed her eyes — pressed her lips to his.

He lost it, that hint of increased contact setting him off. He lifted his hand from the wall, fisting it in her hair as he ate at her mouth, tangling his tongue with hers until his lungs burned and he broke away. Not that she gave him much time to suck in some air before she took control, her fingers slipping behind his neck, curling in his hair and dragging him closer until he had her crushed against the door, his chest heaving in sync with hers.

She nipped at his jaw, her breath nearly as rough as his as she stared up at him, that stunning blue looking more like steel in the warm lamp light.

She wet her lips, closing her eyes for a moment before smiling. "That was…"

He gave her a fleeting kiss. "Adequate?"

"Hard to gauge. I think I need you to do that again."

"Your wish, sweetheart…"

He dove in, kissing her harder. Deeper. Taking his cue from every raspy sound she made. A groan, and he increased the pressure. A purr, and he broke off just long enough to nip at the pulse point fluttering at the base of her neck before capturing her mouth, again. Repeating his assault until she had one leg wrapped around his calf, her other hand fisted in his shirt.

He slipped his hand free of her hair then pulled back, trying to calculate how to pick her up and carry her to bed without losing an inch of contact. She looked ready to climb her way up his torso, when both their phones rang, the clashing tones destroying the sensual atmosphere.

She jumped, whacking her head on the door as he nearly fell on his ass, her leg catching him in the knee. He fumbled both their weight, finally regaining his balance enough to palm the door.

He reached into her rear pocket, loving how her breath hitched as he cupped her ass before snagging her phone and handing it over.

She stared at it for a few moments, frowning as he retrieved his. "It's Zain."

Foster glanced at his, ice sluicing through his veins. "Mine, too."

They answered in unison, putting both on speaker as a horn blared in the background, wind and rain echoing through the room.

"Zain?" Foster cursed when nothing sounded but the storm. "Damn it, talk to us."

"Foster, Mac, I..." The line cut out, his voice sounding like a garbled robot before it picked up again. "Need..."

"We'll be there, buddy, just tell us where you are."

More odd sounds, then he was back. Slightly clearer. "On the road up here..." His voice faded into a grunt, his breath coming in rough pants. "Upside down but Chase and Greer..."

"What about Chase and Greer?"

"River. Beckett... Danger..."

Mac gave Foster a shove, but he was already moving. Racing upstairs and retrieving one of his rifles from his gun cabinet before running back down, taking the steps two at a time. He grabbed his coat and his keys as he fumbled with his cell, hitting Kash's number. Mac had her jacket back on and was out the door heading straight for his truck before Kash's phone even connected.

Kash answered on the second ring, sounding as if he'd just gotten home. "Sorry, Beck, but we think you and Mac should—"

"Zain's in trouble. Something about being upside down. Possible threat. And there's something wrong with Chase and Greer. I think they went off the road. Chase's truck is here, so they must be driving Greer's Bronco. It might be in a river. I need you and Nyx in your truck. Two minutes ago, if possible. And Kash... Bring everything."

Kash hung up without saying another word. Foster shoved his cell in his pocket as he did a quick check of his supplies, placing the rifle on the console between him and Mac then jumping behind the wheel. Kash appeared a moment later on the path to the rear of the property, running full out, only slightly slower than Nyx. He practically bounced off the truck when he hit it still sprinting, starting it up and pulling in behind Foster in what had to have been some kind of Olympic record.

Mac had her cell in her hand. "Emergency services says they'll send a response team as soon as they can and to update them with a more accurate location once we know what we're facing. But with the rain, the distance and all the multiple calls, it'll likely be at least twenty minutes."

"I have a very bad feeling they don't have that much time."

Foster roared down the driveway, fishtailed onto the road then punched the gas. They didn't talk as he raced along the slick surface, fast but not reckless. Crashing wouldn't save anyone, and Foster knew the situation had to be pretty desperate for Zain to sound the way he had. That he was probably hurt far worse than Foster wanted to acknowledge because his buddy generally cursed a blue streak when he was in pain.

Rain poured from the sky, the wipers barely keeping up as the fog ate away most of Foster's visibility, threatening to send them over the cliff at every turn. He passed the corner where they'd dealt with the van and kept going, following the twisting road until it finally turned away from the shoreline and headed inland, winding through trees and rocky plateaus as it snaked toward town. He slowed when he reached the section where there was even a possibility of an SUV landing in a river — hoping he'd be able to see just a hint of one of the vehicles in the unrelenting fog — when his heart stopped dead.

Zain's truck. The tires still spinning against the gray sky, the front end pointing down toward the edge of a gully or ravine. Smoke poured out of the hood, a few flames flickering out the side.

Foster had his truck parked and was rounding the flatbed in five seconds flat. He grabbed a fire extinguisher and a crowbar, tossing the first aid kit to Mac. "Get the rifle and cover our six."

He didn't ask her if she could handle his Sauer, trusting that even if the Coast Guard hadn't beaten all that training into her, Atticus had. That she was likely as deadly as any of his buddies.

Kash was at Foster's side and hoofing it over to Zain's truck a heartbeat later, Nyx racing in front.

Kash whistled and twirled his finger once they reached the vehicle and the mutt took off. What looked like a perimeter search.

Mac was scanning the area, glancing over at them, then scanning again. Back and forth until she must have been satisfied the area was clear and moved in beside him. "I'll go do a quick recon to see if I can locate Chase and Greer."

Foster nodded as he went straight for the fire, dosing the entire front section until the extinguisher ran dry. He'd try to find Zain's if the flames picked back up before they'd gotten his buddy out, but for now, he doubted the engine would blow.

Kash was at Zain's door trying to open it before banging on the window. "Zain!"

Zain groaned, then faded, the seatbelt keeping him suspended.

"Damn it, Zain!"

No sustained response had Kash moving — busting out the rear window then crawling through. He placed his jacket between Zain and the driver's window, holding firm while Foster smashed the glass into a thousand tiny squares.

He swept away any pieces still clinging to the frame before going to one knee and placing two fingers along Zain's neck. "Pulse is steady, but he's got a gash across his forehead and blood soaking through his sweater. It might be his shoulder, but I can't be certain with him hanging upside down."

Kash was tugging on the seatbelt, trying to get it

loose. "It's impossible to tell if he simply went off the road or was forced somehow."

Mac darted in beside him, her hair already dripping as she kneeled in the mud. "I didn't find anything. No tracks, no debris trail."

"They've got to be close. No way Zain would just keep driving." Foster rubbed his knuckles along Zain's sternum like he'd seen Chase do in the field, relaxing a bit when his buddy bolted awake, struggling against the belt as he blinked half a dozen times, his breath sounding more labored than normal. "Easy, Zain. You're still in the truck."

Zain turned his head, growling when it must have set off a chain reaction of pain. "Chase!"

"Haven't found him yet. Let's get you—"

"No. No time. The river…" He shouted as he tried to undo his seatbelt.

"Jesus, stop moving before you do more damage. Now, what's this about a river?"

Zain grunted out a few breaths, definitely sounding as if he wasn't sucking in enough air. "On the other side of the road. Greer's Bronco suddenly shot up and flew off, then rolled out of sight. My truck was tumbling the other way a moment later. But I know the terrain along here — been studying it just in case — and there's nothing but raging rivers on both sides of this stretch. So, stop standing there and go!"

"I'll get Zain out then meet up with you two." Kash waved off Foster's huff. "Nyx will let me know if there's a threat. You need Mac to have your six. Go. We'll join you."

Foster stood, staring directly at Kash. "Do *not* make me regret leaving you both here."

"Not a chance. Now go save Chase and Greer."

CHAPTER SEVEN

Mac was on her feet as Foster stared at Kash for a few more seconds, having what she swore was another one of their unspoken conversations before Foster grunted, then took off. Mac raced behind him, shadowing his every move. Still scanning the area in case that danger Zain had mentioned jumped out at them.

Foster stopped to clear the road then darted across and down the slight hill on the other side. He slipped a few times on the wet gravel, catching his balance before he'd actually fallen as he picked his way along the rocky ground, stopping at the edge of a near identical gully. White water churned through the narrow river, the strong current carrying branches and other debris along the winding path.

Mac shouldered up beside him, searching the surface for any sign of Greer's Bronco. She paused at what looked like twin ruts farther up the bank, though with all the rain and mist it was impossible to tell what had made them. She took a step closer, inhaling when she spotted what looked like the top half of a vehicle, the white color blending in with the raging water. "Beckett!"

That's all she managed past the lump in her throat — the fear that maybe they'd wasted what little time Chase and Greer had. That all they'd find was the sum of their failures.

Mackenzie didn't wait for Beckett to follow her outstretched arm, she just took off running, jumping over downed logs and thorny bushes. A few branches clawed at her pants, but she pushed through, stopping on the bank next to the Ford.

The roof was caved inward, a large stump half-buried in the windshield. Chase was slumped against the steering wheel, water already filling the cabin all the way to the dash. Mac couldn't see Greer through the fogged up window but it was obvious they didn't have much time before the river swallowed them.

Foster tried the doors, but they wouldn't budge, everything twisted to the point it would take a spreader to get them open. He banged on the glass, staring at Chase as if he could will the man to reply. "Chase!"

Chase jolted upright, shouting when the movement obviously hurt before glancing around the interior. He blinked, finally nodding at Foster when he banged on the glass again before letting his head tilt backwards. "I hear you."

Foster glanced at her, mouth pinched tight, eyes wary before focusing on Chase. "We'll get you out, just hold on."

Chase mumbled something that sounded like him having nowhere else to go, as the water roared past the vehicle, a thick fog curling in around them.

Mac ran to the rear of the Bronco, pointing at the broken window. "There."

Foster grunted then hopped into the river, nearly getting swept away when a large log hit the back end a foot from where he was standing. The impact tipped the vehicle forward, the sides grating against the rocky slope as it jerked ahead, then stopped, even lower than before.

Foster climbed onto the bumper, clearing any bits of glass from the frame before trying to wedge himself through. But after a couple minutes, it was obvious he wasn't going to fit.

He slammed the crowbar against the back, glancing up at her. "I can't fit. Not with it crushed like this."

Mac held his gaze. "Bet I can."

She placed the rifle on the bank and was in the water then up on the bumper a few seconds later. Praying she didn't send the entire vehicle shooting down the rapids simply by altering the weight.

Foster snagged her wrist, eyes narrowed. His nostrils flaring. "Mackenzie..."

"Not my first rescue."

"But this is different. You're not in a chopper and it's personal."

She swallowed, gagged a bit, but drew herself up. "All the more reason to get this party started. Crowbar."

He handed her the rod, still holding it. "Just promise me you won't trade your life for theirs."

"Would you make that promise?"

He pursed his lips, and she knew he had more honor than to lie to her face. "Be careful."

"Don't go anywhere."

He rolled his eyes as she accepted his help, wiggling back and forth as she tried to shimmy through the narrow space. It took Foster giving her a firm shove before she finally made it inside, more water rushing in with her.

She crawled over the rear seats then up to the front, leaning over the console until she was level with Chase. "Hey."

Chase motioned toward Greer. "Her pulse is thready and she's unresponsive. We're probably looking at internal injuries. You need to get her out. Now."

Mac nodded. "What about you? Can you move?"

"Just worry about Greer, then we can work on me."

Mac frowned, wishing she could see beneath the water — check if Chase was hiding something he didn't want her to know — but there wasn't time. Instead, she reached for the roof panels, using the crowbar until the one over Greer finally gave. Not fully, but with a good amount of pulling and pushing, Chase would *probably* squeeze through.

Foster was there a moment later, bending the jammed panel forward as much as possible. Though, even with him putting all his weight on it, there wasn't enough room for him to get through — to take Mac's place. But at least she wouldn't have to drag Greer out the back.

It took a bit or work to get Greer's seatbelt unbuckled and her chair shifted enough that Mac could ease Greer free. Mac took a breath then plunged beneath the water until she'd wrapped her arms around Greer's waist in an effort to heave her through the opening. Foster reached in, bodily lifting Greer clear once Mac had the other woman's head and shoulders through the hole. He didn't even need any help — just his arms under Greer's and she was out.

Which only highlighted how much higher the water was. How it swirled all the way up to Chase's shoulders as if freeing Greer had created some kind of vacuum.

Mac turned, her hip still braced on that ridiculously narrow console as she breathed heavily. "Okay, your turn."

Chase made eye contact as he sighed. "My left leg's pinned."

The inklings of fear bubbled in her gut, but she pushed it aside. "Then, let's unpin it."

"Mackenzie…"

"No." She leaned in close, their breath mixing. "I'm not leaving you here. Period. So, get that thought right out of your head."

"I'm not sure—"

"I said no. Now, let's find a way to get that leg free."

She reached underwater until she was able to squeeze the crowbar between Chase's seat and the dash, sliding it down enough she was confident it wouldn't slip out the moment she put any pressure on it. Chase pressed his torso into the seat as she pulled on the long rod, grunting when nothing happened.

She stopped, shaking her head as she sucked in some air. "There's no way I can move the steering column."

"I know. That's what I've been trying to say. There's no time—"

"There's still plenty of time, and I bet my ass I can move the chair. Hold tight."

She pulled the crowbar out then shifted back, shoving it between the rails and the rear section of the console. What she hoped would be enough to wrench it back a few inches. Sweat mixed with the water on her brow as she yanked on the bar, using her foot against the door to give some added strength. The seat shook, rocking back and forth before sliding an inch.

Mac stopped, her chest heaving, every muscle aching as she leaned over Chase, again. "Any better?"

He cried out as he did something with that leg, the water above him swirling around. "Not enough."

"Then, I'll move it more."

"Mac..."

"I said no is not an option, Chase." She got impossibly closer. "I wasn't there for Josh. Didn't have his back, but I'm here, now. And I'll damn well have yours. Which means we either both get out of here, or we both drown. And I'd rather not die today, so get ready to move that leg."

The Bronco shook as Foster climbed back on top, poking his head in the hole. "We need to move this along. The river's really rising."

"Just a few more minutes..."

He frowned, and Mac knew she'd been right. That he wanted to take her place. Be the one to rescue his best friend. What would probably be an easy feat for him. But seeing how close Greer had been to the edges of the opening, it was obvious Foster wouldn't fit no matter how hard he tried. In fact, the more Mac thought about it, the less convinced she was that Chase would squeeze through, even with her help, but she'd have to worry about that once he was free.

A rush of water got her moving. Shifting back until she was heaving on that bar. Bracing both legs against the door, this time, aware she'd fall backwards when it finally gave but not caring. Whatever it took to get Chase free.

The seat was rocking again, all that water bubbling up when an eerie groan reverberated through the vehicle before the entire Bronco shifted. It shot forward, bouncing along the riverbed, tossing them around like rag dolls as water surged through the cab, bringing branches and leaves with it.

Some of the debris battered against Mac's side, tearing lines through her clothes before she finally pushed to the surface, gasping in air as the water churned around her. She glanced at Chase, but his chair was completely submerged. Just his hands grasped around the wheel as he tried to lever himself up.

She took a deep breath then went underwater, sealing her mouth on his and giving him whatever air was left. Then she was cresting the surface and moving back. She grabbed the crowbar one more time and pulled. All the anger, the guilt, spurring her on. Her internal clock ticked in the background, slowly counting down Chase's chances of making it out when the seat let loose, sending her careening backwards.

She hit the far window and pain ricocheted through her skull as everything went dark for a moment. Then a hand wrapped around her sweater and yanked her back up.

She coughed, spitting out water as Chase shook his head, dragging her toward the open roof. "You're insane. Now, get the hell out before this whole thing goes."

"You first." She held firm when he glared at her. "You're gonna need a shove to squeeze out that opening and you know it. Even then, it's gonna hurt like hell. Though, judging on how your arm is hanging, that dislocation might just save your life. So, get up there, and I'll give you a boost."

He stared at her, looking as if he wasn't going to listen before he huffed, then reached for the opening. Foster appeared at the lip, blood dripping down his face from a cut across his brow. He didn't speak just grabbed Chase's right arm and started pulling.

Chase shifted back and forth, trying to squeeze his shoulders through. Grunting whenever the left one moved. Mac positioned herself beneath him, giving him that boost until he finally scraped free, his shirt ripping in the process.

He cleared the roof just as something impacted the rear of the Bronco, pitching it forward, again. Burying the entire front end underwater. The force tossed Mac against the windshield, slamming her into the stump still lodged against the frame. Water rushed over her head, quickly filling the SUV as it slid along the riverbed.

Dead.

That's what she'd be in another thirty seconds. When her air ran out because she couldn't move. Couldn't fight against the sheer volume of water holding her against that stump. Like a rip tide refusing to let go. She clawed at the passenger seat, trying to wrap her hand around the side just enough to counter the raging current, when Foster's fingers closed around her wrist.

That got her moving. Had her up and slipping through that opening then out. She crested the surface a moment later, Foster still holding her arm. All that fast-moving water rushing past them as he dragged her over to the bank, his sheer strength stopping her from continuing down the river.

Kash was on the bank, grabbing both their hands and yanking them up. Falling back on his ass in order to get them clear. Mac collapsed on the muddy ground, glancing at the Bronco over her shoulder, but it was already fifty feet away, the back bumper rising out of the water before tumbling over and disappearing around the next bend.

Kash grunted, moving over her. "Are you nuts? If Foster wasn't built like a damn tank with the unrelenting persistence of one, you would have been killed."

Mac snorted. "Never leave a teammate behind, right?"

Kash simply shook his head, looking back as sirens wailed in the distance. "Sounds like the cavalry's finally here. You two okay? Because we're not out of the woods, yet."

She nodded, pushing onto her elbows. She wanted to stand, but she wasn't sure her legs would hold her.

Foster rose beside her, offering his hand. She accepted, and he practically launched her off the ground and against his chest. He didn't speak, just wrapped his arms around her and held her tight. As if he was worried she'd float away.

Mac rested her head against his shoulder, sharing his warmth as shivers raked through her.

He sighed, easing back then tucking a handful of wet strands behind her ear. "You're definitely in the first stages of hypothermia."

"I'm not the only one whose lips are blue."

"But I wasn't pinned underwater for a full minute." His nostrils flared, his eyes wide — as if he was staring at a ghost instead of her. "I distinctly remember telling you to be careful."

She sighed. "I couldn't leave him."

"I know. Trust me, I know." He took a step back and grabbed her hand. "Come on. You need a blanket and someone to check you over. You're bleeding."

"Says the guy with a crater across his forehead."

"I'm fine, you…" He drew her in close then started walking, heading back to where Chase, Greer and Kash were gathered on the bank as emergency personnel swarmed the area. Red and white lights illuminated the misty fog, the eerie glow sending more shivers along her spine.

They hadn't even reached the others before some guy was handing her a blanket — whisking her away toward an ambulance. There was shouting and people running before one of the ambulances sped off, siren sounding above the storm, the lights quickly fading into the distance.

Mac brushed the medic away, moving over to

Foster and Kash as they materialized out of the crowd and the fog.

Foster tsked, arching a brow when she stopped in front of him. "Have you even let an EMT look at you?"

"Have you?"

He leaned in closer. "Can you answer a question, just once, without asking another?"

"No. And yes, some guy shined a light in my eyes. I'm fine. Now, are we going to the hospital or what? Because you're still bleeding, and I know you won't let anyone look at you until you know your buddies are okay."

"Are you sure you don't need to ride in the ambulance?"

She snorted. "I'm cold, and wet, and I think I could sleep for a week. But I don't need some guy taking my blood pressure every five minutes. So, either get behind the wheel or give me the keys."

Foster stared at her, then shook his head as he placed the rifle in a lock box before tossing the other supplies in the flatbed and shutting the gate. "You really are something. Fine, get in."

He walked her back to the passenger side, giving Kash some hand signal when the man drove past, following the other ambulance. The one she suspected had Zain in the back, despite the man's protests she'd heard clear across the road.

Foster opened the door, giving her a boost up

before leaning in close. "And for the record. What happened before…"

She inhaled, unsure whether to nod or just sit there, waiting.

He smiled. "Wasn't a one-off. At least, not for me."

Then he was clipping her seatbelt and closing the door. Leaving her there with her heart hammering against her ribs, her lungs, once again burning, as heat exploded across her skin.

Or maybe she really did have hypothermia, and she'd reached that phase where her body wanted her to strip. Where it was fooled into thinking it was burning up.

Until he jumped in and started the engine, blasting cold air through the cabin for a moment before he turned it down. That had her shivering. Tugging that blanket tighter around her shoulders as Foster checked over his shoulder then pulled onto the main road.

He picked up speed, navigating the winding road like a formula one driver. As if he saw just a few seconds into the future and knew exactly when to turn to bleed the most speed out of his truck.

The rain was still coming down when they finally pulled into the hospital, the entire trip taking less than half the usual time. He was out and at her door before she'd even unbuckled, helping her down then taking her hand.

He sighed, then leaned in. "Are you going to play

nice in there and let them look at you? Or do I have to call Atticus so he can guilt you into it?"

She huffed. "You're seriously going to call my dad instead of trying to guilt me into an examination first?"

"You just saved my best friend's life. Laying a guilt trip on you is the last thing I'd choose to do. But I need to know you're okay, so yeah... I'll call your dad. Let him play the role of bad cop."

She was definitely suffering from that last phase of hypothermia because she was melting just from the way he was staring at her. His blue-tinged lips pursed. Those turquoise eyes staring into her soul. "I'll play nice if you will."

He snorted then started walking. "Fine. But you first."

"Always a counteroffer."

"It's the only way I might win an argument with you."

"Oh, I don't know. I can think of one other way."

Foster tripped a step, chuckling as he regained his balance. "Save that thought for later. Because we're going to be here a while, and I have a very bad feeling we're not going to like whatever Zain and Chase have to say once they're actually coherent."

Mac stopped as they reached the nurse's station. "You don't think this was an accident."

"I think someone doesn't want Greer passing on that intel. And I think this trouble is only going to get worse."

CHAPTER EIGHT

"What the... Son of a..."

Foster chuckled as he walked down the hallway, Mac's hand in his as Chase's voice echoed through the corridor, the expletives impossible to miss. It had been three hours since they'd arrived at the hospital, and they'd finally been given the green light to see Zain and Chase.

Atticus had shown up shortly after Foster had led Mac through the emergency doors, blowing into the place like the cyclone rattling the building. Atticus had marched into the exam room, eyes wary. Back straight. He hadn't even needed to yell — he'd just glared at the intern until the man had all but bolted from the room.

Mac had talked her father off the ledge, but he'd given Foster a firm look that had clearly expressed his sentiment. Either Foster guarded Mac's life like an order handed down from God, or Atticus would make Foster's life a living hell.

Not that Foster needed the extra motivation. Getting tossed off the Bronco after handing Chase to Kash — then having to swim along with the current in order to catch the vehicle before it disappeared for good — had made Foster acutely aware of how much he'd come to care about Mac. How this was more than just lust with a side of loneliness.

That this was the start of the rest of his life.

Atticus had been halfway through his laundry list of questions when he'd been called out on another rescue. He'd begrudgingly left when Mac had all but tossed him out of the room, but not before giving Foster another stare down.

Mackenzie cringed at the next colorful quip echoing through the hallway. "Chase sounds… alert."

Foster laughed again, some of his earlier tension easing. All that fear that this would be a repeat of his last encounter in a hospital, with some of his buddies not making it out alive. And with Rhett still lying in a bed — his mind lost to the trauma as they all waited to see if he'd ever come back to them — Foster knew things could still turn ugly. Especially with Greer in surgery. "Whoever said doctors were the worst patients never treated a pararescue medic. Though, that's largely because Chase is hands down the toughest son of a bitch I've ever met. A few years back, he broke three ribs trying to rappel down this insane cliff to a wounded SEAL. I couldn't get remotely close to pick either of them up or provide any kind of support. Chase still managed to drag the guy back up and carry him five miles to the extraction point."

"That explains a lot."

"Just be prepared for him to use extreme tactics in an effort to get us to spring him loose."

"Do I look like the kind of person who falls for puppy dog eyes or blackmail?"

"I guess it depends on who's involved."

He stopped at the doorway, giving her a once-over. He'd snagged some of the spare clothes he'd had stashed in his truck and given her one of his sweatshirts to go with the scrubs the hospital had provided. And damn if she didn't look like sin wearing it. "Are you sure you're okay? That doctor barely examined you."

Mac shook her head. "That's because I'm fine. Though, I'm not sure why you expected him to hang around when you just stood there, growling."

"I wasn't growling. I was letting him know I wasn't impressed with his lack of enthusiasm. How am I supposed to be sure your head's not going to explode later? Or that the gash across your ribs won't get infected?"

"It's a minor bump, and definitely not the first I've ever had. And he gave me more antibiotic cream. Though, it's hardly a gash." She pointed to his forehead. "That's a gash. This is just a scratch."

"Really sweetheart? Because if it was any larger, we'd have to give it a name."

A hint of blush crept into her cheeks. What he hoped was a reaction to him using the endearment, again, and not because she was suddenly spiking a fever. Another symptom that reckless intern had obviously missed.

Mac snapped her fingers in front of his face, frowning. "I don't think my state of mind is the one we need to worry about. How many fingers?"

Foster cupped her hand and held it against his chest, hoping she didn't notice how the simple touch sped up his heart until it was pounding against her palm. "Three. And I was just thinking."

"About how you lied? Because I swear that other doctor didn't even shine a light in your eyes to see if you'd been compromised."

"That's because she knew I was fine."

"Or because you simply stood there, giving her your death glare until she caved and left."

"My death glare?"

"Don't play dumb. I've been watching, and you all have it. Chase gives it to rescue victims if they try to make the situation more dangerous. Kash and Zain are less discriminating and flash it at anyone they deem as a threat."

She'd been watching?

Foster leaned in, loving how her breath caught as her mouth twitched at the corner. "And when do I give this mysterious death glare?"

"When someone stands between you and your team. Which is why you gave it to both those doctors. You didn't want either of them to delay this reunion."

"You realize that your logic implies you're part of my team."

"Is that what I am? A teammate?"

He reached up and tucked some strands behind her ear. "You're something. I'm just not sure what, yet."

"Maybe if your buddies can stay out of danger for more than a few hours, you might find out." She waved at the doorway. "After you."

Foster glanced at the door then back to her, all that heat and confusion from earlier returning. How he'd been lost the moment she'd walked into his home. And he couldn't help but wonder if their next kiss would be just as explosive. If she'd taste just as wild.

He could find out. He was already leaning in. All he needed was to move a few inches closer — tilt his head — and his mouth would be over hers. Though, between the adrenaline from the recuse — nearly losing her in that damn Bronco — he wasn't convinced he could stop at one kiss. A week's worth didn't seem like enough.

Mackenzie sighed, as if she'd read his mind. Knew he was torn between wanting to talk to Chase and Zain and wanting to pick up where they'd left off. Not that it was an option in the middle of the hospital, but he knew it was written across his face. Probably tattooed on his forehead.

She palmed his cheek like she'd done back at his place. "Earlier wasn't a one-off for me, either. If that helps with your indecision."

"Maybe I'm just enjoying the view for a few moments before I have to face reality, again. Acknowledge that someone tried to kill Zain, Chase and Greer. And that it's likely my fault for asking her to dig deeper."

"Even if that's why she got hurt, it's not your fault. She's a cop and an ex-fed. And not to absolve you of any guilt because who really needs a reason to self-blame, but even if you'd told her you'd uncover the intel by other means, she would have dug deeper. That's who she is, and she doesn't take anyone threatening her friends lightly, either."

"So, we're all friends now?"

"That's kinda how it works. Friends by association. And it's a good thing, Beckett, in case you were having doubts. Now, are we going to hear what Zain and Chase have to say or just stand out here until they march their asses out against doctor's orders?"

Foster smiled. "I'm starting to think that you're really just a pain in my ass."

"Sounds like I'm doing everything right, then."

"More than you know." He straightened, pushing all that heat and unfamiliar emotion down until he'd locked them away. Or at least, curbed them enough his team wouldn't call him on them the minute he walked through the door.

Mackenzie giggled, schooling her features when he arched a brow at her, before sliding her hand over his. An obvious declaration that there was something brewing between them, as she'd phrased it. And that she didn't care who knew.

"Foster! About damn time." Chase waved him over with his right hand. "What's up with Greer? No one will tell me what the hell's going on. Is she okay? Is there a guard outside her door? Do I need—"

"Whoa, slow down."

"Then, start talking." Chase paled. "God, she isn't—"

"As of ten minutes ago, she was still in surgery. The doctors said she broke several ribs and that the splinters from them caused some limited internal bleeding and a collapsed lung. But they promised to grab Mackenzie as soon as Greer was in recovery. And they said it looked promising."

"Internal bleeding and a collapsed lung is *not* promising. Shit." He speared his right hand through his hair. "I need pants."

Foster glanced at Kash when the man shook his head, blocking Chase from swinging his legs over the edge of the bed. "Why on earth would you need pants?"

Chase glared at Kash. "So, I don't flash my ass to everyone as I walk out of here and over to the sheriff's station to beat some intel out of her fucking colleagues."

Zain grunted as he levered up and tossed the blankets aside. "Hell yeah. If Chase is breaking ranks, then so am I. Especially if it means getting some payback."

"Jesus would you both just stop for a minute?" Foster moved between the twin beds, ready to pounce on whoever's feet hit the floor, first. "No one is going anywhere until someone explains why you want to start a war with the sheriff's office."

Zain snorted, nearly tumbling out of the bed before Kash caught him. "I don't know. But if Chase is going, I'm backing him up."

Foster sighed, staring at Kash. "He already took his meds, didn't he?"

Kash merely nodded. "And they're kicking in right on schedule."

"I'm fine." Zain grinned, motioning Foster closer. "But I do have something I need to tell you."

Foster arched a brow. "What's that?"

"I love you, brother."

"Thanks for the tip." Foster focused on Chase. "Assuming you're not as high as *Major Tom*, here, why don't you start at the beginning."

Chase squeezed his forehead, looking as if he was considering pounding his head through the wall before he huffed. "I don't remember everything."

"Then, tell us what you do remember."

"When we arrived at Greer's office, she was edgy.

Maybe not something everyone would notice, but I did. When I asked her if everything was okay, she simply said she'd explain once we were back at your place. That it wasn't safe to talk about it there."

"Greer said the station wasn't safe?" Foster frowned. "What does that even mean?"

"You tell me because we left, and everything seemed fine considering the freaking weather. Then the next thing I know, you're banging on the glass, Greer's half dead in the passenger seat and Mac's shimmying through some hole as the Bronco's flooding."

"And you think someone at the station was involved with the accidents?"

"All I know is that we asked her to dig deeper, then she says her office isn't safe before she's nearly killed in a car accident. And before you ask, no, I don't remember how the Bronco went off the road, but you know me. I've driven in conditions far worse than these. I wouldn't simply slide off the side. And even if I did, how did we get enough momentum to reach the river?"

Foster held up his hands, keeping Chase from launching out of the bed. "I don't know, but I promise you, we'll find out. Just... try not to worsen whatever's hiding beneath all those bandages. Your shoulder's already been dislocated once. We don't need you knocking it out again because you face-planted on the floor trying to get out of bed."

Chase scowled, clenching his jaw as he let his

head tip back against the pillows before he focused on Mackenzie. "Are you okay, Mac?"

She smiled. "You *do* remember who my father is, right? Because I've been hurt worse on a family camping trip."

Chase shook his head. "Great, another Beckett."

Mackenzie coughed, rubbing her chest a bit as she took a breath. "I'm fine, Chase. Only a few scratches."

"Right." He shifted, again, all but shouting out this time.

Foster edged closer. "Have you taken any meds?"

Chase looked away. "A couple Tylenol."

"You're black and blue, with a separated shoulder and a crater in your left thigh. Tylenol's not going to touch that kind of pain and you know it."

"You know how I feel about narcotics."

"I do, but brother... You're not your old man. He had the problem, not you. And whether you want to agree or not, you're not responsible for his sins. So, take the morphine or the Percocet or whatever. We'll stand watch until you're back with us. Promise."

"If I take the pills, I can't protect Greer."

"You let us worry about Greer. You just need to get some rest so I can bust yours and Zain's asses out of here in the morning. And yeah, you're both staying the night because Zain managed to partially collapse a lung and skewer a piece of shrapnel through his shoulder. Which means, he's as messed up as you are."

"And if whoever's behind all of this comes back while we're all having conversations with the furniture?"

"Then, they'll have to go through me." Kash nodded at the mutt. "And Nyx."

Chase shook his head, another groan rumbling free. "You need to keep Greer safe."

"We'll watch over Greer." Mac motioned to Foster then back to her. "With all those injuries, she'll likely spend the night in the ICU. I know a couple of the nurses and I'm sure I can convince them to let us stand watch. They know how we like to take care of our own. And I'll call my dad. He knows that ex-deputy ranger guy, Page, who Beckett's dad hired. If you guys agree he's trustworthy, we'll arrange for Page to provide security until Greer's ready to be discharged. Then, she can stay at Foster's if needed until this is settled. Okay?"

Chase pursed his lips, looking as if he was still going to argue before he blew out a rough breath.

Kash nudged him. "Take the meds."

Chase eyed Kash. "You promise you won't let me out of this bed until I'm coherent again?"

"I swear on Sean's grave."

Chase inhaled, glancing at Foster before begrudgingly nodding. Kash gave his good arm a pat then darted out of the room, returning a short while later with one of the nurses. The guy merely shook his head as he injected a syringe into Chase's IV then left, mumbling something about medics and how stubborn Chase was.

Kash shuffled over to Foster. "What I just said about Sean…"

"Was the only response that was going to get Chase to actually take those meds. We both know what demons lurk inside his head, and he needed to believe we'd have his six."

"Still…"

"It's all good." Foster turned to Zain. "Zain? I know you're already floating up in the clouds, but do you have anything to add?"

Zain chuckled. "Did I mention I love you jerks?"

"Twice, now."

"Then, nope." He closed his eyes, drifting for a bit before he inhaled and opened them, again. "Other than you should probably look into that truck."

Kash perked up. "Truck? What truck?"

Zain grinned. "Where's Nyx? I love that furball."

"Standing guard. What truck, Zain?"

Zain hummed, eyes drifting closed. "The one that was on the side of the road just before the Bronco exploded into the air and my Chevy went flying."

Kash inched closer. "Do you remember what kind of truck it was? Who was driving?"

"It was white. Tacoma, I think."

Kash frowned. "I don't suppose it had California plates, did it?"

"I don't know, but the white guy driving it was jacked. He was standing in front of the grill…" Zain's voice trailed off for a moment. "Is the room spinning for you, too?"

Kash grabbed the remote and lowered the bed. "Sleep buddy."

Zain made a show of shushing everyone before sighing and closing his eyes.

Kash arched a brow. "A white Tacoma driven by a white guy. And jacked definitely sounds like the type of dude who'd have a military-type crew cut. Any of that sound familiar?"

Mac inhaled. "That's the description Jordan gave Greer that day at the café."

Kash nodded. "And you know how we all feel about coincidences."

Foster raked his fingers through his hair. "Yeah, there aren't any."

"We need whatever intel Greer was going to share." Kash kicked at the floor. "And I don't think we can afford to wait until she's vertical."

"Agreed. Which means, I need to make a call."

Kash crossed his arms over his chest. "Keaton?"

"Florida's about as removed from here as possible. And his buddy Dawson is chief of police. Even if it's outside his purview, he has the kind of connections that can acquire the information without alerting anyone local."

"You think Dawson will be okay with that?"

"I think Dawson's an ex-SEAL who sees loyalty and the brotherhood the same way we do. And I bet my ass Keaton has a few cards he could play if Dawson has any *reservations*."

Kash laughed. "Nothing like your best friends having secrets they can exploit at a moment's notice."

"Keaton knows I'd never ask him or his buddies to do something blatantly illegal."

Kash scoffed and Foster sighed.

"Not without being up front about it, first. And only with lives at stake. And I'd leave them out of this and march over to the sheriff's station and get in Sheriff Thompson's face if Chase hadn't shared that bit about Greer's concern regarding security."

Kash nodded. "You think Thompson's involved somehow?"

"It's possible. He did brush off all those incidents my father reported. Or it could simply be Greer didn't want anyone knowing what she'd uncovered in case it got out. That rumor mill Chase commented on. But we'll err on the side of paranoia, just to be safe. Which means ensuring Greer isn't left without protection."

Kash slapped him lightly on the chest. "Guess you two are spending the night in the ICU."

Foster sighed when Nyx growled a second before a voice sounded from the doorway.

"Or, you could let me handle that and you two can go home and get some rest like your doctors ordered."

CHAPTER NINE

Foster snapped his head around, staring at the man standing in the doorway. He was large, maybe an inch or two shorter than Foster but what Foster guessed was easily the same weight. And the man carried himself in a way that clearly broadcast he could handle himself without being overt about it. Add in short hair and a scruff, with black boots, black cargo pants and a black hoodie and vest, and the guy screamed ex-military.

He nodded at Foster. "Even if Atticus hadn't described you, it's obvious you're Foster Beckett. You're the spitting image of your dad." He extended his hand. "I'm Bodie Page."

Foster took the few steps separating them then grabbed the man's hand. "You're the ex-ranger, right?"

"Ten years until an IED put enough shrapnel in

my right leg, I can set off the metal detectors from twenty feet away. I eventually got the mobility back, but..." He shrugged. "I'm sorry about your parents. They were good people."

"Thanks, and yeah, they were. Why didn't you come by the house and let me know you'd been providing security on the place?"

Bodie coughed. "John didn't tell you?"

"Not a word."

Bodie shook his head. "That's odd because he swore he was going to call you — talk it all through. Though, that was right before the accident so maybe he hadn't gotten the chance. But I assumed you knew and you'd stop by my office if you had any questions. When you didn't..."

Bodie shoved his hands in his pockets, finally looking at Mac and Kash. "Where are my manners? You must be Mackenzie. Your dad talks about you non-stop. And you're either Kash, Zain or Chase."

Kash gave Nyx a scratch, still eyeing the guy. "Kash. The guy on my left is Chase and Zain's in the other bed. So, Atticus called you?"

Bodie smiled as he motioned toward Mac. "As soon as Mackenzie kicked him out of the exam room to attend to that emergency, he gave me a ring. Thought you might need some extra security, though he didn't elaborate."

Mac snorted. "Only my father would assume none of this was purely an accident."

"Based on what I heard when I walked in, neither do you."

Foster sized the man up. He'd missed being played once before and he was *not* going to make the same mistake twice and trust someone simply because they'd been a soldier. "What we said?"

Bodie held up his palms. "I only caught the last part about keeping an eye on Greer. But you wouldn't be worried about her safety unless you thought those accidents had been manufactured, and she was still at risk."

Foster glanced at Kash, and he knew his buddy was thinking the same thing. That this could be Stein and Adams all over again.

Bodie alternated his gaze between them, finally blowing out a rough breath. "I get it. You guys are coming off a rescue, your adrenaline's high, your friends are hurt, and here I am, barging in, just offering to help right out of the blue. But you don't know me, and you certainly have no reason to trust me. So, call Atticus. I ran a few JSOC missions under his command before getting medically discharged and I've told him he can be as candid as he likes. And, if I check out to your satisfaction, I'm hoping you'll let me at least watch Greer for you. She's my friend, too, and with half your team injured, it looks like you could use some backup."

Mac jumped when her phone went off a second later, the noise overshadowing the constant beeping in the background. She grabbed her cell, shaking her head as she stared at the screen. "I swear, it's like simply mentioning his name out loud conjures him in one form or another." She swiped the screen, motioning that she'd take it in the hallway. "Dad…"

Foster inhaled, curbing his urge to follow her out. Have her six despite the fact she was only a few feet away, her left side still visible through the doorway.

Bodie chuckled.

Foster focused on him, again. "Something funny?"

"Nope."

Foster ignored the way the guy stood there, grinning, as Mac talked to Atticus, too softly for Foster to make out any of the words. Another male voice joined in a few minutes later, but just when Foster was about to bolt to the door, Mackenzie strolled back into the room.

Bodie turned to face her. "Well?"

"First, that was the doctor. Greer's in recovery. They managed to stop the bleeding and put in a chest tube. She'll be in the ICU until they're confident her lungs are clear and she's not going to pop any of those bleeders back open. But he said she should make a full recovery and be back busting balls in a few weeks."

Foster nodded when Kash slapped him on the back. "Thank god. And your dad?"

Mac held up her phone. "As usual, he said he was *too damn busy* to hold our hands through this and that all you need to know about Bodie is he was involved in Black Canary."

Foster coughed then scrubbed his hand across his face. "That was your Ranger unit?"

Bodie sighed. "Which means it was your team who pulled us out."

"Talk about a small world." He gave Bodie a clap on the shoulder. "We'd love some backup until Greer's ready to be discharged. After that, I have a feeling Chase will insist on her staying with us until this is all sorted out. And before you ask, we don't really know what this is, yet. But we're damn sure gonna find out."

"I won't let anything happen to her. You've got my word on that." He turned then stopped at the doorway. "Give me a shout if you need anything else. I've got a pretty decent setup. And I've got Mac's number. I'll send updates. Until then, I'll be parked outside of recovery then in the ICU."

Mac cozied up to Foster, bumping his hip with hers. "I assume that whatever happened on that mission means we can trust him?"

Foster sighed. He couldn't say too much but he could put any doubts at rest. "That's when he got that injury he mentioned. He went back when two of his teammates got pinned down. Damn near died, but he got them clear. Men like that can't be bought."

She simply smiled, leaning against him a bit as the room fell into an odd silence.

Kash broke it first as he gave them both a shove. "Go home."

"No way." Foster widened his stance. "We'll spell each other off."

"Is that before or after you both pass out from exhaustion?" Kash scoffed when Mac went to interrupt him. "You're both still blue and you both took blows to the head. I'm fine. I didn't end up trapped in a Bronco or swimming in a river. And I've got Nyx with me if I need to close my eyes for a moment. Nothing gets past her. So, go. Call Keaton, and I'll expect coffee in the morning."

Foster glanced at Mac and damn, she did look cold. "You'll call if there's even a hint of trouble, right?"

"Scout's honor."

"You're such an ass." He grabbed Kash's hand as he gave him a pat on the shoulder. "Call if you need us back here."

Kash shooed them out then plopped down on a chair between Chase and Zain's bed, Nyx circling twice before lying at his feet. Foster took one last look around the room, searching the shadows, just in case, before palming Mac's back, again, and walking with her down the hallway. They didn't talk, just continued along in a comfortable silence until they jumped in his truck then headed toward home.

She kicked her seat back a bit, twisting toward him. Staring with what he could only describe as a dreamy smile lighting up her face.

He waited a bit then shook his head. "I'm starting

to think that doctor was way off, and you need to be under observation for a while."

She laughed, the easy sound skittering along his nerves until he swore the truck must be overheating. "Why's that?"

"Because of the way you're looking at me. Either you're having an aneurism, or you took some of Zain's meds when I wasn't watching."

"You think I'm high because I'm smiling?"

"Smiling while *looking* at me." He shrugged. "Usually, women scream and throw things."

She laughed again, and it had the same effect only far more intense. As if she'd lit every inch of him on fire. "Guess I'm not like other women."

"Amen, to that, sweetheart." He groaned when the endearment slipped free, again. He'd never been one to use pet names, but the word just formed on his tongue regardless of whether he was thinking it or not.

Mackenzie leaned in, getting dangerously close. "Call me crazy, but I kinda like the way you say that."

"Amen?"

"You're so not what I expected." She drew her finger along his arm. "And I meant sweetheart. It's…" She inhaled. "Jesus. Foster. Pull over!"

He tensed, checking the mirrors then angling onto the shoulder. His headlights cut a path through the darkness, outlining the edge of a ravine as the limbs of the bare trees snapped in the wind. His wipers swooshed across the windshield, giving him fleeting views of the foggy landscape.

"What the… Are you okay? Do you need to go back to the hospital? Should I call—"

She cut him off with that finger over his lips. "Kill the lights."

He frowned but turned them off. "You're scaring me."

She shook her head, leaning in even closer. "There's someone on the edge of that ravine. I saw their silhouette when you came around that bend."

He scanned the tree line, frowning. "Are you sure? I don't see anything."

"They darted down toward the river as soon as your headlights hit them."

"Do you think they need help?"

"I think it might be our guy because this is where Greer's Bronco went off the road." She looked Foster dead in the eyes. "And he was wearing night vision goggles."

* * *

Mac stared at Foster, noting how his lips pinched tight as he focused on the patch of land they'd left only hours earlier. Where he'd nearly lost his best friend. His eyes narrowed as he pushed out a few rough breaths. A hint of blush colored his cheeks before he simply flipped a switch.

She knew the moment he'd changed from the

charming man she was quickly falling for, to the hardened warrior whose loyalty and determination seemed limitless.

This was the Foster Beckett her dad had sent on various missions. Who defied orders if it meant saving a life. Who had risked his own life so his brothers would come home. And she knew, without a doubt, he wasn't going to simply drive past.

He rolled his right shoulder, grimacing a bit as it obviously pulled on those plates and screws he'd mentioned before he steeled his resolve. Any hint of uncertainty fading away as he turned off the ignition.

He looked over at her, tilting his head as if he was considering what to say. If he should accept the help he knew she'd offer or find a way to insist she stayed in the truck. That maybe he'd only trusted her to have their backs earlier because he'd been worried about Zain — had wanted to get to his buddy as quickly as possible.

Until he simply blew out another rough breath. "Do you prefer a handgun or that rifle?"

The question caught her off-guard, and she stared for a moment before she broke into a broad smile. "What are we talking for the pistol? A Sig like your buddies?"

"It's our weapon of choice."

"Then, I'll stick with the Sauer rifle. I'm assuming you've got a forty-five in the back, and that's a bit more kickback than I'm accustomed to. You'll be the better shot if it comes down to that."

"Let's try to see that it doesn't but..."

He was out of the truck and at the back in under five seconds. Just like before. Five more seconds, and he had a couple containers pulled to the edge of the flatbed. He rummaged through one, removing two ballistic vests along with a couple flashlights, some extra ammo and two multitools.

Foster handed her the slightly smaller of the two vests. "Put this on."

"It's too big."

"Big beats nothing, though you have a point." He grabbed another spare hoodie he had in the back. "Put this on first then the vest. It'll take up a bit of the room. And no, this isn't up for debate. You want to have my six, then you wear the appropriate protective gear."

She didn't argue, just tugged the hoodie over her head. It smelled like pine and cottonwood, and she couldn't help but wonder how often he changed out his gear. If he still saw the world as a series of endless threats.

Which, of course he did. He'd been in the military for twenty years. That kind of training never went away.

Foster gave her a thorough once-over after she had the vest secured and the rifle in her hands. He pursed his lips again, looking as if he might change his mind before he nodded. "You sure you're okay with this? We have no idea what we're up against. If it's one person or a freaking gang."

"All the more reason to have backup."

"Until all hell breaks loose, and you get hit."

"You're not going searching alone. And maybe I'm wrong. Maybe it's just someone looking for junk to grab."

"Right. It's simply a run-of-the-mill upcycler who's out in the middle of an apocalyptic storm wearing night vision to search through a bunch of debris for some spare parts."

"Well, when you put it like that..." She snorted. "Regardless, I've got your back."

"We'll stick together, go slow, and we won't fire unless it's life or death. This isn't the service, and we're not the law. This is strictly info gathering, though if we get the chance to have a chat..."

He patted down his vest as she was sure he'd done a thousand times in the service. Some kind of ritual that ensured he was fully armed and ready to wage war. Then, he rolled that shoulder one more time, shaking his right hand out before he took off. Not fast. More of a quick side-step from his truck, down the short hill then over to a group of trees.

He darted behind the thickest one, waving her in behind him. "I don't see anything but without using our lights, he has the advantage."

"I can't imagine there's much natural light for his goggles to amplify. But if we turn on the flashlights..."

Foster merely nodded as he wiped away the rain running down his face. He gave her a quick signal then was out and moving toward the riverbank. Staying low. Silent. No broken twigs, no scuffing the gravel. Just him moving over the ground like a ghost.

She'd definitely underestimated his skill level. Hadn't considered that he'd either elected or been forced to engage in ground maneuvers. That maybe he'd seen the kind of action she'd only touched on with the TACLET units.

Sure, she'd been under fire. Had faced off against drug lords and weapons traffickers. But she'd never done anything like this.

Good, because I'd prefer a partner.

That's what he'd said in his house that night — without hesitation, and he'd proven he trusted her to have his back twice today. There was no way she was letting him down.

Mac shadowed Foster's movements, constantly checking their six. She wasn't sure where he was headed, but she wasn't going to let anyone get behind them.

Foster pulled up short, ducking behind a large stump. He motioned off to his right. "Tango. Two o'clock."

She peeked out, spying the same figure she'd spotted from the truck. What looked disturbingly similar to the silhouette she'd encountered in Foster's house and who fit the description Zain had given of the guy he'd seen standing in front of that white truck prior to the accidents. The perp was rummaging through some debris at the edge of the bank, stopping to check his surroundings every ten seconds.

Foster leaned in. "Stay close."

She wanted to tell him she wasn't getting more than a foot away when he started moving, again. Quickly closing in on the guy as Foster kept them hidden behind brush and trees. They got within twenty feet when the guy froze, tilting his head their way before he turned suddenly, a nine millimeter aimed their way. But Foster already had his flashlight directed at the man's eyes, the bright light illuminating the fog with an eerie glow. The bastard clawed his goggles off his face, losing any advantage as they all stood there, that jerk's weapon pointed toward the ground.

"Uh, uh." Foster motioned to the guy's weapon with his Sig. "Put it on the ground before I decide it's definitely worth another trip to the ER."

The man scowled, looking between them for a few moments as he stood there. Staring.

Foster inched closer. "Call me crazy, asshole, but I have a feeling that even if I do shoot you, you're in no position to report it. So, either put the fucking gun down, or I'll call your bluff."

He snarled this time but allowed his weapon to rotate around his finger before he held it up. He made a show of bending over, when a canister bounced down the hill, each impact emitting a shrill tone until it spun to a halt between the three of them.

Mac had barely registered it was a grenade when Foster had his arms around her — was launching them behind a log. They hit the muddy ground a moment before the flash bang erupted, lights and smoke and ear-piercing wails exploding around them. She squeezed her eyes shut, wondering how Foster didn't puke when he took the brunt of the attack, shielding her with the sheer size of him.

But he had her on her feet and racing behind the perp in after what seemed like only a second or two. Though, it was more staggering than actually running but just being on her feet seemed like a medal-worthy accomplishment.

Foster kept moving, his strong grip preventing her from tripping. Their perp was already jumping into a white truck when they crested that small rise, the taillights quickly fading around the far bend.

Mac palmed her knees when Foster finally eased up, nearly tipping onto her ass before he had her braced against him, keeping her from simply collapsing in the mud. She scrubbed her hand down her face when she was finally able to straighten, shaking her head at him in awe. "How the hell are you upright and steady? I swear I'm gonna puke."

He sighed, encouraging her to bridge more of her weight against him. "Practice."

"You practiced getting assaulted by flash bangs?"

He stared at her, looking as if he wasn't sure how to answer — probably how much he could answer —

before sighing. "How much do you know about Flight Concepts?"

"Not nearly enough because I had no idea you trained for *that*. Though, it all makes sense, now. How you move like Zain and Kash and Chase. Why you're so comfortable with weapons. I'm just not sure if I'm impressed or intimidated."

He snorted. "Says the woman who's faced off against cartel and mafia assholes."

"Sure, in the air. It's a lot creepier down here."

He laughed. "You really are something else. And I agree. Way creepier. Which is our cue to get out of here before we push our luck and tempt fate one too many times."

"What about the debris? That canister? Don't you want to have a look?"

Foster glanced at the spot then back to her. "You're exhausted and cold."

"And yet, not dead. Come on. Ten minutes, then we'll hop back in the truck."

Foster huffed but nodded, covering her six as they trekked back down the hill and over to the pile where the tango had been picking through bits of metal and plastic. Foster didn't talk, just started rummaging through his half of the junk as she took the other side. Her internal clock was closing in on those ten minutes when Foster inhaled, the rough breath sounding loud in the surrounding silence.

She shifted over to his side, crouching beside him. "Did you find something interesting?"

"I'll say." He held up part of a small black box with some frayed wires and what looked like a circuit board. "More than interesting, really."

Mac frowned. "You're excited because you found half of a garage door opener?"

"That's what it looks like, but Greer's Bronco had a built-in one. And seeing as she's tech savvy, why would she have a manual one, too?"

She inhaled. "Wait. Do you think it's some kind of detonator?"

"That would explain how Greer's Bronco had enough momentum to suddenly fly off the road and roll all the way down here. Why that guy was standing out on the side. He needed to be able to activate it."

"But if they used an explosive, why aren't Chase and Greer dead?"

"The right explosive in the right amount... Or maybe they used the wrong amount, and it didn't go as planned. But I guarantee this is what our mystery guy was looking for."

"Because you might be able to lift some prints off the inside."

"If we're lucky." He shoved it in his pocket, glancing over at her before doing a double take. "Crap. You're more than just cold and wet now, even with the scrubs and the borrowed hoodies. Which means, it's time to get you into some dry clothes."

"Or at least, out of these wet ones."

Foster coughed, shaking his head as he took her

hand, grabbed the spent canister as they passed by then trotted back to the truck, giving her a boost inside before slipping behind the wheel again, and pulling back onto the road.

Mac buckled in, glancing at the area as it faded behind them. This was far more than some sophisticated burglars. And she had a bad feeling Foster had been right, and it was only going to get deadlier the longer they played the game.

CHAPTER TEN

Two o'clock in the morning, and they were just locking the door behind them as they staggered into Beckett's place, the rain and wind still raging outside. Foster had made the drive home fairly quickly, but simply pulling into the driveway — parking beside Chase's truck — had brought the night's events into sharp focus. And he knew he'd never settle until he'd done a thorough sweep of the property.

He'd glanced at Mac, wondering if he should ask her to stay in the truck or make the rounds with him, but she'd simply smiled and asked him which one of his buddies' houses he wanted to clear first.

And just like that, he'd fallen a bit harder.

They'd spent the next hour scouring every inch of the other buildings and surrounding area until he felt confident they were alone before heading back to his place. He'd disarmed the new system Zain had installed then whisked Mac inside, rearming it as soon as he'd locked the door.

Mackenzie removed her wet hoodie, her teeth chattering as she attempted to hang it on one of the hooks only to drop it when her hands didn't seem to work quite right.

Foster tsked. "Why didn't you tell me you were freezing? We could have scrapped searching the other homes and just come straight inside."

Mac scoffed at him. "As if you would have been able to relax without knowing the property's clear."

"Better me courting a stroke than you slipping into a hyperthermic coma."

"I'm not that bad. But some dry clothes would be nice." She tilted her head, staring at him for so long he thought she'd fallen asleep on her feet before she sighed. "Who are we kidding? Even after searching everything — with Zain upgrading everyone's security systems — there's no way you'll be able to go to bed and sleep. So, why don't you plant your butt on one of the chairs, make that call to Keaton if it's not too early or too late, and I'll be right back." She arched a brow. "Assuming you don't mind me rummaging through your closet and grabbing a few things."

Mackenzie smiled when he nodded then turned on her heels and headed for the stairs. Her hips swayed hypnotically as she climbed the steps, turning right at the top before disappearing down the hallway.

He could catch her. Race up the stairs and scoop her into his arms then take them both into his room — have her stripped and on his bed in record time. What he'd been itching to do since that earth-shattering kiss at the front door.

Except where she was right. The warrior in him whispering how that tango could be outside, right now, biding his time. Waiting for them to drift off before breaching the house.

He glanced at the new security system. Zain had gone overboard, though Foster had to admit, he hadn't expected any less. And something he should have allowed his buddy to do the moment they'd moved in. But he'd hoped Raven's Cliff would be different. More like his rose-colored memories of his parents never locking their doors. The *Andy Griffith* vibe it gave off.

He'd gotten lucky. And after having to watch Mac battle to get Chase free — knowing there wasn't a damn thing he could do to help — he knew his mind wouldn't quiet until he was convinced they were safe.

He didn't need to stay alert for hours. Just one or two — until he was sure the bastard with the night vision goggles wasn't going to make a surprise visit. Then, he could put his faith in Zain's tech and get some sleep.

Foster stripped down to his boxers and tee, kicked off his boots and padded over to a winged-back chair, sinking into the comfortable cushion. His shoulder ached from the cold and the strain, every screw feeling as if it was trying to burst free. He scrubbed his hand down his face as he hit Keaton's number, waiting for his cousin to appear on the small screen.

The video winked into view, Keaton's sleep-weary face appearing amidst the darkness. "Foster? Jesus what's wrong? Are you hurt? Trapped? Need bail money?"

"If I was hurt, I'd be calling emergency services, and if I was trapped, I'd have my team on the line. As for bail money..." Foster chuckled. "Do you even have any?"

Keaton blinked then carded his fingers through his hair. "Well, something's wrong because it's five o'clock here, which means it's two freaking a.m. there. Wait, you're not drunk dialing me, are you?"

"Do I look or sound drunk?"

"Honestly, you're one of those guys who you just can't tell."

"I'm not drunk. And before you ask, I'm not high, either. But I need your help, and it couldn't wait. There's been an incident. A few actually, but tonight's..."

He swallowed, Sean's ghost mocking him from across the room. Just like he'd done throughout the entire rescue. Always hanging over his shoulder like a beacon of all Foster had to lose. Everything he'd already lost. And now that the adrenaline was starting to wane, it seemed all too real.

"Foster? Cuz, you'd better start talking because

the color just drained from your face, and you look like crap. Is everyone okay?"

"They will be. Zain and Chase had their trucks go off the road. Actually, Chase was driving one of the deputy's — Greer Hudson's — Bronco. She took the brunt of it. She's stable but in the ICU. The guys are spending the night under observation, but they're mostly just pissed."

"Damn. What the hell happened?"

Foster used the hem of his shirt as he reached into his pocket and removed the device before holding it up for Keaton. "This."

Keaton squinted then inhaled. "Is that part of a bomb?"

"I think so. I've got a connection here who I'll have take a look at it in the morning to confirm, but…"

"So, someone put a bomb on Zain's truck?"

"It was Greer's Bronco, actually. Though, I didn't look at Zain's Chevy. It was already towed. I'll scour it tomorrow."

Keaton frowned, turning his head to talk to someone on his right. Trinity, Foster supposed. Keaton's girlfriend and the woman Foster knew Keaton was going to spend the rest of his life with. "Maybe it's because we had a late night, and the wine's still kicking my ass. Or maybe it's because it's five a.m., and my brain's not fully functioning, yet, but why would someone put a bomb on a deputy's

SUV? And what has this got to do with you and your team?"

Foster sighed, giving Keaton a quick rundown of what had happened. How Foster was pretty sure this revolved around whatever intel Greer had been planning on sharing. And while it had seemed like a stretch when they'd been sitting in the café, the whole Carrington connection appeared much more viable now.

Keaton scratched the back of his head. "I gotta give you credit. You and your team don't do anything half-assed. So, I'm guessing you're hoping Dawson can unearth whatever Greer had uncovered regarding this Carrington guy and GeneTide — if there's any remote connection to Raven's Cliff and your manor house, specifically."

"In a nutshell, yeah. I don't know how long Greer will be sidelined, and the last thing she needs is me hounding her for information. Possibly putting her life at risk again. And before you hyperventilate, we've got a fellow soldier guarding her until we can move her here, but I need to keep this from getting back to anyone else in her office. Hell, in town."

Foster arched a brow as he leaned back. "You think Dawson will play along? Maybe call in a few chits if needed?"

Keaton coughed. "Are you kidding? He lives for this spy stuff. And we actually have an in with a fed down here. If she's in town, she might be willing to help too."

Foster nodded, turning when the stairs creaked. Nearly falling off the chair when Mackenzie rounded the bottom of the staircase dressed in one of his massive tees with a pair of wool socks. She glided over the old wood floors, the hem of his shirt swaying seductively across her thighs. She stopped beside him and tossed him a shirt and his pajama pants. He smiled, wondering if he'd ever seen her look sexier than she was right then, when she glanced at the screen then back to him, arching her brow.

Keaton cleared his throat, gaining Foster's attention. "What was that?"

Foster frowned. "What was what?"

"The look on your face. You're obviously not alone and whoever just walked in..." Keaton whistled. "What's her name, cuz?"

"Bugger off."

"So, it's serious." Keaton leaned in closer. "Her. Name."

Foster groaned, waving Mackenzie over. "Keaton, this is Mackenzie Parker. Mackenzie, this is my cousin Keaton Cole. The man I'm going to throttle the next time I see him."

Mac·smiled, and Foster's heart flipped over hard in his chest. Stealing what little breath he'd gasped in. "Nice to meet you."

Keaton grinned like a freaking Cheshire Cat. "Parker. Any relation to that JSOC guy Foster ran a number of missions for? Who's been trying his damnedest to get him to join his search and rescue unit? Atticus, I think?"

Mac chuckled. "He's my father."

Keaton broke out laughing, dabbing at fake tears. "Oh, man, this is better than reality TV."

Mac met Foster's gaze. "I can definitely see the resemblance. Does he share a brain with his team, too?"

Foster nodded. "More than you know."

"What's wrong, cuz?" Keaton leaned closer to the screen. "Getting a bit frosty there because hell's freezing over? That is when you said you'd fall for a lady, right?"

Foster groaned. He'd known Keaton would tease him the minute he introduced him to Mac. But he hadn't anticipated that he wouldn't care. "I see you have the same amount of tact as Chase, Kash and Zain."

"Sounds like I'm in good company."

"If you can stop smirking long enough to actually give me a hand, there's one more thing I'd appreciate Dawson looking into."

"What's that?"

"My parents' accident."

"Well, crap." Keaton raked his hand through his hair. "Are you concerned you didn't get the whole story?"

"Let's just say, things aren't adding up like they were before. But I can't exactly walk into Thompson's office and demand more without tipping our hand."

"I'll see what Dawson can uncover."

"Thanks. I'll let you go. Tell Trinity I'm sorry I woke you up. Hope I didn't interrupt anything."

"Not here, but over there..."

"Goodbye Keaton. And buddy..."

Keaton paused with his hand hovering over his cell.

"Thanks. I owe you."

Keaton looked at Mac. "I think you've already paid me for this one. I haven't been this entertained in a while. I'll call you as soon as I have anything."

The video winked off, leaving an odd silence in the room, Keaton's obvious assessment of the situation hanging between them.

Mac walked over to a basket positioned beside the couch and grabbed the blanket they'd used that first night, along with another fluffier one. "So, that's your cousin? The ex-SEAL?"

Foster chuckled. "Trust me, I continually wonder about that. Though, he's tough as nails. And ridiculously smart. Like embarrassingly so."

"And yet, still a five-year old."

"That's just being a guy."

"I'll keep that in mind. Now, get out of those clothes while I get this ready."

Foster stood, holding the pajamas to his chest. "This is stupid. We can just go upstairs—"

"And have you hyperventilating while you lie there, staring at your phone in case you get a message that one of your new shiny alarms has gone off? I don't think so. At least down here, you'll feel as if you have more control. And if that creep happens to show up and looks through the window, he'll be less likely to try anything if we're right here."

She shook out one of the blankets, glancing at him over her shoulder. "Because that's what you're worried about right? Him coming here in the first couple hours that we're back?"

"Do you read minds on the side or am I just crap at keeping anything hidden?"

"Even I know that if he was going to strike, it'd be pretty quickly. Which means spending at least a few hours down here. So, go change."

Foster ambled past her, taking a moment to admire the expanse of creamy smooth skin showing beyond the edges of his tee before darting into the bathroom. He tore off his remaining clothes, piling them on the counter to deal with in the morning then slipped on the ones she'd given him. A couple minutes to get everything else done, and he was walking back to the couch. Forcing himself not to launch onto the cushions when he took in the view.

Mackenzie snuggled beneath the blankets, her long brown hair cascading over her shoulders as she fluffed up a pillow. She turned when he got within a few feet, inhaling as she let her gaze drift over the length of him. And if the way her pupils dilated as she drew her tongue across her lower lip was any indication of what she was thinking, the woman would likely give him that stroke he'd mentioned earlier.

He rounded the coffee table then settled in beside her, lifting his arm when she turned and burrowed against him. He was about to ask if she was comfortable, but she was already humming as she drew lazy patterns across his chest before drifting off. Just like that first night.

Only now, it seemed dangerously more intimate. As if those few kisses had shifted the playing field. Made every move a possible game-changer.

He tugged her closer, inhaling the subtle scent of lavender. What he assumed was from a lotion she'd found in the washroom. It soothed some of the rawness still tensing his muscles, allowing him to relax on the sofa as a clock ticked softly in the background. Rain still pelted the windows, the wind rattling the old wood frames.

Foster let himself drift. Not sleeping but not sitting there at attention, either, until his internal clock gave him a nudge. He shifted on the couch, checking his watch. Almost two hours had passed without so much as a hint of incursion, which meant it was probably safe to actually try to get some sleep. While he wanted nothing more than to wake Mac up, hike her over his shoulder and head to bed, watching her sleep — the adorable way she kept snuggling against him as if she couldn't get close enough — satisfied him in a way he hadn't experienced before. That seeing to her needs meant as much if not more than tending to his. And if that meant spending the next four or five hours on the couch, he wasn't going to complain.

Until she twitched, tensing against him as her breathing sped up. She mumbled Josh's name a couple times, the raspy sound sending shivers down his spine. He rubbed her arms, hoping to ease whatever dreams were playing in her head when she screamed and bolted upright. She fought against the blankets, nearly socking him in the face when he tried to calm her before she seemed to come to her senses — was able to look at him with focused eyes.

Foster gave her a moment, staying close but not to the point he was touching her until she groaned and placed her elbows on her knees, scrubbing her hands down her face.

He eased forward, matching her position as he gave her a gentle nudge. "You okay?"

She pushed out a rough breath. "If I ignore the fact that I seemed destined to embarrass myself in your house, I'm great."

"Having a nightmare isn't embarrassing."

"It is when you nearly punch the guy beside you. And I'm sure I probably said something damning first, right?"

He shrugged. "Just your brother's name a couple times."

Mac merely nodded, staring at her hands as she sat there, shaking.

Foster sighed. "Do you want to talk about it?"

She slid her gaze his way. "I think it's pretty self-explanatory. He's dead. I'm not."

"It wasn't your fault, though."

She huffed then stood, untangling the blankets as she took a few heavy steps away before spinning. "Hate to break it to you, Beckett, but you don't hold the monopoly on guilt. Justified or not."

He rose, eyeing her as she stood there toeing the floor as more shivers raked through her. Though, he was fairly certain she wasn't cold. "I was sitting in the helicopter beside Sean when he died. You were a few thousand miles away on deployment when Josh was killed. One of those feels remarkably more justified."

"Why? The end result's the same. You couldn't save Sean, and I couldn't save Josh. Sacrifice doesn't care whether or not you're in the room or if they gave their life for yours or for the greater good." She choked out a laugh. "Trust me, ghosts aren't that discriminating."

Foster froze, her words sinking in. He glanced at the window, fully expecting Sean's apparition to be standing there, openly mocking him. Seeing nothing but the hint of the tree line in the distance was oddly surprising and he did a double take before rounding the table — closing in on her. Mac didn't move, standing there with her arms wrapped around her, his shirt riding high on her thighs.

He lifted his arm, softly tucking some of her wild

hair behind her ear. "I doubt either of them would want us to be stuck treading water."

"Then they shouldn't have died."

"Can't argue with you there, sweetheart."

The corner of her mouth quirked at the endearment, and she stared up at him with the same fiery look in her eyes she'd had when he'd had her pressed against the door and she'd dared him to deny the spark between them. That whatever was brewing had been more than chance. More than convenience.

That this really was some sort of cosmic destiny.

Foster kept his hand poised at her neck, his fingertips teasing the soft skin at her nape. Waiting for a sign she wanted more.

Mac smiled, nuzzling against his hand before stepping forward and palming his chest. "Are you still worried that creep might bust through the door?"

"Not tonight."

"And will Zain's new system let us know if anyone breaches the perimeter?"

"It'll let us know if anyone so much as breathes on it, let alone tries to gain access."

"Then, what are you waiting for?"

He forced himself to hold his ground and not toss her over his shoulder before taking the stairs two at a time. "I don't want you to think I'd take advantage—"

Mac cut him off with a delicate finger over his lips. "Do me a favor?"

He nodded.

"Shut up and make love to me."

CHAPTER ELEVEN

Either she was certifiably, insane and this would turn out to be an epic mistake, or she was finally finding her footing.

It only took one look at how Foster's mouth curved into a stunning smile beneath her finger for Mackenzie to acknowledge he was the reason she'd stay sane. Why civilian life would be far more rewarding than she'd counted on.

That maybe she'd finally be able to move beyond Josh's death and make peace with his ghost.

Foster tsked, his hand sliding back to cup her head as he leaned in. "Are you sure you want this? Because you seem a thousand miles away."

She laughed, then jumped into his arms, laughing harder when he caught her as she wrapped her legs around his waist. "Just thinking…"

"That this is either one hell of an epic beginning or a disaster in the making?"

"Pretty much."

"And?"

She cinched her arms around his neck as she leaned in, nipping at his bottom lip before teasing him with a soft kiss. "I say we let this dark horse run."

He closed his eyes, exhaling a raspy breath before smiling as he brushed his mouth over hers. "Hell yeah. Which means, you'd better hold on. This is gonna be one hell of a ride."

He kissed her. Not soft and gentle. This was desperate. Hungry. The kind of kiss that started wars. She ate at his mouth, moaning when he cupped her ass and started walking, somehow getting them up the stairs without tripping. Foster bumped them down the hallway, pausing every few feet to press her against the wall and reclaim her mouth.

His bedroom door bounced open as he carried her through, pausing just long enough to kick it shut behind them before continuing to the bed. He barely slowed as he placed one knee on the mattress then followed her down, landing them mostly in the middle.

Mac stared up at him, loving the way his hair teased his eyes and how he seemed to be focused on drawing air in then forcing it out. As if she'd pushed him past some internal limit, and he was fighting not to simply strip her down and thrust inside.

She lifted her hand and palmed his jaw. "Foster."

He groaned, resting his forehead on hers. "The

way you say my name. It's a nice change from Beckett."

"Then, you're gonna love the way I scream it."

His muscles tensed, his breath escaping in a harsh rasp. "Mackenzie…"

But she was already yanking on the hem of his tee — dragging it up his back and over his head. He tucked his chin enough she managed to pull the fabric off and toss it to one side before he dipped down — took her mouth with his.

His kisses were heaven. Or maybe hell. Some fiery combination of both? Or maybe it was lust wrapped in a promise. A glimpse of the future without losing the intensity of the moment.

Need burned across her skin. She lifted her head when he skimmed one hand up her side and across her shoulders, taking her borrowed shirt with him. A flutter of white cotton momentarily obscured her view, then he was back. Mouth pinched tight. Nostrils flaring.

He eased away until he was able to give her a long, slow sweep before those kissable lips curved into a brilliant smile, that same hand tracing a line across her collar bone. "Damn."

One fingertip danced lower, circling her breast before inching across her ribs. He frowned at the bandage taped along her side, huffing out a rough breath.

Mac shook her head, palming his jaw until he looked at her. "I'm fine."

"I saw the cut before they covered it up, and it's massive."

"Foster, it's really nothing."

"What you did tonight." His left eye twitched before he leaned in close. "I know you're a seasoned pro. That you've likely saved more lives than my team put together. But you risked everything for Chase. And I'll never forget how you were willing to die to get my best friend out of that Bronco. So, no, sweetheart. This isn't nothing."

He brushed his mouth over hers, giving her a hint of a kiss. "It's who you are. And I'm having a hard time seeing any reason why falling for you would be an epic mistake."

Her breath hitched, the hand palming his jaw trembling as she stared into his eyes, the truth of his statement gleaming back at her. Heating her skin until she swore wisps of smoke were curling off her.

Mac urged him closer, holding his gaze as she brushed her thumb across his cheek. "Then, stop worrying if my ribs are sore or whatever else your mind's conjuring up, and make this one hell of a beginning."

Foster inhaled, then he was moving. Crushing his mouth to hers as he pressed her into the mattress. Pinning her to the bed until she thought her lungs would explode. Foster didn't seem to care if either of them could breathe, barely giving her a second to gasp in some air before he was back. This kiss deeper. Far more desperate.

Her heart rate jacked up, her pulse echoing inside her head as he finally paused, grinning down at her as if she'd exorcised some of his demons. Lifted a massive weight off his shoulders.

He nipped at her lip, then kissed his way down her neck and along her shoulder, licking and sucking until she wanted to scream. She speared her fingers through his hair, tugging on the strands, but the brute didn't move. Just took his time, slowly making his way down her body until he was poised between her thighs.

Mac pushed onto her elbows, eyeing him as he teased her with a hint of penetration. "God, Foster. Do you know how long it's been? One more touch and…"

She let her head fall back on the bed when he swiped his tongue along her flesh, moaning as if he couldn't get enough of her taste. Was equally invested in her pleasure. Maybe more so because he made a second pass, humming this time.

That unraveled her. Had her fisting his hair as she pressed into his touch, all but grinding herself on him.

Foster laid one massive forearm across her hips, holding her captive as he devoured her, taking her to the brink only to ease off until the feeling ebbed before starting all over. Taking her right back to the edge of that abyss. Daring her to fall over.

Was she chanting his name? Begging? Or was that only inside her head?

Whatever it was, it seemed to set him off. Had Foster humming and licking as he added another finger, making her thighs shake when all that heat swirling inside her stalled.

She inhaled, poised on that edge. Waiting. Her chest squeezed tight. Dots eating away her vision.

Until he increased the pressure, nipping at her sensitive flesh, and she broke, riding out her release as she shattered into a thousand pieces.

Time stopped, or maybe it was only the two of them that seemed frozen. Nothing registering beyond his warm breath against her skin and her heart thundering in her chest.

Mac wasn't sure if it was minutes, hours or days later when she finally opened her eyes, her muscles lax. Feeling as if she might sink through the bed if given the chance.

Foster slid over her, brushing some hair back from her sweat-dampened face as he smiled. "Now that was epic."

She laughed, eating at his mouth when he put his lips on hers. Her lungs were burning again by the time he finally pulled back, all the muscles in his neck and arms straining.

Mac wrapped her legs around him, waiting for him to thrust inside when he groaned. She pried open one eyelid, frowning at the pained look on his face. "Foster?"

He grunted when she tilted her hips and all but pressed an inch of him inside her. "My wallet's downstairs with my wet clothes, not that I think I even have any condoms in it. And there's none up here, either."

She blinked, still trying to process the words when he sighed.

"I can go down and check…"

The thought that he hadn't been planning this messed with her head. Had her starting to believe that this really was the start of an epic beginning from a new perspective.

Mac palmed his cheek, loving as his stubble grazed her fingertips. "You weren't expecting this?"

Foster's eyes rounded, and he exhaled a rough breath. "Sweetheart, in a million years I never could have anticipated finding myself in this position. Here, with you. So no, I never saw this coming. Never thought I'd ever fall…"

His voice drifted off, but the unspoken words hung between them.

She nodded, any doubts or reservations that this wasn't forever in the making faded away, leaving only red-hot need in its wake. "I've been on birth control since I was seventeen, but I've never had sex without the guy wearing protection. Never really trusted anyone enough to take the chance. Or maybe I was just never that invested."

Foster tensed, every muscle flexing. "Understood—"

She slid her hand forward, cutting him off with a finger across his lips, again. Just like downstairs. "So,

I guess it's a good thing this isn't just sex. That I trust you with more than my life, and that I've never been this invested."

Foster froze, looking at her as if he wasn't sure if he'd heard her correctly.

She smiled, levering up to plant a scorching kiss on his mouth. "So, in case it's not blatantly obvious, I'll say it again. Shut up and make love to me."

He blinked, staring at her for what felt like forever before he closed his eyes and rested his forehead on hers. And she knew, everything had changed.

He started slow. A tentative rock of his hips that eased just the tip inside her. More like a promise than him staking a claim. She inhaled, falling back on the bed as she slid her hand behind his head, pulling him down until his mouth was only a breath away.

Foster grinned, then he was kissing her. Eating at her mouth as he thrust inside, stealing any breath she had left. He bottomed out, taking her to the brink in a single stroke. Whether it was his size, the unspoken words or all the ways he'd shown her he cared over the past few weeks, she wasn't sure. But she knew that this one night would alter her to the core.

The bed creaked as he picked up the pace, matching his movements to the shaky beat of her heart. Rain pelted the window in the background, as the howling wind added the perfect amount of ambience.

She wasn't sure how long they'd been entwined on the bed, her body strung tight as the inklings of what she knew would be a life-altering climax built low in her belly when Foster suddenly stopped, staring down at her as he shook his head.

He leaned in, nipping at her shoulder before staring her dead in the eyes. "You're holding back."

She blinked, her chest heaving, all that heat swirling beneath her skin. "I'm holding back?"

He raised an eyebrow as if daring her to lie to him.

She swallowed, staring at him as she pursed her lips. "If I give you that piece…" She wasn't convinced she'd survive if he walked away.

He shifted his weight onto one elbow as he gently cupped her face. "I'll keep it safe. And I'll give you mine, in return."

Mac inhaled. From the easy tilt of his head to how his mouth quirked at the corner it was obvious these weren't just words.

She closed her eyes as any remaining walls crumbled around her, leaving her lying there, exposed. Raw. Her heart pounding so hard she fully expected it to burst out of her chest.

Foster nuzzled her neck, peppering kisses across her collar bone then up the side of her face. "Now, we can make love."

Was she crying? Screaming his name? Having a stroke? Because it all hit her at once. Him starting up that punishing rhythm while claiming her mouth. How he lowered until every inch of their bodies was touching. The raspy way he whispered her name once he finally allowed her to breathe.

It pulled her under. Had her clinging to him as a lifeline. Her only tether keeping her from flying apart. And when he sucked at her pulse point, palming her ass as he tilted her hips and hit that sweet spot…

She broke. Died. All but burst into flames as the heat billowed out, taking her with it until she was floating in a blissful haze. Foster gave a few more jerking thrusts then he was emptying inside her, her name sounding around them like a benediction before he collapsed onto his elbows, bridging just enough weight that she could breathe.

She tugged him tighter, shaking her head when he mumbled something about crushing her and aggravating her ribs. She didn't care about her ribs or if her lungs could expand. She needed him. Grounding her. Keeping her sane when the sheer immensity of her feelings threatened to ruin her.

Foster sighed, dropping a kiss on her forehead until she finally managed to open her eyes and look into his. He brushed his thumb across her cheek, smiling at what she realized were tears. "Now, *that* was epic."

She laughed, though it came out wrong. Shaky. Borderline hysterical.

But he didn't seem fazed, just claimed her mouth in a soul-searing kiss as he placed his forehead on hers, again. "Me, too. Come on. Let's get you cleaned up so you can actually sleep, then we'll come back to bed, and I promise I'll hold you all night."

"Foster you don't have to—"

"Would you shut up and let me take care of you?"

She was definitely crying, now. Though, he took it as some weird form of approval and rolled off the side, then scooped her into his arms, crossing the short distance to the bathroom. He set her gently on her feet, ensuring she was steady before twisting on the taps as he grabbed a couple of clean towels off the shelf. Steam fogged the glass as he placed the towels on the counter then took her in his arms.

She smoothed her palms up his chest, along his shoulders then behind his head, teasing the hair at his nape. "I hope those muscles aren't just for show, because I'm liable to fall flat on my face."

"Are you questioning my virility already?" He shook his head in mock disappointment. "That hurts, sweetheart. Though, for the record, I'd never let you fall."

He shuffled backwards, angling them both into the shower. Hot water soothed any remaining rawness, the strong spray finally taking away the last of the chill. She stepped into his arms, closing her eyes as he grabbed the soap then ran it across her skin.

She smiled against his chest, laughing to herself at the way he hummed as he smoothed the suds around, easing her back in order to get the rest of her. She clenched her jaw, trying not to react as his fingertips danced across her skin, but between the strength of his touch and the lingering high from her orgasm, it was futile.

Two minutes in, and she was already strung tight. Another two, and he had her pinned to the wall, her ass balanced on a ridiculously small grab bar as he wedged his massive body between her thighs then plunged home.

Foster paused, grunting in seeming pain as he mouthed her shoulder, sucking at her skin as he forced air in and out. What she assumed was him gathering back a semblance of control.

But she didn't want him controlled. She wanted him raw. Unfettered. All but blind in his need.

Mackenzie braced her arms along his shoulders, biting at his jaw. "Now who's holding back?"

He snapped his head up, his gaze seizing and holding hers. He furrowed his brow, looking as if he was going to deny her claim before lowering his head as his chest heaved against hers. His breath mixing with the steam billowing around them.

Foster cocked his head to the side. "Are you sure you really want what's inside of me, sweetheart? Because it's nothing but shattered pieces."

She palmed his cheeks, tugging him in even closer. "'That just makes it easier to put us both back together because I feel broken, too." She brushed a soft kiss across his lips. "Except when I'm with you."

He froze — his eyes wide as his breath stalled in his

chest. Nothing but those turquoise orbs staring at her as the water echoed around them. Then he was leaning in, claiming her mouth as he crushed her into the tiled wall. He started a hurried rhythm, their combined heat adding to the thick air hanging around them.

She held on, meeting each thrust with a tilt of her hips. Trusting him not to let her fall as she used his shoulders to lever up and take his mouth. Needing that connection to keep her grounded.

Until he groaned against her ear, the desperate sound sending her over.

She arched into him, pulling him as close as possible as her climax shook through her, every muscle squeezed tight until her strength waned, and she collapsed against the shower wall.

Foster kept moving, muttering a raspy version of her name before he stiffened, inhaling a shaky breath. Then, he was emptying inside her, each stabbing thrust sending her higher until everything faded. Leaving only that red-hot pleasure and the firm weight of Foster pressed against her.

Mac came back to her senses realizing she was wrapped in a towel, Foster smiling victoriously at her as he carried her back to bed. She frowned, looking up at him as he placed her on the mattress. "Did I seriously pass out for a few seconds?"

"More like minutes." He shrugged. "Guess you really were exhausted."

"You don't have to look so proud of yourself."

He leaned in, dropping a kiss on her lips. "We both know I kinda do."

"Remember that when I bring you to your knees in the morning."

His eye twitched, the muscle in his temple jumping. "Deal."

He gave her another kiss, then grabbed the shirt she'd been wearing off the floor along with his pajama pants.

She arched a brow when he handed the shirt to her before pulling on the pants. "Something wrong with being naked?"

"Generally, no. But on the off chance we need to adapt to a dynamic situation, it might be wise to at least have the minimum on."

"The way I feel, a grenade could go off in the hallway, and I wouldn't even hear it, but if it means you'll sleep..."

"You're the reason I'll sleep, but Zain would have my ass if I wasn't still a bit prepared."

"Like the Sig that's probably in the nightstand?"

"Exactly." He climbed onto the bed shuffling them around until she was snugged against him, her head on his chest. "Comfy?"

Mac smiled up at him. "Perfect."

"Sleep. I'll wake you when it's time to go back to the hospital."

Mac burrowed against him, his steady heartbeat lulling her back into that warm haze. Tonight's events had definitely changed her future. She just hoped they'd figure everything out in time to enjoy it.

CHAPTER TWELVE

Foster bolted upright, taking Mac with him as his alarm app echoed through the room, his cell dancing across the nightstand. He reached for it, blinking away his blurry vision as he stared at the screen — back door.

Mac mumbled something that sounded like, "What the hell," before staring up at him. It only took one glance before she was rolling off the other side — meeting him at the foot of the bed. She moved with him to the door, cursing under her breath when his phone blew up with a series of chirps before going eerily silent. "Where?"

He huffed as he shoved his cell into one of his front pockets. "It started with the back door followed by a bunch of motion sensors activating before it cut off."

"Kash and the others?"

He placed his ear against the door, straining to

hear even a hint of movement. "It's not even seven. That's a bit early for Chase and Zain to be discharged, and I'd like to think they'd shoot me a text, first, to let me know it was them, but…"

He wouldn't count on it being his teammates. Not after the night they'd had. And with only a hint of light beyond the windows, it could be that same asshole hoping he'd caught them sleeping.

Mac waved her fingers at him. "I need a weapon."

Foster grunted then motioned toward the bed. "There's a spare twenty-two duct-taped to the bottom side of the boxspring at the end of the bed."

"Of course there is." She darted over and bent low, ripping the gun free. "Do I want to know why it's taped under the bed?"

"In case I ever had to hide under there."

She shook her head as she moved in beside him, again. "You're not the type of guy who'd ever hide. But even if you wanted to, you're too big to fit under the damn bed and no one hides there. It's the first place anyone checks."

"Which is why there's a freaking gun taped to the bed frame." He froze when the floor creaked outside. Not much noise, and definitely something most would chalk up to the quirks of a century-old house. But he knew the sound of a footfall anywhere.

He motioned to the other side of the door, then shuffled over, staying far enough back he wouldn't be instantly visible if the door opened. Mackenzie held her ground, looking far too comfortable with his Beretta as they stood there, waiting.

Foster was just starting to think he'd been wrong when the door swung open, a dark silhouette stepping through. He moved forward, but Mac already had her gun at the guy's head.

"Give me a reason, asshole."

The guy froze as her voice sounded through the room, the tension thickening the air. There was nothing but silence for a few moments before the guy tsked.

He glanced behind him at Mac before meeting Foster's gaze. "Was it something I said?"

Mac inhaled then grunted. "Chase? Seriously?" She gave his buddy a light shove, shaking her head as she took a few deep breaths. "I could have shot you."

He simply shrugged. "I would have countered if I'd thought you were actually going to fire."

She crossed her arms over her chest. "You're pretty cocky for a guy whose brains were in my crosshairs a second ago. No one's that fast."

Chase grinned. "I'm glad we don't have to put that theory to the test. You two sleep well?"

Foster walked over, staring Chase down. "Why aren't you still in the hospital?"

"Because they're loud and uncomfortable and smell like lemon-scented death."

"And yet, it's where you're supposed to be when you've separated your shoulder among other things."

Chase blew off the comment. "I've been hurt

worse rock climbing with Zain. Besides, Keaton called Kash thirty minutes ago and said he and his buddy Dawson would have that intel you wanted within the hour, so we came back."

"Why did my cousin call Kash?"

Chase chuckled, motioning toward Mackenzie. "He said you might be otherwise engaged, and he didn't want to interrupt a morning love fest."

"I'll kill him. It's that simple."

"Foster!" Kash's voice echoed up the stairs. "Keaton's on video. You and Mac need to get your asses down here."

Chase swatted Foster in the chest. "Keaton's nothing if not punctual. Get dressed." He ambled back out the door only to stop a foot into the hallway. "And before you think about blowing us off, I'll be waiting right here."

Foster shut the door, leaning against it as he met Mackenzie's gaze. "I'm starting to think I need new friends."

Mackenzie laughed. "Please, those are your *ride or die* guys. Though, I'm starting to think they're the real reason you suggested I wear your tee to bed."

"Busted. Though, you do look incredibly hot wearing my clothes. Guess you probably need some sweats, huh?"

"I'm pretty sure everything from last night is still wet."

"We'll do laundry, but in the meantime..." He

sorted through his stuff, tossing her some track pants. "That's the smallest I've got."

She waved off his concern, shimmying into them. "As long as they're dry."

Foster walked over to her, thumbing the waistband. "Way hotter than I imagined. Especially knowing I get to remove them, later."

"Careful what you wish for, or I might not care that Keaton and your team are waiting for us downstairs."

He grunted, then snagged her around the waist before spinning and backing her against the wall. He fisted her hair as he lowered his face level with hers. "Challenge accepted."

He ravaged her mouth, groaning when she shifted enough to ride his thigh, yanking him back down once he'd paused to catch a breath. Foster upped the ante, smoothing his hand beneath her shirt before cupping her breast. Grinning at how her nipple beaded against his palm. He was already working through how to get her naked, again, in record time, when Chase banged on the door.

"Still waiting, you two."

Foster clenched his jaw, rolling his right shoulder as he shook out his hand then concentrated on stepping away from Mac. It took a few tries, but he managed to untangle his body from hers before grabbing her hand. He shook his head, then headed for the door, huffing at Chase when his buddy smirked at them. "We're good."

Chase laughed as they stepped into the hallway. "Mac doesn't look as if she agrees, but it'll have to do."

Foster snapped his gaze to her, and Chase hadn't been joking. Her eyes were dilated, her lips still kiss-swollen as she took several deep breaths, clenching her jaw until he thought her teeth would crack. But she managed to rein it in, nodding at him a moment later.

He leaned in close. "Just a delay. Promise."

She rolled her eyes but followed him along the hallway then down the stairs, toward the kitchen. Kash and Zain were at the counter chatting with Keaton or Dawson. His buddies looked up, grinning at Foster when he stopped next to them.

Zain laughed, and Foster flipped the man off, offering Mac a stool before taking his.

He claimed the one next to her, running his hand down his face. "At least tell me you've got coffee."

Kash slid a couple cups their way. "Fresh from the Lighthouse Café. It appears Jordan remembered how you both order it. Which means we either go there far too often, or there's something unique about her."

Mac exhaled. "You mean more unique than those Krav Maga moves she unleashed the other day? Classes at the Y, my ass."

"Agreed." Kash angled the phone so it faced Foster and Mac. "And not what you apparently asked Keaton and Dawson to look into, so I'll turn the conversation over to them."

Foster focused on the screen, groaning inwardly at the smug smiles Keaton and Dawson flashed him. "Do you two need to get any razzing off your chests, or can we get down to business?"

Keaton chuckled. "I'm thinking that's what we interrupted but..." He nodded at Mac. "Nice to see you, again, Mackenzie."

She took a swig of her coffee. "I'd say the same, Keaton, but I had big plans for this morning, none of which involves an audience."

Foster choked on his sip of coffee, glancing over at her. He fell even harder at the way she smiled at him, and how she didn't seem the least bit fazed that their changing relationship had been outed.

Keaton whistled. "Straight for the jugular. But that's what you Coasties do. I find it interesting that Foster neglected to mention you were former Coast Guard last night."

"It isn't related to the current issue."

"Everything's related to the current issue, but I'll let Dawson have the floor."

Dawson shifted in his seat, accepting a coffee from someone off-screen before sighing. "Foster. I thought you retired to that blip of a town to get away from all this tangos-on-your-ass crap?"

Foster shrugged. "I can't help it if the crap finds me."

"Right. Well, neither of you are going to like what I have to say."

Mac scoffed. "Not to belittle anything, but why

won't I like this other than because it involves people I care about?"

Dawson looked at Foster then back to her. "Because it also involves your brother, Josh."

Mac straightened, teetering on the edge of the stool. "What?"

"Just, do me a favor and let me get through this before either of you lose your shit."

Foster placed his hand on top of Mac's, nodding when she snapped her attention to him before focusing on Dawson. "No promises, but we'll try."

"Good enough." Dawson took another swig, looking as if he was settling in to be court marshaled rather than to discuss some intel. "It turns out Greer was right to question the Carrington angle because this all revolves around him and his drug, Vexarin."

Foster grunted. "Why am I not surprised?"

"Well, you'd better buckle up, because it's far worse than anyone thought. But before I start, you need to know that Greer's 'friend' in the Bureau she reached out to happens to be a mutual one. And since Chloe's still an active special agent and this could get her fired—"

"Everything's hush hush and doesn't leave this room." Foster crossed his arms. "We know the score, Dawson."

"Wow, you Air Force guys are always so impatient."

"That's because we worked for a living instead of

sitting on our asses for weeks on end waiting for the Navy to give us the green light."

"And yet, you still need our help."

Foster chuckled. "Point noted. Do you need me to grovel a bit or…"

"Save it for the next favor you'll undoubtedly need." Dawson rested his elbows on the table. "Back to your drug problem. As you know, Carrington and his company, GeneTide, were denied FDA approval of Vexarin due to its extreme side effects. But instead of destroying the remaining stock, Carrington vanished with it, only to have it pop up a few months later on the black market. Turns out all those undesirable traits are extremely useful if you're a cartel looking for a performance-enhancing drug for your enforcers. However, even Carrington knew it was way too hot for him to be directly involved in the distribution, so he outsourced it. Want to guess who his distributors were?"

Foster inhaled, praying he was wrong, and it wasn't the two men who'd been accused of killing Mackenzie's brother. But that was the only way he envisioned this linking back to Josh Parker. "Please don't say it was Daniel Shaw and Brad Newport."

"Not saying their names doesn't make it any less true."

"Well, crap."

"Greer and Chloe's contact was able to *acquire* a list of all the soldiers involved in Carrington's trials, and they were two of the first to take the drug. Which makes sense. Ex-Army Rangers with impressive records, no one would have considered they'd turn. But being addicted to Vexarin obviously changed them."

"This is crazy. I can wrap my head around them switching sides but how did they even know about Raven's Cliff?"

"Oh my god. My dad." Mac scrubbed her hand down her face as her skin blanched white. "He was searching for ex-military personnel to work for Raven's Watch. He figured they'd be the most trustworthy. Called a bunch of buddies and organizations. He practically handed them the perfect location to run their operation."

Foster gave her shoulder a squeeze. "They should have been trustworthy. And there's no way Atticus could have known. Their medical records were sealed, and even with his rank and connections, that's not a line he would have crossed."

"We can't tell him any of this. If he thinks that he's in any way responsible—"

"The only people responsible for Josh's death are the men who killed him. Period." Though, Foster doubted that would stop either Mac or Atticus from bearing the guilt. All those undiscriminating ghosts she'd talked about.

"That's not how he'll interpret this intel."

"Then, I guess it's a good thing it can't leave this room." Foster shuffled closer, then focused on Dawson. "None of this makes any sense. Why kill

Josh? And why are mercenary assholes nosing around my place a year later unless..." The pieces started falling together, the obvious answer screaming inside his head. "Crap. You seriously don't think they used this house to store their drugs, do you?"

Dawson shrugged. "It's the perfect spot. And there's an abandoned airstrip not too far down the coast."

"But Shaw and Newport are in jail—"

"They're dead, actually."

"Since when?"

Dawson nodded when Foster and Mac asked in unison. "Last night. Apparently, they were involved in a riot and were killed during the armed assault to retake the prison wing. At least, that's the official story."

"So, the only two men who actually know all of Carrington's secrets get killed the same night Greer, Chase and Zain are attacked? When Greer was bringing this exact intel to us?" Foster raked his hand through his hair. "And that's not suspicious at all?"

"Preaching to the choir, brother. And sadly, I don't have all the answers. But I can tell you that based on the snippets from Josh's emergency call before he passed out and what investigators found at the scene, it was very obvious Shaw and Newport had someone else working with them. Now, there some chatter about it being the caretaker who was overseeing Raven's Manor before your father bought it, but nothing concrete, and definitely not something that would have garnered local police a search warrant. Regardless, our source thinks this third guy got into a deadly shootout with a cartel gang when their drug deal went sideways. Bleeding and near death, he called Shaw and Newport for an extraction. Not wanting their operation to be outed if authorities somehow linked them to this other guy, they passed it off as a rescue call. The only problem was, Josh Parker had worked for the Portland Police Department for several years and knew a damn drug deal gone bad when he saw one."

Foster blew out a rough breath. "So, they killed Josh then made a run for it."

"Authorities never found that other guy, but someone left a lethal amount of blood at the scene. And what's even more interesting is that when Shaw and Newport were apprehended later that same night, they didn't have any drugs on them. And there hadn't been enough time to relocate them, which suggests..."

Foster groaned as he pinched the bridge of his nose, hoping to stem the pain creeping across his temples. "They're likely still in the house."

"Which explains why Carrington attempted to purchase it. He knows the drugs are there, but since he wasn't directly involved in the distribution, he has no idea where on the property Shaw stashed them."

"And when he wasn't successful, he sent his goon squad to uncover them."

Dawson nodded. "But by the time they got there,

your parents had taken possession and Carrington's people couldn't risk another questionable death with Josh's murder still hanging over the area like a dark omen. Which is why they tried a bunch of covert searches."

Foster drew himself up, knowing the answer to his next question but needing to hear Dawson confirm it. "Then they realize my parents are renovating the entire estate and will likely discover the drugs before they do. They still can't risk outright killing them, but if my parents die in an accident, there won't be an investigation, and Carrington's people would have more than enough time to search the house. Hell, tear it down."

"But that goon squad hadn't counted on the security company your father hired maintaining their vigil until you arrived." Dawson motioned toward Keaton. "Keaton told me about that piece of hardware you found at Greer's crash site. The cops found something similar in some debris on the edge of that cliff where you parents went over, but local law passed if off as a garage opener. I suppose it could be a coincidence… "

Foster arched a brow.

Dawson nodded. "I know. I don't put much stock in those either. Which suggests Carrington's men are getting tired of treading water."

Foster nodded, the bitter truth weighing heavily on his shoulders. He should have known something was off. The way his dad had been preoccupied the couple of times Foster had called in the months prior to his death. Or how he'd wondered if Foster was going to visit soon. Not a question his dad had usually asked, especially when he was all too familiar with how deployments worked. But Foster had been too busy worrying about his job to make the connections.

Dawson cleared his throat. "You two okay?"

Foster glanced at Mac, noting her pinched lips and pale complexion. "Ask us after we nail these bastards. Speaking of which, any intel on who we're up against?"

"Remember that part where I said I didn't have all the answers? But maybe you'll get lucky and the detonator piece you picked up will pan out."

"Right, because we've been nothing but lucky so far."

"You're all still breathing. I'd say that's about as good as it gets."

"Noted. And thanks for going the extra mile. I owe you."

Dawson nodded. "Put these assholes in jail, or better still, in the ground, and we'll call it even."

"Hooyah." Foster straightened, then stopped. "Hey, one last thing. I don't suppose you checked out the local sheriff's office? Greer hinted they couldn't be trusted, and I find it suspicious that Carrington and Vexarin were never mentioned regarding Josh's death. That it was left as simply an assumed drug-related incident."

"That's because the Department of Defense has been actively covering up anything Vexarin related. They don't want anyone knowing their wonder drug went dark side, and they let Carrington waltz off with it. As for Sheriff Thompson, I called around but couldn't find any evidence that he or his other deputies were involved in this. Though, that doesn't mean they're clean. They could just be good at hiding their connections."

"I'll keep that in mind. Thanks, again, buddy."

Dawson gave Foster a quick salute then the screen winked out, leaving an eerie void in the room. Kash, Zain and Chase shuffled on their seats then stood, quietly excusing themselves as they muttered something about performing a quick perimeter check. Though, Foster knew they were trying to give him and Mac some time to quietly deal with the new intel.

Mackenzie trudged across the room before spinning and leaning against the wall. She looked up at him, her eyes glassy as she speared her fingers through her hair. "This is crazy."

Foster picked his way over to her. "We'll get whoever's behind this."

"Before or after they hurt someone else we care about?" She shook her head. "Josh is dead, Greer's in the ICU, and your teammates look as if they just survived a few rounds inside the Thunderdome. If I'd just agreed to be part of this business when my father first kicked it off, maybe—"

"What? Josh would still be alive? Because there was no stopping that train, Mackenzie. Your father still would have needed medics and rescue crew, and Shaw and Newport still would have been his best option."

"You don't know that."

"Yeah, I do. And you do, too. But I suppose it could have been you who was killed, instead. Which is really what this is all about. Wanting to be the one who made the sacrifice. And yeah, I'm *intimately* familiar with that scenario — have been living it every day since my last mission. But all this guilt and second guessing doesn't change the facts, regardless of how much we want them to."

Her chin quivered as a few tears welled in her eyes then spilled down her cheeks.

Foster wiped a couple away then gathered her in his arms, holding tight as she took a few shuddering breaths.

"I know nothing will bring your brother back. But maybe stopping Carrington and his enforcers will help ease the burden. And we will."

She nodded, giving him a hint of a smile before pursing her lips into a tight line. "We're going to find those damn drugs and tear down Carrington's entire empire."

"Hooyah."

She snorted, glancing at the door when his buddies reappeared. "I guess this means my big plans for the morning are on hold."

Foster sighed. "Trust me, I'm not happy about that either. But I need to get that device to Bodie. See if he can get any prints off it that might give us a clue as to who we're up against—if they're just your average mercenary or more."

"I'll do that." Chase ambled over to them. "I told Bodie I'd spell him off and watch over Greer for the day. I'm sure the guy needs some sleep, but he could get the process going."

"We can go and have Greer's back. You need to rest—"

"Sorry, Foster." Chase tapped his chest. "Greer's my responsibility. I was driving. I'm the reason she got hurt. And I got more than enough sleep last night."

"If our hunch is right, someone put a bomb under her Bronco."

"And I didn't notice."

"Chase..." Foster speared his fingers through his hair, aware he likely wouldn't win this argument. "So, the fact your arm's in a sling?"

"Won't affect how I shoot with my other hand. And that way, you two can scour the house looking for drugs."

Kash gave Foster's shoulder a pat as he moved in on Foster's other side. "You know he's not going to back down, so just let it go."

Foster huffed. "Fine. But I want hourly check-ins."

"Okay, *Dad*." Chase rolled his eyes as he grabbed a Ziplock bag and put the device inside it. "I'll tell

Bodie to call one of you when he has any news, so don't get so hot and heavy that you miss his call."

Foster shook his head, snagging Kash when he and Zain made a move toward the front door. "Where are you two going?"

Kash glanced at Zain then back to Foster, brow furrowed. "Home."

"Oh, no. Everyone's staying here until we nail these bastards. There're plenty of rooms on the other side of the house."

"This is payback, isn't it?" Kash nudged Zain. "We'll grab some supplies then we'll be back to help look for buried treasure."

"The three of us will look. Zain can sit on his ass and keep an eye on those cameras he installed."

Zain huffed, obviously less than amused at the prospect of being sidelined. "And you thought I was being paranoid."

"You were, but like always, we need paranoid."

Mackenzie moved in beside him, nudging his side after Zain and Kash headed out. "Do you really think there're drugs hidden beneath the floorboards?"

"Probably not the floorboards, but someone seems to think that stash of Vexarin's still here." Foster turned and brushed his thumb across her jaw. "Sorry about this morning."

"I've had worse wake-up calls."

"Knowing Zain, he'll insist on monitoring the security tonight if you'll give me another chance."

She smiled, and it hit him just as hard as earlier.

"I think that can be arranged." She arched a brow. "They will be a few walls away, right?"

"More than a few. Promise."

"Deal. Now, do we have five minutes to make-out before Kash and Zain get back or..."

Foster snagged her around the waist and tugged her in close. "I'm betting on ten, so, take a breath. I'm using every single one."

CHAPTER THIRTEEN

Mackenzie sat in Foster's truck as he drove toward town, fatigue weighing heavy on her mind. They'd spent the day searching the areas of Foster's home that hadn't been renovated but had come up empty. While they still had a few more rooms to go, each unsuccessful search had been like a punch to the gut. A reminder that Josh and Foster's parents had been killed for a stash of drugs that might not even be there.

That maybe none of this would end in justice.

Foster tapped her thigh, tilting his head when she glanced over at him. "You're unusually quiet."

She laughed. "Is that your polite way of saying I talk too much?"

"It's my polite way of asking if you're okay without you getting defensive about it."

She shrugged, pausing to look out the window. Thick gray clouds raced across the sky—the promise of more rain heavy in the air. "I think we both know that I'm not, but that's been true since Josh was killed. Dawson didn't really tell me anything new, he just connected your dots with mine. Which means, I should be asking how you are because you're the one who just learned your parents' death wasn't accidental. That's got to be a hard pill to swallow."

Foster's left eye twitched as he focused on the road. "Just something else I missed that could have been prevented."

She frowned, shifting over until she was as close as possible. "Foster. There's no way you could have known any of this was going to happen. Which suggests that whatever else you think you should have spotted and stopped was probably beyond your scope, too. And I have a pretty good idea it involved your last mission. Why Sean died."

She held up her hand when he slid his gaze her way. "I don't expect you to talk about it. Classified or not, I know firsthand some demons are better left buried. Though, if you ever want to. I'm here."

Foster stared straight ahead as a heavy silence fell over the cab for several minutes before he sighed and rolled his right shoulder. "I haven't mentioned it because it's eerily similar to what happened to Josh. A rescue mission that was more of a setup. Rogue agents who opened fire inside the helicopter. Same end result. Only Sean died because he shielded me. Thought I was the only one who could get everyone else back in one piece."

He grunted then pounded his left hand on the steering wheel. "And all because I missed how edgy those bastards were getting. The increased tension. Not to mention flying in weather I had no right chancing." He gave her a quick side-eye. "So yeah, sweetheart, I should have realized the increased stress in my dad's voice meant something was off. That I needed to ask questions instead of just believing he was tired. That they simply missed me and wanted a chance to visit."

Mackenzie inhaled. She hadn't thought he'd actually talk about the mission. Though, it explained a lot. She studied him for a few moments before softly placing her hand on his shoulder. "Nothing I say is going to sway your line of thinking with respect to your parents. Though, from everything my dad's told me about them, and your dad in particular, he didn't strike me as the kind of man to dance around a subject. I think if he really thought there was something nefarious happening, he would have told you, if for no other reason than to get your opinion. As for Sean... Did he shield you before or after you were hit?"

Foster frowned.

Mac smoothed her hands over the marks she'd noticed on his skin last night. "Those scars on your shoulder and back from all those plates and screws you had implanted. They can't be more than a few months old."

"You noticed them, huh?"

"We were naked last night, and you definitely had my full attention. Which suggests you're only telling me the part of the story where you feel you failed."

She eased back, giving him some space. Though, based on how he was staring at her — eyes narrowed, and chest heaving — he didn't seem as if he wanted any space. "Which I also get because Josh outright told me he thought the new recruits were too twitchy for ex-special forces. To which I told him he was reading too much into it. That adjusting to civilian life took time, and they just needed to acclimate. Pretty sure that makes me responsible, too."

Foster drove for a bit before blowing out a rough breath. "Are you always going to use logic against me? Because if that's the case, I'll have to change my strategy."

"Only when it's really important."

"Why do I get the feeling every discussion will be important?"

"Because you're paranoid." She smiled at him then eased back over. "I *am* sorry about your folks. I was overseas on a TACLET mission when my mom died of cancer. Still haven't really forgiven myself for missing those last few months."

Foster shook his head. "We're quite the pair." He nodded at a nondescript building not too far from the hanger. "That should be Bodie's place. Here's hoping he didn't ask us to stop by because it's actually some kind of intervention your dad arranged."

Mackenzie laughed. She had to admit, she loved

Foster's sense of humor. Though, she had a nagging feeling it wasn't the only thing she loved about him. In fact, the more she thought about it, the more obvious it seemed.

She'd been completely honest when she told him that being with him had been the first time she'd felt whole in what had probably been years. Flying was the only thing that ever came close, and even that had been lacking lately — as if she was missing a piece.

A Foster-shaped one.

Mackenzie groaned inwardly. The nonstop threats and lack of sleep were obviously getting to her. And she needed to rein in her emotions before she made a complete fool of herself.

Foster parked the truck outside the office door, looking over at her as if he knew she was having an internal conversation. And she had a bad feeling she wasn't hiding those emotions nearly enough. As if it was written in the lines of her forehead that she was falling hard.

That she *had* fallen hard.

He chuckled, and she knew she was right. "Come on. The faster we talk to Bodie, the sooner I can get you out of those clothes."

She nearly tripped as she jumped out of his truck, shaking her head before meeting him at the front. The jerk just smiled and placed his palm on the small of her back, glancing over his shoulder several times on the short walk to the entrance. Even after they'd walked inside, he scanned the gravel lot one more time.

Bodie strode through another doorway a moment later, his hair disheveled, smudges beneath his eyes. She doubted he'd gotten any sleep.

"Foster. Mac. Thanks for coming over."

Foster shook the man's hand then gave him a slap on the shoulder, the same way he did with his other teammates. What Mac assumed was some unspoken show of kinship. "It sounded important and likely something you didn't want to discuss over an unsecured line."

"You could say that." Bodie walked past them, locking the front door before waving them through. "Let's go where it's a bit more secure."

Foster placed his palm on her back, again, leaning in close. "I really hope this isn't an intervention."

Mackenzie gave him a playful swat, following Bodie down the hallway then through a set of doors. He motioned to a desk on the other side of the room, closing the doors behind him.

He walked straight to the chair on the far side, sliding onto it then tapping on his keyboard. Ten seconds flat, and the machine was humming, the blue light reflecting off the far window. "You two look as if you might fall down, so pull up a chair."

Foster held one out for her, giving her shoulder a squeeze before taking his. "This is quite the setup. Bug-proof room?"

Bodie grinned. "That obvious?"

"It's got that feel about it."

"And before you say anything, the glass has a coating that makes it impossible to see through from the outside."

Foster nodded. "Are the doors blast proof?"

"Depends on the magnitude. But it'll stop a fair amount. And I've got an armory behind that wall, so…"

Foster nudged her. "And you think I'm paranoid."

Mac leaned in. "I'm pretty sure Zain has all of this and more at his place."

Foster merely grinned, laying his arm across the back of her seat as he focused on Bodie. "I'm really hoping that all of these precautions mean you uncovered something interesting."

The corner of Bodie's mouth lifted slightly. "I guess that depends. Let's start with that device. In a nutshell, while it looks innocuous, it's a freaking art piece. Small. Unobtrusive and virtually undetectable. I haven't seen anything like this outside of the military. Hell, it might be beyond what they're using. Which makes sense considering my next point. Does having an ex-Green Beret on your ass count as interesting?"

Foster was out of his seat a second later. "I knew that guy was way too cool to be some run-of-the-mill mercenary. And the way he countered that flash bang…"

Bodie arched a brow. "There a flash bang involved?"

Foster waved it off, reclaiming his seat. "Old news. So, who's the name at the top of my shit list?"

Bodie tapped a few more keys then turned his monitor. "Meet Captain Jack Voss, aka Striker. As I said, former Green Beret turned mercenary for hire. The man left the service a year ago on very unfriendly terms. I can't confirm a dishonorable discharge, but something went seriously sideways because he was essentially booted overnight."

Foster leaned in, studying the man's image on the screen. "Any idea who he's currently working for?"

"Now, that's another interesting part. My sources say Striker's only had one employer — one Dr. Elias—"

"Carrington?"

Bodie frowned. "You know the man?"

"His name keeps popping up and not in a good way. I assume you know about his botched drug, Vexarin?"

"That wanna-be wonder drug that's creating evil *Captain Americas* instead? I read about it." Bodie eased back in his chair, steepling his fingers. "You know about the trials, right?"

"Only that anyone involved started exhibiting extreme paranoia and aggressive behavior and that it failed to get FDA approval. Which explains why it's now a wanted commodity on the black market by mainly cartel bosses."

"Can't let all that unbridled aggression go to

waste. But I was referring to the black-ops unit that tested Vexarin in the field before it was shut down."

Foster sat up straighter, glancing at her before frowning. "There were actual missions?"

"Several months' worth before it became apparent that the men no longer considered orders their top priority. Which I think is the real reason it was shut down. The JSOC commander couldn't control his own operatives."

Mackenzie shifted on her chair. "Is this where you tell us that Striker was part of that unit?"

Bodie sighed. "The guy wasn't just part of it. He was in charge of it. Which means, he knows, firsthand, the brutal effects of the drug and the horrifying advantage it gives to anyone taking it. There's just one problem. According to my contact, the longer the men took it, the more they needed to sustain the same level of enhancement. And men like Voss don't give up that advantage without a fight."

Mac nodded. "You think he's still addicted to it."

"I think Voss is batshit crazy with extreme tunnel vision. From what I understand, Vexarin has been noticeably absent on the black market for several months. That timing alone is suspicious, and it makes me wonder why he's targeting both Greer and your team, Foster."

Foster scrubbed his hand across his jaw as he glanced at her. He arched a brow, motioning to Bodie. Silently asking her how much she thought he should share. Which she had to admit, sent a few shivers along her spine — that he valued her opinion enough to ask.

She shifted over and gave his hand a squeeze. "You already know he can't be bought, so no sense in withholding intel, now."

Brodie chuckled. "And here I thought the interview was over."

Foster grunted. "You're an ex-Army Ranger. You know it's never over. But Mac's right. The gist of it is that we believe the men who were distributing Vexarin for Carrington were using Raven's Manor as their warehouse."

Bodie pursed his lips, looking directly at her. "The only drug dealers who went down at that time were Shaw and Newport."

Mac closed her eyes for a moment before nodding. "We think they killed Josh when a Vexarin deal went bad."

"Well, shit." Bodie huffed. "Let me guess, Carrington believes his stash of Vexarin is somewhere on your property."

Foster nodded. "And we get the feeling he's done trying to be covert about acquiring it."

Bodie nodded. "That's the intel Greer was going to share that night."

"Which is why Voss blew her Bronco off the road, along with Zain's truck. He was trying to keep his involvement on the down low because he knew once she shared everything involving Carrington, it was only a matter of time before it circled back to him."

"Not to make matters worse, but I don't think it's just the drugs that might be hidden there. It's all his research." Bodie placed his forearms on the top of the desk. "Think about it. If Carrington had the formulas, he'd simply make more rather than chance getting caught trying to steal whatever Vexarin is left. But when he originally went dark, he couldn't risk keeping the research with him on the possibility he was discovered before he arranged new lab space. His only choice was to deep six everything in case anyone came knocking. No better place than with his secure drugs."

Foster groaned. "This just keeps getting better." He motioned toward the room. "I don't suppose you have anything in here that can see through walls?"

Bodie laughed. "I *might* have a Range-R in my office supply room, but that won't help you narrow down where those drugs are. Though, I'm trying to get my hands on one of those new Nighthawk devices. For study purposes, of course."

"Of course." Foster frowned when his cell pinged. He took a quick glance, smirking when he read whatever was onscreen before shoving it back in his pocket as he stood and extended his hand. "Thanks, Bodie. I owe you."

Bodie waved it off. "About time I repaid you for saving my life."

"I just flew the chopper, brother. You did the hard part. And I'm serious. You need a hand with anything, you call."

"This sounds like the makings of a very dangerous friendship."

Foster laughed. Hard. "Wouldn't have it any other way. Are you okay watching Greer tonight? Mac and I can spell Chase off."

Bodie waved him off. "Got it covered. Besides, you guys have a house to rip apart."

Foster shook his head, chatting with Bodie as they made their way back to the door then out to his truck. He gave the man another pat on the shoulder. "Thanks, again."

Bodie gave him a small salute. "Anything for you, Major. But get some sleep. You two look exhausted. Though, maybe that's not from Voss."

Mac rolled her eyes as Foster chuckled then slid behind the wheel. "Why do I get the feeling I'll be the one flying his ass around when he needs a favor?"

Foster shrugged. "Like you wouldn't jump at the chance. Though, don't count me out, just yet, sweetheart. Maybe I just need the right motivation to get behind the controls, again."

Though she suspected he'd meant it to sound casual, she didn't miss the tightness in his voice. Or how he clenched his right hand and released it a couple times.

Mac slid closer and brushed her hand along his arm. "You know it's okay if you decide that part of your life is over, right? That you don't owe anyone, anything."

"Other than your father?"

"Foster…"

"It's fine. Atticus means well and hell, maybe everyone's right, and I just need to man up. I'm just having a hard time compartmentalizing what happened that night. How to sit in the damn chopper without seeing all the blood. Hearing Sean…"

He swallowed, looking as if he wanted to puke before shaking it off. "But seeing as you already sold your soul to Greer when you promised to fly her anywhere she needed to go…"

She swatted him, noting the shift in topic away from him. "In for a penny, I suppose." She frowned when Foster turned onto the road leading to the Raven's Watch parking lot. "Foster? Why are we at the hanger?"

Foster merely grinned as he parked the truck out front before twisting to face her. "I thought since we were going past and your dad hadn't seen you since last night, you might want to drop in and say hi."

Mac snagged his arm before he could slip out the door. "Beckett. You did *not* stop by on a whim. So, why are we really here?"

He stared at her for a few moments, then grabbed his cell, unlocking the screen before holding it out to her. "Your father wanted proof of life. I thought this was easier than explaining why I was taking your photo."

She stared at the screen, heat burning through her cheeks as she read the message. "I'm going to kill him."

"You're all he has left. And after that insane rescue yesterday, I can't fault the guy for worrying."

"Christ, you're going to be sending me the same damn proof of life messages when I'm out on a call and late, aren't you?" She held up her hand. "Don't bother answering, it's written on your face, and I'd hate for you to lie to me when I still have all these big plans floating around inside my head."

"I wasn't going to lie. I absolutely will be demanding proof of life if you miss your check-in time, so make peace with that now, sweetheart. And no, it's not because I don't think you can handle any situation. It's because I care."

"You make it extremely hard to argue with you."

"Funny, you haven't had issues with that before." He jumped out, waving to her over the hood. "Come on. Kash and Zain will be demanding food on the way back."

She met him at the front, smiling when he took her hand and headed for the door. Her father opened it when they were still a few feet back, crossing his arms over his chest.

Foster merely walked past. "She's still breathing, so stop scowling at me, Atticus."

Mackenzie stopped and faced her father. "Why on earth did you text Foster and not me?"

Atticus shrugged. "Because I knew he'd answer. You would have ignored me."

"I used to hunt cartel. I think I can handle a few cuts and scrapes without needing to check-in."

"And that's why I texted Beckett." He looked between them. "Is that his shirt?"

She smiled. While Foster had washed and dried her clothes, she'd elected to keep wearing his stuff. "And his sweatpants. Is that a problem?"

Atticus muttered something under his breath. "Saylor's here. You might as well say hello before you take off." He walked off, giving Foster those creepy "I'm watching you" fingers.

"Saylor's here?"

She grabbed Foster's hand and dragged him into the hanger, smiling when her friend came barreling across the room, nearly bowling her over. She grimaced against the pressure on her ribs, not that she'd complain.

Her friend eased back, giving Foster a thorough once-over before grinning at her. "I was starting to think your dad had lied about you signing up just so I'd join."

Mackenzie laughed. "Which he would, but no. I'm just not working today."

Her gaze narrowed as she looked at Foster, again. "I heard you were involved in some sort of bizarre rescue." She leaned closer. "On the ground!"

"You say that like it's the first time."

"It probably was." She eyed Foster. "I don't suppose you're *Beckett*?"

Foster sighed. "Glad to see the trend regarding my last name continues."

"You're the one who's pissed off Atticus."

"All I said was no."

"Exactly. Why do you think I'm here? The ornery goat said he'd call my dad if I didn't base my tour company here and help out with water rescues whenever he needed me."

Mac groaned. "Which translates into you working full time for him within a month or two."

Saylor shrugged. "It's not like I left the Coast Guard because I was over the adrenaline rush."

Mac nodded. "Is all of that resolved?"

Saylor sighed. "I got out. He's hopefully going to jail. That's what's important."

"There shouldn't be any *hopefully* involved."

"We both know that's not how the military works. Even with all the proof, he was a captain. I was just a lieutenant commander. Rank matters."

"It's bullshit. And you shouldn't have had to leave."

Saylor grabbed her hand and squeezed. "I couldn't stay. You know that. Besides, when my best friend tells me to haul ass to her ridiculously small town to keep her company, I haul ass."

"Did that marina space work out?"

"It's perfect. And I love the loft space above." She grinned. "Do I want to know where you're staying? Because those are clearly not your clothes."

"No. They're not. And technically, I rented a cabin at the Lighthouse Lodge just outside of town. But I'm staying at Foster's for…" She paused, unsure how to answer. Was it just for a few nights? A week? Until they decided where this was going?

Foster palmed her back. "Until she decides she'd rather shoot me in the ass."

Saylor nodded. "So, any day now."

"Ouch." Foster shook his head. "Another one with claws. You should drop by some time."

"I will. After I get sorted." She stuffed her hand in her pocket and grabbed a couple of business cards. "What do you think?"

Foster smiled. "Raven's Nest. Cute play on words. Are you as crazy on the water as Mac is in the air?"

"More so." Mac shushed her friend. "Please, I've seen you pilot boats through conditions Poseidon, himself, wouldn't be caught out in."

"Only because I was backing you up."

Mac scoffed, but she didn't miss the way Foster merely shook his head. "We're going to grab some food and head back to Beckett's if you'd like to join us."

"Next time. I only dropped by to get your dad to stop calling me every hour. But ring me in a few days once I'm human again and we'll grab coffee, and you can tell me all about how you came to wear those clothes."

Mac gave her a playful shove then headed for the door, waving as Saylor drove off. Foster followed Mac around to her side, crowding her once she'd jumped in.

He motioned to where Saylor had been parked. "Are all your friends ball busters?"

"Are all yours ex-Spec Op?"

"Fair." He leaned in. "I should have asked you if you were okay with people assuming we were…"

"What? Sleeping together?"

"Basically, though it's so much more than that."

She grabbed his shirt and dragged him close, eating at his mouth until she finally needed to gasp in some air. "Does that answer your question?"

"Perfectly." He eased back, then closed her door, disappearing for a minute as he ducked out of view before hopping in his side.

She nudged him as he started the truck. "Did you just look for any sign of a bomb?"

"Hell, yeah. I would have searched at Bodie's, but the man has cameras everywhere." He reversed then turned the truck. "I'm not getting played, again. And since we have a habit of putting our cards on the table, I'd love for you to stay for the foreseeable future."

Her heart kicked up at the thought, and she couldn't stop from leaning over — kissing him again. Mac wiped her thumb across his mouth once she'd pulled away. "Me, too. So, drive, Beckett."

CHAPTER FOURTEEN

"Why do we always end up traveling along this section when it's dark and creepy?"

Foster smiled. Mac had been staring into the darkness for the past five minutes. Ever since they'd turned onto the long winding road up to his place. And he hadn't missed the way she'd scoured the tree line. Likely looking for a glimpse of Voss amidst the foliage.

He winked at her. "Luck?"

"You're hilarious."

"Greer regained consciousness. We had to alter our plans and pay her a visit. Especially since I put her in the crosshairs. And no, you explaining, again, how she would have gone digging regardless won't make me feel less responsible. I'm just not sure if her temporary amnesia regarding that day is a blessing or a curse."

"I'd call it a win, for now. Because I have no doubt

she'll be out hunting Carrington and likely Voss once she remembers even a fraction of that night."

"Chase might have something to say about that. He takes the whole medic thing pretty seriously."

"I think he's taking Greer pretty seriously. Was it just me or did he look like a love-sick puppy?"

"It wasn't just you. I think…" He let his voice trail off when headlights appeared behind them, following along for a few moments before winking out.

Mac nudged his arm. "Foster?"

"There's a Sig in a lockbox under your seat. Code is one-seven-two-four."

Mac's eyes widened, then she was shuffling until she had the box open and the weapon in her hands. "What's going on?"

"Not sure, yet, but there were headlights behind us, then they vanished." He glanced at her. "There aren't any dirt roads back there, so where did they go?"

She looked out the rear window, scanning the area. "I suppose they could have pulled off onto the shoulder, but it's really narrow. If they waited a minute, it opens up."

"Right where Chase and Zain went off the road."

"You think it's Voss?"

"I think we can't be too careful." He nodded at the gun. "Are you okay handling that if it comes down to it?"

Mac huffed. "I said Sigs weren't my preferred weapon, not that I can't use one."

"Good, because I'm not sure it would be wise to stop and change... shit."

Foster dodged his vehicle to the left when a white truck barreled around the corner, crossing over the white line and flashing on their headlights in what was likely an attempt to blind him. But he was already sliding across the slick grass, fishtailing back onto the road a moment before he would have clipped a tree. What would have either stopped them dead or rolled them over.

Mac was tracking the truck as it spun around behind them, those headlights reflecting off his mirrors. Foster hit the gas, taking the next curve faster than he should, keeping the truck on the road by letting the back end skid around the corner.

Unbuckling, Mac opened her window and leaned out, aiming down the road. "Hold it steady, and I'll see if I can hit something important."

"We've only got a few seconds of straight road."

She didn't even flinch, nearly falling out when he had to swerve out of the way of another oncoming car. He grabbed her sweatshirt, holding her secure as she fired off a round the moment the other car was gone.

The truck veered one way, bouncing along the rough shoulder before finally steering back onto the road.

Foster glanced at his mirrors, still holding Mac's sweatshirt. "Do you have a death wish? You nearly fell."

"I knew you'd grab me."

"That makes one of us." He skidded around another corner, getting way too close to the edge. "Did you hit anything important?"

"Left tire, but the bastard must have run flats. I can try and land a few in the grill—"

"Or you can get your ass back in the seat, and we can try another approach." He pointed to a spot on the nav screen. "There's an old two track around here. We can veer off and try to put enough distance between us I can spin this baby, and we can deal with this issue head on."

"You want to play chicken with this asshole on a deactivated dirt road?"

"Whatever it takes so I can have a chat with our friend. Though, if you've got any better ideas…"

She grunted then buckled up, his Sig still at the ready. Foster followed the pavement, going as fast as possible without tipping them over when the old track appeared on his left side. He didn't even slow, just took the gravel road going insanely fast. The suspension creaked and groaned as the truck bucked along the path, tossing everything not belted down scattering across the interior.

Mac didn't complain, focusing on the rear. She tapped him as they went around a bend. "He just reached the gravel, but it looked as if that tire I clipped wasn't playing as nice on the dirt. That might be our advantage."

"Then, let's see how far we can push it."

Foster slowed enough to pop the transmission into four-wheel drive, eating up the mud as he followed the overgrown trail. Stones flew out the side, some pinging off the undercarriage as he kept the speed up, taking the corners fast and tight.

He was starting to wonder if they'd run out of useable road when Mac tapped his thigh.

"He's gone, Foster."

That's all Foster needed to spin his truck and turn off the headlights, leaving them sitting there in utter darkness. The overcast sky blocking any hint of star shine.

Mac remained vigilant beside him — gun at the ready as the road brightened a moment before the truck bumped around the corner. Foster punched the gas, then hit the lights, setting off the white Toyota in sharp relief as he quickly ate up the distance between them.

He didn't know if Striker was driving, but the figure veered off the path, careening down a small incline before bouncing to a stop, the tires spinning against the mud. Foster hit the brakes with every intention of racing down the hill before Voss could react — hopefully ending everything right there — when an SUV bounced around the corner. What looked like the same shaped headlights he'd originally noticed behind him.

Someone leaned out the window, an assault rifle aimed their way. Foster hit the gas, narrowly missing the SUV when it sped past, a barrage of bullets striking his truck. He reached for Mac and shoved her head below the dash, somehow keeping the truck racing along the track without hitting a tree or getting stuck in the mud on the side. Those lights appeared behind him, but they faded a few moments later, nothing but dark forest staring back at him.

He waited until he'd reached the paved road and fishtailed onto it before easing up on Mac. She arched a brow once she could look at him.

He sighed. "I didn't want you to get hit."

"And I'm touched, but it would have been hard to counter whoever fired at us when I can't see to shoot."

"You not getting shot is a hell of a lot more important than throwing a few bullets their way." He glanced in his rearview, still heading toward home. "I could call Kash and we could go on the offensive."

Mac scoffed. "Call me crazy, but I doubt even your rifle is a match to that AR-15. Now, if I had my chopper…"

"Easy there, *Airwolf*. Sadly, I'm certain we'll get another chance. Though, I'm not sure what they hoped to achieve." Which was what concerned him the most. Eliminating Greer, Chase and Zain had made sense. Especially if Voss wasn't sure how much she'd already shared. But this felt more random. Or was it desperate?

Mac stared out the back before shaking her head. "You're worried they're escalating."

"I don't like putting the people I care about in the crosshairs."

"Not to kick you while you're down, but we were already there. And maybe Voss, or whoever that was, just wanted to scare you. They didn't fire until one of them was at risk of being caught."

"Let's hope that's the case."

He glanced in the rearview, again, as he shook out his right hand. But even after he'd parked in front of the house, the road was deserted behind him.

Mac met him behind his truck. "I suppose this means more patrols tonight."

"At least, we've got backup." He frowned at the couple bullet holes in his quarter panel. "I doubt they can buff that out."

"I think it gives the truck character."

He shook his head, taking her hand as she grabbed the food. They carried it into the kitchen, looking over at Kash and Zain when they ambled in.

Foster gave them a twirl of his finger. "Did you guys clear the perimeter or should I go check?"

Zain gave Foster that death stare Mac had talked about in the hospital. "You did *not* just ask me if the property was clear when my paranoia level far exceeds yours."

Foster held up his hand. "Sorry. My adrenaline's still a bit high." He gave them a rundown of the day's events, ending with the chase.

Zain all but growled, fisting one of the napkins as

he placed his burger back on the plate. "I'm really starting to hate this guy."

Kash gave Zain a slap on the back, avoiding his left side. "I'm pretty sure you're way past hate and well on your way to plotting revenge."

"He tried to murder Chase and Greer *and* make it look like an accident. Hell, we're pretty sure he actually murdered Foster's parents. We need to end this. Preferably with me looking down my scope."

"You're in no condition to use your sniper rifle." Kash arched a brow. "Unless you were hoping to mess up both shoulders?"

Zain pouted, picking at his fries as the room fell into a heavy silence. Nyx paced back and forth across the room, seemingly sensing the ever-growing restlessness

Foster pushed his half-eaten burger aside. "As much as I hate the thought, we should definitely up our security tonight. Mac and I'll take first watch. One of you jackasses can spell us off."

"I can handle security." Zain tapped his chest. "All night."

"Sorry, brother, not this time. We're a team, and we'll go in shifts. Your system's solid. I'd just feel better if there were eyes on the property all night. For all we know, Striker's next escalation will involve C4."

"No one's getting that close without me knowing about it. Period." Zain clenched his jaw as he stood, closing his eyes for a few moments before blowing out a rough breath. "Midnight, Beckett. Not a minute longer."

Kash sighed as he watched Zain march out, holding his elbow despite wearing a sling. "I'd hoped civilian life would smooth some of his hard edges, but he's as intense as ever. And before you volunteer to stay up all night or get your panties in a twist, I'll be keeping watch *with* him — that whole team thing. I know you two barely got any sleep last night, and it's been full-on ever since that chat with Keaton and Dawson. And I doubt tomorrow will be any easier. We still have a stash of drugs to find."

Foster eased back in his chair. "Looks like Zain's not the only stubborn intense soul here."

Kash laughed. "Yeah, you're a real hardass, too. I'll go close my eyes for a bit, but I'll see you at midnight." Kash whistled to Nyx, and the dog trotted off, totally focused on Kash.

Mac shuffled in beside Foster, laughing when he snagged her around the waist and pulled her into his lap. "Is it odd that I'm a bit jealous of the way Nyx looks at Kash?"

"You're not the only one." He dropped a kiss on her neck. "If you're tired, you can head up. I can handle the shift alone."

"And give you something to gloat over, later? I'm tired, not stupid. Besides, if I wanted to sleep alone, I would have gone back to my rental."

"Even if we just sleep?"

She brushed her lips over his. "Especially if we just sleep, which is increasingly possible with each passing hour. And at the risk of you walking around, pounding on your chest like some kind of caveman, last night was the first time I actually got any quality sleep. Even if it only lasted a few hours."

"Sounds like another challenge."

"That comes after we sleep." She stood, offering him her hand. "Come on. Let's get comfy because I'm sure we'll be traipsing around the perimeter far too soon."

"At least it's not raining, yet."

"And now, you've jinxed it."

Foster tugged her close as they made their way into the living room. Mackenzie had insisted on clearing the house and grounds before they settled on the couch. Her head resting on his shoulder as they watched some sappy old movie. Time ticked past, Mac dozing a bit before they made another round of the property. Zain and Kash were waiting in the kitchen when they finally trudged through the back door.

Zain looked at them over the rim of his coffee mug. "Well?"

Foster hung their jackets on a hook. "Nothing so far but the promise of another impressive storm."

"Storms I can handle. Having some ex-Green Beret asshole trying to kill my family? That's another story."

"All the more reason to find those damn drugs

tomorrow." Foster placed his hand on Mac's back and studied his teammates. "You two sure you're okay? We could all hang out."

Zain scoffed. "Please, there's already a third wheel. You two would just make it awkward."

Kash gave Zain a shove. "Nyx is not a third wheel."

"I was talking about you, sunshine."

Kash rolled his eyes. "Just wait until we're out scouting the area. Nyx might accidentally tackle you."

"She likes me too much." Zain gave the dog a scratch then motioned toward the stairs. "Go, before we have to carry your sorry asses up there."

"You'd better be storming my door if Striker so much as looks at the property line."

"Still bossing us around." Zain pointed at the door, this time. "Go."

Foster headed for the door, glancing back at Zain one more time before taking the stairs then turning down the hallway. He closed his bedroom door behind him and Mac, leaning against it as she made her way over to the bed, practically collapsing on top as she flopped back on the mattress. He smiled, studying her until she must have felt him staring and turned to look at him.

"Why are you looking at me like that?"

Foster pushed off the door and ambled over. "Like what?"

"Like you've never seen me before."

"More like I was admiring how damn beautiful you are."

She chuckled. "If you like tousled hair and bloodshot eyes."

"Funny. All I see are brilliant baby blues and thick hair I want to gather in my hands."

That got him a smile. "And suddenly, I'm not so tired."

"Oh, no. Sleep, first. Then, we'll see."

"I'll sleep better if you make love to me." She sat up and fisted the front of his jeans, lowering the zipper then tugging them and his briefs down. She inhaled then ran her tongue along the seam of her lips as she gently fisted his length. "Damn."

Foster gathered her hair in his hand, just like he'd been envisioning, prepared to ease her back, when she leaned forward and took him in her mouth. No teasing or preamble. Just all that wet, hot pressure engulfing him as she took him to the back of her throat before slowly easing up.

"Christ." He made a mental note not to yank on her hair, failing miserably a moment later when she repeated her assault, pausing with him lodged deep, this time.

Heat burned beneath his skin, threatening to push him over in record time when she hummed, the low vibration completely wrecking him.

Foster wasn't sure if he started moving his hips by chance or by design, only that he was thrusting into her mouth a minute later. Reveling in the way she moaned around his length, sounding more than pleased with herself.

He closed his eyes, trying to stave off the inevitable release, aware it hadn't been anywhere close to long enough. That a lifetime might not be long enough where she was concerned. Mackenzie didn't seem to be strung tight. Wasn't obviously poised on the edge like him, clawing at anything that would give him a hint of control, until she faltered.

Prying his eyelids open took a few attempts, but he finally managed to stare down at her. And damn, she seemed as wrecked as he felt. Her chest heaving nearly as much as his as she worked his length, looking as if she was ready to explode.

His chest tightened, a deep warmth spreading up through his core. He stopped thrusting then tugged on her hair, waiting until she finally met his gaze. "Mackenzie."

That's all he managed around the lump in his throat — the thickness making it hard to form the right words. Three in particular he feared would change everything.

She furrowed her brow, then eased free, pushing to her feet a moment later. Foster kept his fingers buried in her hair as he tilted her head and ravaged her mouth, drinking in every hushed rasp that seemed to scratch its way free. She was gasping for air when he finally pulled back, using the brief pause to tear off their clothes before wrapping his arm around her waist and shuffling her onto the bed.

Her thick brown hair fanned out across the sheets as he settled above her, bridging his weight on his elbows. He stared down at her, memorizing the fine curve of her jaw and how her skin blushed pink. She was beyond stunning.

Mac palmed his cheek, smiling up at him. "Foster."

God, the way she said his name.

He nuzzled her hand. "It's not that I wasn't thoroughly invested in you sucking me off, I just needed..."

More? Her?

Her smile widened as she slid her hand behind his neck and dragged him down to her. "Then, what are you waiting for? Love me."

Had she read his mind? Knew he was teetering on the edge of that cliff, ready to throw himself off? Did she feel remotely the same?

He held her gaze as he slowly sank inside her. She inhaled, her breath stalling as her head tilted back. Her eyes rolled slightly, a breathy moan escaping her full lips as the tendons in her neck corded. She dug her fingertips into his back and side when he finally bottomed out, holding himself fully seated.

Mac took a few panting breaths, clenching her jaw before meeting his gaze, again. "Foster, please..."

Her voice trailed off as he pulled back then slid home. A bit harder. Faster. Only pausing for a few moments before thrusting, again — loving the way she cried out his name.

She urged him closer, eating at his mouth as he kept his pace slow and easy. Building the heat between them until his muscles started cramping.

Mac panted against his ear, every ragged breath fraying the one thread of control he had left. "God, Foster. I need…"

She cried out as he slammed home, her voice shattering the last of his willpower. He let loose, pounding into her as the headboard knocked against the wall. Mackenzie scratched at his back, her heels giving each stroke an added boost until everything collided, and he cracked, emptying into her in a series of stabbing thrusts.

Heat tore through his veins, sending him into a numbing haze until his strength waned, and he collapsed on top of her. The room faded, nothing but their rough breath sounding above the pounding in his chest. What was likely a heart attack in the making.

It wasn't until all that heat started to cool that he was able to open his eyes — take stock. Mackenzie's face was scrunched up, her chest still heaving as she drew in a shaky breath then pushed it out. Tears dotted her cheek, but it was the dreamy smile curving her lips that made his heart skip a beat.

Love.

That's what it looked like. Staring up at him when she finally opened her eyes. And he couldn't stop from dipping in and kissing her mouth. Drinking in the softest of sighs.

He shifted his weight to one elbow, brushing his thumb along her skin. "You okay?"

She laughed. "That depends. Are we dead? Because I can't imagine anything being better than this."

"Pretty sure we're both still breathing."

"Then, that should be illegal because... damn."

"Think you can sleep now?"

Another laugh, the easy sound bubbling up all those emotions until he had to physically stop himself from shouting out those three words he'd been thinking about earlier. "I hope Kash and Zain don't need us because I'm not sure I can move."

"So, no shower?"

"Only if you're carrying me and doing all the work."

"Challenge accepted."

Mac wrapped her arms around his neck after he'd rolled off and gathered her in his arms. "You're going to hold me all night, right?"

"All night."

She smiled, somehow staying conscious until he had them back in the bed, her head tucked against his shoulder.

He pulled her closer, smiling at how she burrowed against him. "Sleep. I've got you."

She dropped a kiss on his chest. "Remember. All night."

He nodded, chuckling when she drifted off a moment later. As if someone had flipped a switch. Foster glanced at the door, hoping Kash and Zain were okay. Not that he questioned their skill, but Jack Voss wasn't their typical opponent. And Foster had a bad feeling that the worst was yet to come.

CHAPTER FIFTEEN

"No!"

Mackenzie bolted awake, fighting against the covers until Foster freed her arms, staying lover-close as she whipped her gaze toward him, her rough breaths sounding loud in the early morning stillness. A hint of gray light brightened the window, sunrise still a while away.

Foster eased her against him, holding her waist as his other hand combed through her hair. "Josh, again?"

"Yeah." She sighed, smoothing her hand across his chest in an effort to still the shaky roil of her gut. "Which I know is insane. I wasn't even there."

"Which is exactly why it haunts you."

She nodded, listening to his heart beating against her side as he rocked her back and forth. "So much for sleeping in."

"Sleep's overrated. And I'll never pass up an opportunity to hold you."

"Good to know." She grinned against him. "Since Zain and Kash didn't wake us, I guess Voss didn't show last night."

"I suppose we have to take the wins wherever we can get them. Though, finding the hidden drug stash would be nice." He groaned when his cell pinged. "I swear if that's Atticus, I'm sending him a selfie of us in bed just to shut him up."

"You wouldn't."

"Hell, yeah, I would." He grabbed his phone off the side table.

"And?"

He laughed, sending back a quick text. "Just Kash asking if he and Zain are needed because they heard you shout. I told them I've got it covered."

His cell buzzed again.

"Do I want to know what Kash replied?"

"Not something I'll repeat, the bastard."

She looked up at him. "At least, they didn't just barge in."

"I'm sure Chase already warned them about your penchant for putting guns to people's heads who stroll in uninvited."

"I thought Chase was one of the bad guys. Besides, I didn't actually shoot him."

"Again, we'll take the wins where we can." Foster chucked his cell back onto the table. "Other than the nightmare, you sleep okay?"

"I don't think I moved." She nudged him. "I could get used to this."

Foster grinned, rolling them until he was looming over her. "Me, too. Especially if we get to do this every morning."

He dipped down, giving her a long, slow kiss when his phone chirped a third time. He grunted, glancing at it over his shoulder. "Now, that's probably your father wanting us to stop by the office or something."

Foster checked his phone, shooting off another text to Kash or Zain — hell, maybe her dad — when Mac inhaled, the obvious answer to why they hadn't found the drugs slamming into her head.

She gave him a light swat. "The office. That's it."

Foster frowned before placing the back of his hand across her forehead. "You don't feel like you have a fever."

"Funny." She motioned for him to move then rolled off the bed and made a dash for his closet, reappearing a few moments later wearing more of his sweats. "What are you waiting for? We've got drugs to find."

Foster was on his feet and snagging her arm a second later. "Mac? Sweetheart, you're starting to scare me. Did you hit your head when we were bouncing along that gravel road last night?" He held up his hand. "How many fingers?"

"Three and I don't have a concussion and I'm not crazy. I just figured out where they hid the drugs."

His frown deepened. "Judging by your comment, I assume you think they hid them in my dad's office, right? And not to put a damper on your enthusiasm, but that's one of the few rooms that didn't need to be renovated. In fact, I don't think he changed anything."

"Exactly." She crossed her arms over her chest. "If you wanted to hide something you hoped no one would find, would you stash it behind a wall that obviously needs to be gutted in the future? One that could possible just rot away? Or would you put it someplace that's already perfect? That won't likely be touched."

Foster glanced at the door. "Son of a bitch."

He darted to his closet, grabbing jeans and a long-sleeved shirt before tugging them on. He snagged her hand, pausing long enough to drop a soul-searing kiss on her mouth before heading for the door. Foster practically jogged down the stairs, along the hallway and over to the rear of the house. He didn't even answer Kash when his buddy asked if he'd *killed the mood*, continuing on until they were standing in the doorway.

Zain and Kash appeared behind them, looking as if they couldn't decide if they should question Foster or call Chase for medical guidance.

Mac sighed when Foster stood there rolling his shoulder as he shook out his right hand. She hadn't stopped to consider why they'd shied away from the office yesterday. That maybe it triggered a bunch of those unwanted memories he was trying to shove down. All those demons she'd agreed were sometimes better left unchallenged. Only now, she'd forced his hand.

Kash shifted on his feet, glancing at her then back to Foster. "Are we staring at the study because we're having a moment or…"

Foster gave his buddy a roll of his eyes. "I'm not having a mental breakdown, Kash. Mac suggested that the drugs might be hidden in my dad's office." He swallowed, coughing a bit after. "My office, I guess."

Mac gave his hand a squeeze. "I kinda like the idea of keeping this as John Beckett's office that you just borrow from time to time. And it's just a hunch, which I'm already starting to question."

Foster looked at her then leaned over and kissed her. Hard. "Thanks. And I think you've got a point."

Zain groaned. "I think I might be sick."

Foster gave him a light shove, staying clear of his shoulder, then waved at the stack of boxes. "I'll admit. I haven't really given this room a hard look. I just packed up some of my dad's stuff and put it in here."

Zain clapped him on the back "None of us are questioning your motives, Beckett. So, let's make this a team effort."

They dove in, moving all the boxes to another room until just the furniture was left. And it was impossible not to see John Beckett's mark on the place. From the antique desk and thick padded chair, to the collection of photographs hanging on the walls, the room was definitely a tribute to his and Foster's lives in the service.

Kash tapped one of the photos. "I had no idea your dad had a copy of this shot. It was in Syria, right?"

Foster laughed. "Just before we went on that furlough in Berlin." He nudged Kash. "Are you still banned from ever going back?"

"It wasn't that bad."

"It really was." He sighed at the photo hanging next to Kash of Foster and his dad shortly after Foster had been recruited to Flight Concepts. "I had no idea my father was such a sentimental pack rat."

Mac cozied up to him, slipping her hand over his. "I'd say he was extremely proud of you."

Foster merely nodded, looking more than a bit lost, when her phone pinged, followed a moment later by Kash's.

Mac groaned inwardly, glancing at Kash before stealing a look at her screen. "Damn."

Foster huffed. "Obviously, that's work if both yours and Kash's are going off."

"My dad just sent a nine-one-one. Hold on. I'll get more intel."

Zain grunted. "How come mine's not going off?"

Kash rolled his eyes. "Because your damn shoulder got skewered with a piece of metal,

Einstein. You're offline for at least another week. And standing there, growling, won't change that."

Mackenzie shook her head as she hit her dad's number. "Got your text. Hoping you can elaborate for me."

Atticus scoffed. "I'm fine, Mac, thanks for asking."

"Of course, you're fine. I just saw you twelve hours ago."

"I'm old. It changes hourly."

"You're not old, you're ornery. There's a difference. The call?"

"Apparently, a couple hikers managed to get off a call to emergency services before their phone died. I've got their relative location. They're out in the Cascade Head area, and there's a suspected broken leg involved. Seems they completely disregarded the closure on the forest service road and now they're pretty much cut off. Ambulance services can't access them, and with the incoming storm, there's only an hour, maybe ninety minutes, to get them before they'll be waiting a day or two for help."

"Doesn't anyone in this damn town have common sense? That section of Cascade Head hasn't been maintained since that landslide a few years back. Everyone knows it's risky, especially this time of year."

"You know they don't." Atticus snorted. "I assume you're with Beckett. Is his buddy Kash able to accompany you? Charlie's out of town, and Remington and Everett are still on the disabled list.

Though, you should be able to land close enough you two can hike in and grab our injured hiker without needing the hoist. It's a bit too overgrown, anyway."

"Kash is good to go. And we'll definitely have to land and hike in." She arched a brow when Foster crossed his arms and simply stared at her.

Atticus huffed. "I'm guessing by your sudden silence Beckett has a few thoughts on the matter. You can tell him, he's welcome to join in. I'll have the appropriate papers waiting for him to sign, and I'll put him into tomorrow's rotation."

"Dad. You're not helping."

"Having him pitch in when it was life and death on the side of the road was one thing. This is different, and he knows it. Which is why he's probably glaring at you, right now."

"If he's glaring, it's at you, not me. We'll be there in fifteen. Have her pushed out and ready to go." She scoffed. "If your advanced age allows for that kind of thing."

Her dad grumbled something she couldn't make out before ending the call.

Foster was still staring at her when she tucked the cell into her pocket. "Weather's coming in fast, sweetheart. Are you sure you'll have enough time before it gets to the point even I would have reservations?"

Kash laughed. "In all the years I've flown with you, I've never known you to scrub a mission due to weather. And that's saying a lot."

Foster shrugged. "I'm a bit less discriminating than most. But just because I did, doesn't mean it was the right call to make."

Mac gave his arm a squeeze. "It should hold off long enough to get the job done. And they really don't have any other options. Kash."

"I'll go grab my kit and Nyx's and meet you at your Jeep in two minutes."

Kash raced out, Nyx hot on his heels. Mackenzie darted upstairs, changing into her clothes before heading for the door. Foster handed her a jacket then followed her out to her vehicle.

He opened the door, leaning against the frame when she rolled down the window. "I'm guessing Atticus was resistant to having anyone else join in."

Mac sighed. "Something like that."

"I'm welcome if I sign on the dotted line, right?"

"Basically."

She reached for him, cupping his jaw when he bent low. "We'll be fine. I've got excellent backup. And we'll be back before the really bad weather rolls in. Though, there's always a chance we get stuck at the hospital."

"Have the old man call me if that's the outlook, and I'll meet you there."

"Oh, I'd love to eavesdrop on *that* conversation."

"I'm sure yelling will be involved." He straightened as Kash and Nyx came racing down the path. "All Atticus, by the way."

"You're a big boy. You can take it." She looked in

her rearview when Kash opened the back, tossing stuff in before getting Nyx to jump up. "I'll text you before we leave and then again when we land at the hospital. Now, go find those drugs."

"Be safe."

"I'm not the risk taker."

He rolled his eyes, staring at Kash until the man flipped Foster some kind of hand signal. What she assumed was Foster doubling down on how he expected his friend to have her back. Not that Kash needed reminding. All of Foster's buddies took guarding their teammates to the extreme. And she knew they'd all gladly sacrifice themselves for each other without hesitation.

Mackenzie made the drive in record time, Kash keeping the conversation light. Though she suspected he was dying to grill her about her intentions with Foster, he avoided the topic, jumping out before she'd even put the Jeep into first.

She trailed behind, shaking her head at her father when he held the door for her. "I'm starting to wonder if you're having me followed."

Atticus smiled. "No need. I know exactly where you'll be."

She stopped. "Foster's a good man."

"He's an exceptional man. Which is why I need him to grow a set and sign on." Atticus held up his hand. "I know. He's retired. He has demons. He's broken." Atticus sighed. "His words, not mine. But I still think he'll come around given the right motivation."

"And you think, what?" She cocked her head to the side. "That *I'm* the right motivation?"

Her dad simply smiled. "Coordinates are already in your nav. And I've got the latest weather reports waiting, too. Just be careful, and for god's sake don't risk both your lives if that storm cell moves in quicker than anticipated. I know how you feel about rescuing people and not leaving any behind, but you can't help folks if you're dead."

"Thanks, Dad. I hadn't thought of that."

Mackenzie headed out, shooting Foster a text as she jumped behind the controls then donned her helmet. She checked out the location and the weather reports then rolled on the throttle. The chopper started rocking, the instruments quickly springing to life. She glanced back at Kash, waiting for his thumbs up before calling out her intentions across the airwaves then lifting the bird into the air.

The gusting wind buffeted the chopper, thick dark clouds filling the horizon. The first inklings of fog dotted the coastline. Nothing substantial but it was shaping up to be one hell of a storm.

Kash clicked on his mic, his voice rasping over the comms. "That's quite the front baring down on us."

"Definitely not something we want to get caught in. Though, I assume you're accustomed to that with your comments about Foster."

Kash laughed. "Beck's crazier than most. And he

never could say no if there was a fellow soldier at risk. Part of his charm."

"I'd say you all share that trait. And thanks for coming along. I know I'm not Foster."

"Nope. But just as crazy." Kash grinned. "And just as good. I've got everything ready. Let me know when we're getting close or if you need any help spotting a place to put this baby down."

"Will do. And Kash?" She smiled. "Thanks."

Mac followed the coastline, eyeing that front moving in along the horizon. It was larger than predicted and she doubted they'd have any time to spare. Not that she hadn't flown in extreme weather with the Coast Guard, but this was different. She didn't have the same chopper, the same tech, despite Foster buying her damn near every advanced piece of avionics available. And her dad was right. Dying wouldn't save anyone. Still, she'd give it her best shot.

Rain started dotting the bubble as they came up on the edge of the reserve, the thick foliage standing tall and green against the cliffs. A few colored leaves still clung to the scattering of deciduous trees, granting fleeting glimpses of the forest floor.

Kash leaned in between the seats. "Even at this time of year that canopy is impressive."

"Not that I could fly *and* work the hoist, but it definitely means we'll be walking." She pointed to a small clearing not too far from the edge of the cliff as she did a low pass. "I'll put her down there. We're a couple of clicks from the approximate coordinates. But they should have heard me go over, so hopefully they'll be making noise."

"Right, because safety is obviously their top priority."

"It might be now."

Kash laughed, reclaiming his seat as she brought the chopper around then lined up the landing site. The rain kicked up a bit as the gusting wind seemed to hit them from every direction, shaking the aircraft as she flared off a bit of speed, then placed the machine down in the center of the space.

"Nice. Beck would be proud." Kash hopped out, slipping a huge pack over his tactical vest before clipping Nyx's leash around his waist. "Nyx will source them out once we get close. And I've got enough first aid supplies to at least stabilize our patient's leg. I'm not Chase, but I can handle the easy stuff. Are you okay carrying the rescue stretcher?"

Mac secured the controls, then jumped out, scanning the area before nodding at Kash. "Hell, yeah, especially if my other option is that bag. Do I even want to know how much it weighs?"

"About half as much as Chase carries, so, we'll keep that between us. The guy's nuts."

"Right. He's nuts, but you're sane."

"I'm glad we agree."

She motioned to his vest. "Do you think you have enough ammo for a rescue mission? And since when do you wear a ballistic vest to a rescue?"

Kash merely shrugged. "The real question is, where's yours?"

"I don't have a vest, Kash."

"Pretty sure you were wearing one the other night."

"That was Foster's, and it was about five sizes too big."

"Big beats dead." He reached for the straps. "You can have mine."

"Kash, stop. I get Striker's on all our minds, but this isn't a covert mission. We're just picking up a couple of weekend warriors who thought they were bulletproof."

"Assuming shit still won't go sideways is always the first mistake. And I'm the first to admit, Zain, Chase and I have allowed ourselves to get complacent these past few months. But we'll be sure to rectify that for next time. From now on, you don't get in the chopper without being prepared for serious resistance. Which reminds me…" He grabbed a pistol and holster from around his left ankle, though she suspected he had another on his other leg, then handed it to her. "If you don't have a vest, then I doubt you came armed."

She nodded her thanks, clipped the holster on her pants then followed behind him. Nyx tugged gently at the leash, leading the way before suddenly stopping. The hairs rose down her back as her ears flattened against her head, a low menacing growl sounding around them.

Kash reacted before Mac even registered the threat, firing off several rounds as he managed to dance around her, blocking two shots from behind. He hit the ground, nearly yanking Nyx onto her side, before he rolled. Somehow gaining his feet and shoving Mac beneath him in the space it took her to draw her weapon.

Footsteps sounded around them before a dozen men stopped in a lopsided circle, semi-automatic weapons trained on them. Mac glanced up at Kash, inhaling at the two slugs lodged in his vest. What had possibly damaged some ribs or at least bruised the hell out of them. Not that Kash showed it — kneeling above her, Nyx alert but still at his side, his Sig sweeping the gathering of men.

She shifted her focus to the assholes surrounding them. Of the crew, she knew three. Thompson and a new deputy — Baxter, she thought. But it was the other bastard standing slightly in front of everyone else that held her attention. Cold. Focused. He looked as if he wasn't quite sane, a slight twitch arcing through him ever so often.

Jack Voss.

Thompson edged forward, motioning at the men to hold their ground. "I have to say, Sinclair, you're impressive. I didn't think you'd get off a shot let alone down two of my men and catch a couple more in their vests before we even got two shots your way. I bet your ribs are killing you. Guess you black op guys live up to the hype."

Kash didn't move, his weapon still trained on everyone. "Which one of you has the broken leg?"

"Enough talking." Voss inched forward. "You've got two choices, Sinclair. You can holster your weapon and lock your dog in the chopper, or things can get bloody. Either way, there's no scenario where you come out on top. Maybe if we weren't locked in, you'd have a chance. But we don't even have to aim this close. And your buddy's girl won't last long if you choose poorly."

The corner of Kash's mouth quirked, his hand tightening around his gun. Mac squeezed his arm, shaking her head when he glanced at her. She mouthed, "He's not worth it," motioning toward the chopper.

Kash held his ground for another minute before easing up. He holstered his pistol then tossed the whole thing towards them, doing the same to hers after she handed it to him.

Voss grinned. "Good choice. Now put Cujo in the damn chopper. I have this thing against killing dogs, but I will if I have to."

Kash offered Mac his hand, helping her up then keeping her glued to his side as he walked back to the chopper and put Nyx inside. "Good girl. Stealth mode."

Nyx immediately crouched low, alert but still. And Mac knew Kash had given her some kind of covert command. One that would likely activate when their enemies least expected it.

He closed the door, still keeping his body in front of Mac's. "This isn't going to end well for you."

Voss shrugged. "Why? Because of your teammates? Two of them are lucky to be breathing, let alone capable of going on the offensive. And Beckett?" He laughed. "He's just a fucking Prima Dona who's too broken to do the one thing he was good at. So sue me if I'm not *worried* about your teammates. Though, you're definitely worth being concerned about."

He struck, hitting Kash across the side of the head with the butt of his rifle, knocking him into the helicopter. Kash hit the back panel then bounced onto the ground, still trying to shake it off before Voss hit him, again.

Mac dove at the bastard, tackling him to the ground before he could get in a third strike. She managed a few hits before Thompson and his half-wit deputy yanked her off. She tripped the deputy onto his ass, catching Thompson in the groin, but Striker was already on his feet.

He grabbed her around the neck then pulled her in close, cutting off any chance at breathing as he tightened his hold. "Be nice, or Thompson will have one of his other men drive by the hanger and shoot your father."

He shoved her off, and she gasped in a breath. "Now, let's get this party started."

CHAPTER SIXTEEN

Foster leaned against the far wall, shaking his head as Zain ran his fingers along the shelving units, pressing anything that might be a switch. They'd been searching the office since Mac and Kash had headed to the hanger but hadn't found any evidence of a hidden compartment, let alone a secret room. Not that Foster was fully focused on the task. In fact, he'd been restless since she'd texted that they were getting airborne.

"Earth to Beckett."

Foster blinked, snapping his attention to Zain as the man waved his hand in front of him. "What?"

"I said, I thought for sure one of those bookcases would slide open." Zain tilted his head. "Where were you?"

"Just thinking."

Zain sighed. "She'll be okay. Kash is a beast.

Maybe more hardcore than the rest of us. He just fakes all that Zen shit better."

"It's not Kash. I just..." How did Foster admit he had this churning in his gut without confessing he was head over heels for the girl?

Zain frowned. "You think they're in trouble?"

"You think who's in trouble?"

Foster turned toward the door, cursing under his breath at Chase leaning against the frame. "Jesus, buddy. I damn near threw my dad's ugly ass paper weight at you. It's an actual rock. I should know. I painted that thing in kindergarten."

Chase laughed. "I texted you this morning that I'd be back within an hour or so, and I wasn't exactly quiet. Where is everyone, and who's in trouble?"

"They got a rescue call. And no one's in trouble. I'm just on edge."

"I didn't get paged."

Foster crossed his arms. "I can't imagine why."

"Shut up." Chase looked at Zain then padded his way across the room. "You realize you're gonna have to let her go to work, right?"

"She's out on a mission, now, isn't she?"

"And you're here, working yourself into a lather."

Foster flipped off his best friend. "That's because we're trying to find the damn drugs. And sue me for being concerned because there's an ex-Green Beret asshole on our tail and a weather system reminiscent of the great flood about to swallow the entire Oregon coast."

Chase simply shook his head. "All you had to say was that you're hopelessly in love with her, and we'd get the point."

"You're an ass."

Chase winked. "I know. But that doesn't make what I said any less true." He dodged Foster's attempted slap. "So, we're down to looking for some kind of secret hideaway? In the bookcase?"

Zain waved him off. "Don't question, brother. Just look."

Chase studied them as if he was questioning their sanity before heading for the far wall. He scoured the shelves then went to one knee, poking around the outer piece of molding before something clicked and it swung open. "You guys so owe me."

Foster peered at the small lever inside. "This is crazy."

"I think you mean insanely cool." Chase pulled the lever down. There was a swoosh and an odd grating sound, then the back panel slid open, revealing a compartment behind the shelf. "Well, I'll be damned."

Foster removed the contents, picking up one of the bottles of pills as Chase flipped through a series of papers. "Definitely Vexarin. Is that Carrington's research?"

Chase nodded. "It's insane, is what it is. Do you know what he spliced together?"

"That's your wheelhouse, not mine. And I assume it isn't good."

"More like deadly. Christ, I can't believe it ever went to trial."

"Maybe—"

A blast of music cut Foster off, and he removed his cell, frowning. "It's Mac on a video chat."

Zain was at his side a heartbeat later. "No way they got all the way to Cascade Head and back in forty-five minutes. Which means this isn't good news."

Foster drew a deep breath, then hit the button. "Mac? Sweetheart is everything..."

Dead.

That's how he felt. Standing there, staring into Striker's wild eyes as he smirked into the camera.

Voss laughed. "I guess that depends on your perspective, Beckett. I'd say your buddy and your girlfriend have had better days."

"Where are they?"

Voss angled the camera. Thompson had Mackenzie beside him, his gun jabbed in her ribs. Kash was braced against the side of the chopper, blood trickling down the side of his face with more matted in his hair. What was obviously a brutal head injury. "Do I have your attention, now?"

Foster clenched his jaw. "If you wanted to talk to me, Striker, all you had to do was knock on my door."

"I prefer a more incentivized method. Since you know who I am, you know what I want."

He held up the bottle. "You mean this?"

Striker's eyes widened, and Foster swore the man actually licked his lips. "And the research?"

"It's here, too."

"Then, it looks like we can make a deal. The drugs and research for your friends." He distorted the view for a moment then Foster's phone pinged. "I just shared your girlfriend's location. You've got one hour to get here. I'd suggest you fly, but I have the only chopper in town. And rumor has it, you're not that man, anymore. You might want to consider a boat, seeing as it would take nearly double that to drive. And that doesn't count all the hiking you'd have to do."

"There's an inbound storm cell, and I'm not a boat captain."

"Then, I suggest you find someone who is. There's a rough trail up the cliff. You might make it without falling. You can bring the medic, but that's it."

Foster's stomach dropped. "Is Kash that bad?"

"Not yet. But I'm getting the sense you're not fully committed, so…"

Striker turned, raised his gun and fired, hitting Mac in the upper left shoulder. She jerked out of Thompson's grasp, landing on the ground with a resounding thud.

"No!" Foster hit the screen, wanting to punch right through it — save her. But all he could do was watch. Just like that night with Sean. No other recourse but to play along. Pray he reached her in time.

"You fucking son of a bitch." Foster fisted his hand. "I swear to god if they're not still breathing when I arrive, there won't be a rock on this earth you'll be able to hide under that I won't find you."

Striker merely grinned. "Now, you're motivated. One hour, Beckett. Because I really don't think she'll last much longer than that."

He ended the call, leaving Foster standing there. Frozen. His heart more like a dead weight inside his chest.

He closed his eyes, shoving down all the fear and uncertainty until all that was left was stone cold determination. Then, he was moving. Yelling at Chase and Zain to pack everything up then get all their gear and meet him at his truck. He detoured to his room, grabbing two rifles, his vest and all the ammo and gear he could carry before hoofing it down the stairs. He tossed it all in the back of his truck then jumped behind the wheel.

He grabbed Saylor's business card from the day before, tapping in her number as his buddies rounded the building, arms loaded with more supplies.

Saylor answered on the third ring. "Raven's Nest, but we're not—"

"It's Beckett. Please tell me you're at your loft at the marina."

"Yeah, but... Are you okay?"

"Not even close. I'll explain everything once I'm there, but I need a boat and a captain, and I needed it five minutes ago. And Saylor..." He swallowed the roil of fear bubbling in his stomach. "This is going to be ugly."

Saylor breathed heavily into the phone before she huffed. "I'll share my location. I'll have everything ready in five. This had better be life and death, Beckett."

"It always is." He ended the call then hit Bodie's number, already reversing the truck with Chase and Zain still buckling in.

Bodie answered immediately. "People are gonna get the wrong idea about us, Beckett, if you keep calling me at odd hours."

"Are you at the hospital with Greer?"

"Actually, no. She's at my place. She's as stubborn as everyone else and insisted on leaving. Against doctor's orders, no less. Chase was going to get a room ready over there and catch a few hours of sleep, then drop by and grab her. Why?"

"I need a favor, brother. It's big and it's dangerous."

Any hint of humor left the man's voice. "Name it."

"Greer should be safe at your place until we get back. But tell her not to let anyone in, even if they're wearing a badge. I'll have Chase send you Saylor O'Conner's address. She's ex-Coast Guard, and she's readying a boat as we speak. I need you to meet me there in ten. Five if you can swing it. And Bodie... Bring as much as you can carry."

Foster disconnected the call, taking the roads faster than he should, not that Chase or Zain called him on it. In fact, they looked as if they were willing the vehicle to go faster — skid around each turn a bit quicker. They were hitting six minutes when he turned onto the small marina road, the wind already blowing over fifty. A couple boats rocked against the dock in the small cove, the rough waves spraying water across the shoreline.

Saylor waved them over once they'd parked, arching a brow as they chucked a number of bags onto the main deck. "Is this some kind of invasion?"

"More like a tactical assault." He gave her a quick rundown of the situation, doing his best not to scream. Because if he thought, for one second, that Mac was out there, bleeding along with Kash, he'd lose it.

Saylor schooled her features, simply nodding. "Then, let's go get this bastard. And Beckett? You'd better have a weapon for me in there."

Then, she was off, doing something to the nav at the helm when Bodie roared down the road and skidded to a halt in the middle of the parking lot. He didn't bother parking the truck properly, just jumped out, grabbed nearly as much gear as they'd brought and loaded it onto the boat.

Chase took one of the bags, nodding toward town. "Is Greer secure?"

Bodie snorted as he arranged some of his supplies. "She took one of my semi-automatics, two handguns and three smoke grenades. Then I locked her in what's likely the most secure building in town with a buddy of mine arriving as backup within the hour. I think she's good for now. I assume this involves Striker, and he's got leverage."

Chase clenched his jaw, glancing at Foster. "Kash, Mac and Nyx. Kash has a head injury, and Mac's got a GSW to her upper left shoulder. They're both still alive, but time isn't on their sides. We didn't see any sign of Nyx, but I swear if they hurt her…"

Bodie looked over at Foster, then nodded. "Then, what are we waiting for?"

Bodie grabbed one line and tossed it onto the deck before heading for the second. He waited for Saylor to give him the go-ahead then launched the line before jumping onboard. He didn't ask any other questions, just moved up beneath the canopy as Saylor hit the throttle, deftly maneuvering them out of the secure harbor and into the raging ocean.

Water sprayed over the bow, the wind howling around them as she checked her instruments then gunned it. The boat nosed up, plowing through the white caps at some insane speed, each bounce into the next trough threatening to tip them over before the vessel finally leveled out.

Saylor headed south, keeping the boat angled into the large swells. "I really hope you boys have a plan because this inbound system is going to sink us if we don't play this right."

Foster held out his phone, showing them the flashing blue dot, before spreading out the map Saylor handed him. "There's a beach, if you can call it that, north of where they're waiting. Assuming you can get us remotely close, I was hoping Bodie could jump out there. It's going to be a beast of a scramble up those rocks to a heavily wooded plateau, but it should be close enough you can reach us in time, but far enough away they won't spot you, even if they have some kind of overwatch." Foster arched a brow. "You are skilled with a sniper rifle, right?"

Bodie scoffed. "Now, you're just being mean."

Zain gave Bodie a slap on the back. "No worries, Beckett, because I'm definitely skilled with a sniper rifle and I'll be backing Bodie up."

Bodie motioned to Zain's arm. "With that arm in a sling?"

Zain merely grinned then slipped his arm out before tossing the material onto a spare seat. "What sling?"

"Zain." Beckett shouldered up beside him. "I appreciate what you want to do, but I'm not willing to trade your life for Mackenzie's. Mine sure, but that's different. And no, you don't get to challenge that."

"I'm not trading my life. I'm doing my job." He waved off Foster's attempt to correct him. "I've rescued entire squads hurt worse than I am, now. So, stop arguing, and lay out the rest. Because, brother, we're gonna need one hell of a Hail Mary to walk away from this. Assuming we don't die before we even get there."

Saylor gave Zain a not so gentle shove. "Piss off. I'll get us there in one piece. Anything after that is up for grabs, but one way or another, we'll get there."

Foster smiled his thanks. "Then, listen up. Because we've only got one option, and it's going to be one hell of a ride."

* * *

"Hey."

Mackenzie blinked, finally bringing Kash's face into focus as he knelt in front of her, that huge medic bag opened beside him. His hands were zip tied together in front of him, though whoever had bound him hadn't been very thorough, leaving enough room he might be able to break them given a chance.

She frowned, glancing at the blood still dripping down his cheek. "Jesus, Kash, your head."

He gave her a small smile. What she assumed was his attempt to reassure her he was fine. Though, judging on how much his hands shook, he wasn't close to being fine. "Just a love tap. Unlike your shoulder. I need to put on some Quick Clot before you pass out from blood loss. But it's not going to be fun."

She looked over at Striker. He had his gaze focused on them, avidly scrutinizing every move Kash made. "I'm surprised Voss allowed it."

Kash merely shrugged.

She grunted as he cut away part of her sweatshirt. "He needs us alive until Foster gets here, right."

She hadn't posed it as a question, and Kash simply nodded. "How the hell is he even going to make it? The weather's closing in, and—"

Kash silenced her with a gentle finger over her lips. "You worry about staying conscious. Foster's far more resourceful than Striker thinks. And that's why the bastard's going to fail."

She clenched her jaw, somehow swallowing the scream tearing at her throat when Kash pushed on the wound. Hard. "Do you think Striker knows Foster was Flight Concepts?"

"I doubt it. That kind of shit is generally scrubbed from anything he could get his hands on."

She nodded, closing her eyes as pain shot through her shoulder then into her chest, stealing whatever breath she'd had.

Kash sighed. "I know. It hurts like a son of a bitch." He poured on the clotting powder, then applied more pressure, finally wrapping it all with a few layers of gauze. "It's not perfect, but it should buy you enough time until Chase gets here. The guy's a wizard."

"I hope so. But I have a feeling even he has his limits."

"Then, let's stay within them."

Mac nodded at his head. "Let me clean that wound—"

"I'm good."

"All right, that's enough chit chat." Thompson grabbed Kash's shoulder. "Get back beside the chopper."

Kash knocked off Thompson's hand. "If you want her to stay breathing, you'll let me keep an eye on her."

Thompson snorted. "You've done all you can. Now, sit your ass down. Unlike Striker, I don't have any issues with killing any of you."

"I'm okay, Kash." She motioned for him to sit beside her, glaring at Thompson as he smirked and ambled away. "I really hope I get to shoot at least one of these assholes before this is over."

Kash chuckled. "Spoken like a true warrior. Now, do us both a favor, and be ready. Because if I know Beck, he'll be coming in hot. Which means, you hit the ground when the bullets start flying."

"Just like you're going to do?"

Kash laughed, again. "I've got a reputation to uphold. And know this. Nyx won't hurt you, no matter what you see or hear. Okay?"

"That's reassuring."

"She can be downright scary when she's fully engaged. But she's the smartest dog I've ever worked with. And she'll have your back."

Mac nodded, fading a bit before jolting back when

Kash gave her arm a squeeze. "I'm sorry I got you into this. You were right. I should have been better prepared. Hell, I should have questioned the damn orders."

"Why? It came from emergency dispatch. Your father authenticated it, himself. No reason to think it was a setup. And I'm just naturally paranoid."

"Foster questioned it."

Kash smiled. "Trust me. Foster's reluctance had nothing to do with suspecting this was an ambush and everything to do with the fact he's crazy in love with you and can't stand the thought of not being your first line of defense — whether the situation warrants it or not. So, stop beating yourself up for doing your job."

Her chest eased a bit at Kash's words. "I think you might be exaggerating just a bit."

Kash turned to meet her gaze. "No, I'm not. The guy's a goner. He just needs more time to work it all out. Allow himself to be happy because he still doesn't believe he should have been given this second chance."

"Because of Sean."

"Sean might have saved Foster's life, but Beck's the only reason the rest of us made it back alive. What he did that night..." Kash leaned against the chopper. "He thinks Zain and I don't remember too much, and we choose to keep it that way. But I remember everything. The storm. How screwed his shoulder was, not to mention the extreme blood loss.

I still don't know how he kept flying. Kept breathing, really."

Mac swallowed, wondering if the temperature was dropping or if it was just her feeling the cold. "I need to tell you something."

Kash shook his head. "You can tell Foster you're stupid in love with him, too, once you see him."

"It's not for him. It's for me. I need to say it out loud, just once. To someone else. So I know it's real."

Kash stared at her then nodded. "Then, tell me."

"I love him. A frightening amount, if I'm honest. He makes me feel whole." She groaned against another stab of pain. "But if you tell him before I do, I'll kick your ass."

"Did you seriously just give me something to blackmail you with?"

"I guess so. Though, I could always just tell Jordan you've got the hots for her." She grinned. "No one needs that much coffee."

"Busted. Stay awake. I really need you to stay awake."

She nodded, though she wasn't quite sure if she actually moved her head or just jerked it once as her chin drifted down to her chest, the world slowly fading to black.

CHAPTER SEVENTEEN

"I hope you guys are part fish because this weather is getting really bad."

Foster gripped the metal frame over his head as the boat raced along the surface, water crashing over the bow with every bounce. The engines whined behind them as Saylor bled every ounce of speed out of them without blowing them up or capsizing the vessel as she pushed the limits.

He scanned the horizon. "Is that your way of saying this is a one-way trip?"

Saylor pursed her lips. "I guess that depends."

"On what?"

"On whether or not my best friend will die if we can't take the boat back. Because if that's the case, then this will be whatever it needs to be, even if I have to dive into the ocean and wrestle Poseidon for his damn trident."

"I see why you're best friends."

"It's far deeper than that. Mac's had my back through some rough seas so, I'll have hers no matter the lengths I have to go to."

Foster nodded. "How about you get us there in one piece, and we'll worry about everything else after we take care of Striker."

Saylor grunted as if she wasn't quite sure how sound their plan was, and Foster couldn't blame her. He was putting a huge amount of faith in his team. In believing Kash was still able to fight.

That Mackenzie wasn't beyond saving.

Thunder rumbled overhead. A stark reminder that reaching her would be the easy part, and everything else that followed would be insane.

Saylor studied the nav, pointing to a spot off their port side. "That's our first marker. It looks like there are a number of underground rocks all over this shoal. And with the waves this high and the current raging like a hormonal teenager, it's going to be more luck than skill avoiding all of them. So, everyone should be ready to abandon ship if things get hairy."

Bodie moved in beside them. "Because the ocean is obviously far safer than a sinking boat."

Saylor merely grinned, working the throttle until she had the boat bobbing along the surface, timing each burst of speed with the next wave until they were within a few feet of a large outcrop.

Bodie and Zain climbed over the rail, bags strapped on their backs as they waited for the next large swell before launching themselves. Zain landed first, grabbing Bodie's jacket when a rogue wave nearly washed him off the rocky surface. The guy scrambled up the side, giving Zain a hand up once he'd reached the next level.

Saylor didn't wait for them to continue climbing. Instead, she spun the boat and gunned it. She barely beat the next cresting breaker, shooting out from the frothing spray as the water curled over, the droplets distorting the view of the horizon. What would have sent them crashing into the jagged shoreline if she'd been even a second late.

Foster rolled his shoulder, shaking out his hand as his buddies vanished into the spray and mist. God, he hoped he wasn't sentencing them to death. The climb, alone, was crazy. Adding in they were going up against unknown forces — that he was counting on them eliminating enough of the peripheral men, he'd be able to tackle Striker, head-on — only highlighted how tenuous his idea really was.

Chase moved in beside him. "They'll be fine. This is a walk in the park for Zain, and Bodie's an ex-Ranger. You've seen him in action, firsthand. The guy's hardcore."

"In the field. With overwatch, and a team backing him up."

"We have a team."

Foster grunted. "You know this is way outside my comfort zone. It's been a hot minute since I was in Flight Concepts and did anything remotely like this."

"I'd put my life in your hands any day, brother. Whether it's in the air or on the ground."

"Let's hope you're still that enthusiastic when bullets start flying." He nodded at Chase's shoulder. "You gonna be okay?"

Chase waved him off. "Golden, Pony Boy."

Saylor cleared her throat. "Not to interrupt the bromance, gents, but we're coming up on our final destination. And this looks like it's going to be even worse than the first. There's a freaking rip tide causing all sorts of mixed messages. My only option might be running her ashore."

Foster froze. "If we run the boat onto the rocks..."

"Yeah, it could make our return trip a bit more difficult. Unless you'd both prefer to swim to shore?"

Foster looked at the crashing waves as they shot twenty feet into the air, the black rocks a stark contrast to the thick clouds. "Not sure that's a viable option. Even if I was a SEAL, which I'm not. You do whatever's necessary. We'll adapt."

Though, that meant either hiking it out and borrowing whatever vehicles those bastards used to get there or flying the chopper. And the weather was getting to the point even he was questioning if it was doable. Adding the fact he hadn't flown in months — had all but hyperventilated the last time he'd been in a cockpit —the situation only looked bleaker.

Foster pushed aside the doubts. If Mackenzie needed him to man up, he'd sit his ass in that seat and be the warrior she needed him to be. Period.

Not having Chase or Saylor call him out on the viability of him actually piloting the helicopter saved him from having to say the words out loud without choking on them. That, all his tough talk aside, he simply wasn't sure if he could get behind the controls without puking. Hell, passing out. Not that he wouldn't try, but...

Saylor cursed when the wind abruptly kicked up, blowing them off-course as the waves crested higher, breaking over the bow and sweeping one of the life buoys overboard. She spun the wheel, fighting against the current as rain burst from the sky, instantly cutting their visibility in half.

She focused on the nav screens, somehow avoiding a scattering of rocks when they appeared out of the mist, the jagged surfaces rising above the water like death-colored monoliths. The hull scraped over a reef when the next wave bottomed out, the eerie sound sending shivers along his spine.

Saylor huffed as she pounded her fist on the wheel. "Looks like we're taking on a bit of water. I'll make for the least rocky section. Be prepared for a rough landing."

She worked the throttles again, pulling back when the vessel hit another shoal, likely busting more holes in the hull, before she gunned it. The bow tipped up, the boat leaping forward as the next breaker lifted them higher, carrying them over the last part of the reef then crashing them onto the shore.

The impact sent them tumbling across the deck,

the next wave surging over the side and dragging them to the edge. Foster grabbed Saylor's outstretched arm, preventing her from getting washed overboard as the water receded, the next breaker already inbound.

But Foster was up and moving — yanking Saylor to her feet. They grabbed what gear they could, then jumped over the side, landing in the swirling surf. The receding water clawed at their legs, tripping them a couple times as they raced for the shoreline, Chase hoofing it beside them. They reached the base of the gravelly sand as the water broke against the shore, swiping them off their feet then rolling them up the beach. Foster managed to grab some roots, stopping him and Saylor from getting dragged back into the surf as it retreated along the slope, lapping against the wreckage as it waited for the next deadly surge.

Chase scrambled up beside him once the tide ebbed for a moment, getting Saylor upright and moving as Foster dragged his ass to higher ground. Salty spray misted through the air as rain blanketed the cliffs. Another boom of thunder rang out in the distance, the thick bank of clouds drawing closer.

Foster leaned against the cliff. "Saylor? Are you okay?"

She grunted, glancing at her boat over her shoulder. "Not my finest hour."

Chase scoffed. "We're all still breathing. That's a win in my books. And it's not like you had any other options. Those waves would have torn us apart if you'd tried to go farther out to sea. Sorry about your boat, though."

Saylor shrugged it off. "You do realize that by leaving her here, anyone can salvage her."

Chase nodded, scouring the horizon. "Yeah, they'll be lining up any second now."

Saylor crossed her arms. "Not funny. And, at least, she got us here. That's honestly more than I expected. And while it pains me to walk away, boats can be replaced. People can't."

Foster leaned in close. "Try to remember that when we're facing all those guns. And don't make me regret asking for help. Mac will have my ass if you get hurt on my watch."

"Relax, big guy. I can handle myself."

Foster simply nodded, then started toward the hint of a trail way off to their right. He resisted running the rest of the way, keeping his pace metered. He needed to remain calm. Collected. Until the time was right to break loose.

Chase kept Saylor between them, constantly checking their six, though Foster doubted Striker would bother having someone circle around and trail them. Not when he held the cards. Or, thought he did.

Actually reaching the top without falling to their deaths was a nice surprise. Not getting shot on the spot, another. Not that Foster had thought Striker would simply kill them the moment they appeared.

The guy wasn't naïve, and he wasn't stupid. He'd suspect Foster would have a plan, and Striker would want to know what he was up against before he permanently eliminated anyone.

Foster checked over his shoulder before heading off. Saylor had reluctantly agreed to stay just out of sight until their plan was underway. Not that she'd liked it, but he'd reminded her she was his and Chase's backup. That he was relying on her to have their six.

The chopper was parked in the middle of the clearing, the rotors flexing in the increasing winds. It didn't look as if the machine was damaged, which meant Kash and Mac had likely been ambushed after they'd started toward the trail.

A lone gunman appeared once they'd reached the halfway point, his rifle pointed directly at them. He didn't talk, just waved them on, following their progression until they disappeared around the tail end of the aircraft.

Foster stopped, his gaze immediately landing on Kash and Mac. His buddy was sitting beside Mackenzie, blood staining his face as he squinted at Foster. Kash nodded once, then nudged Mackenzie, leaning toward her to whisper something.

Mac roused enough to focus on him, and damn, she looked like death. Her skin was several shades lighter than normal, with an almost bluish tinge to it. Someone had bandaged her shoulder, though the wound was already bleeding through, a few dots of red eating through the pristine white. She pursed her lips then sat up straighter, grimacing as she cupped her elbow, fading for a moment before snapping back.

Striker walked toward him, stopping several feet away. "I'm surprised you followed my instructions, Beckett. I expected you to show up with an entire army."

Foster crossed his arms, making a mental map of where Striker's men were located and how far they were from the cliff, before looking at Striker. "The cops are already here, along with half my team. Not sure who you expected me to call."

"What about Bodie Page?"

"He's watching Deputy Hudson. Which I guess was a good call considering she's the only cop in town not in your pocket." Foster looked at Thompson. "Did you kill my parents or just cover it up?"

Thompson didn't even flinch. "What do you think?"

"I think you're a disgrace to the uniform, and I'm going to enjoy watching you burn."

Striker laughed. "That's what I like about you honorable types. You always think there's a way out that doesn't end with you failing." He took a step closer. "I know you're both packing. On the ground."

Foster made a show of removing his Sig then tossing it on the grass as Chase did the same.

Striker waved at his leg. "Backups, too."

Foster pulled up his pant leg. "I didn't bring any. Unless you want my Swiss Army knife."

Striker cocked his head. "Remington can toss any knives he has on the ground, but you can keep yours."

Foster kept his expression neutral. He suspected Striker assumed he was his team's weak link. The one guy who hadn't acquired any real-world tactical experience. Who hadn't fought his way through hostile territory. And that one assumption would be Striker's undoing.

Chase tossed two tactical knives in the mud, staying close as Striker nodded.

Foster stared Striker in the eyes. "We good, now?"

Voss relaxed a bit. "Just saving you from getting any wild ideas that you have a chance at executing some insane plan. As your buddy discovered, no one's that fast when we're already zeroed in. The drugs."

Foster held out his hand to Chase, accepting the bag his buddy handed him before holding it up.

Striker glanced at Thompson then inched forward. "Hand it over. Nice and easy."

Foster huffed, then tossed it a few feet in front of Striker. "You want it. Get it yourself."

Striker glared at him. "This had better not be rigged."

Foster simply stared at the man, sliding Kash a quick glance when Voss diverted his gaze for a moment. Praying his buddy got the message.

Kash scoured the crowd, then gave Foster a curt nod, looking as if he was readying himself to strike. Not that Foster was convinced the man would do more than face-plant on the ground, especially with his hands zip tied. But he'd give Kash the benefit of the doubt.

Striker stopped at the bag, tapping it with his boot then taking a step back as if he expected it to explode. Foster held his ground, not wavering when Striker glared at him again.

This was it. The point of no return. Either Zain and Bodie were in position and ready to strike, or this would be a short and bloody encounter.

Striker stared at Foster, then grabbed the bag. He held it up, checking the bottom before smirking. "You open it."

"It's not rigged."

Striker snapped his fingers, and Thompson pointed his gun at Kash and Mac. "Then, you won't mind opening the damn bag."

"Fine, just everyone relax." Foster walked over, lowered the zipper then spread the sides apart. "Do I have to read all the research to you, too?"

Striker gave him a shove. "I doubt you'll think this is funny when it's all said and done." He grabbed a bottle, opened it then popped one of the pills, shivering in response as he closed his eyes. It took him a moment to snap back, his pupils already looking slightly dilated.

He rummaged around in the sack before frowning

as he pulled out a metal cylinder. "What the hell is this, Beckett?"

"Carrington's research." Foster held up one hand. "Don't look at me. That's how we found it. There's a thumb drive in the bottom, too."

Striker scoffed. "No fucking way I'm opening this."

Foster covered the few short strides separating them. "You realize if I put an explosive inside, it'll kill me and Chase, too, right?" He pried off the cap, holding the canister close to his chest. "Still breathing, Voss."

Striker waved his fingers at him. "Show me what's inside."

"Sure thing."

Foster tilted it toward Voss, waiting until he'd finally inched close enough to peer inside before slamming it against his head. The strike caught Voss in the face, knocking him back as Foster lunged at the man, grabbing his rifle and smashing it into his head just as shots echoed through the clearing, two of Striker's men dropping a second later.

That got everyone running and yelling, bursts of gunfire spraying across the area — one catching Foster in the arm. Chase managed to toss out the mini smoke grenade he'd smuggled in as Bodie and Zain appeared out of the mist like wraiths moving through the ranks.

But Foster was laser focused, using his hold on Striker's weapon to wrap the strap around the bastard's neck as he pulled up and back. Striker's feet lifted off the ground for a moment before he managed to palm his knife and cut the strap.

The resulting snap sent them both tumbling as more bullets whizzed past. Foster scrambled to his feet, hoping to get off a burst of gunfire, but Striker was already on him, brandishing his Kabar in long, arcing strokes.

Foster used the weapon to block the strikes, missing high when the blade sliced a line across his ribs. But the hit brought Voss in close enough Foster countered with a hard jab to his face, the resulting impact knocking Striker off balance.

That was all the advantage Foster needed.

A step and a turn, and he had Striker within reach — the guy's right side completely exposed. A lunge and a kick, and the man's knee cracked beneath Foster's boot, dropping him onto the mud. Another pivot and a hard swing, and the bastard was on the ground, blood pouring from his nose, his leg bent at an unusual angle.

Not that Foster had time to celebrate when Thompson materialized out of the rain and smoke, his service weapon aimed Foster's way. Foster dove to one side when Thompson fired, the second shot grazing a groove across his thigh. He rolled to his feet with the rifle zeroed in on the sheriff when Nyx bounded out of the mist. The canine jumped, all eighty pounds colliding with Thompson in a brutal attack, the dog locking its jaws around Thompson's arm, then dragging him backwards. Kash appeared a moment later, knocking Thompson out with a firm boot to the head.

His buddy leaned over, palmed his knees as he teetered left and right then tripped onto his ass. Foster did a quick sweep of the clearing, wishing he could see more than a few feet in front of him, before rushing over to Kash. Foster took a moment to cinch Thompson's handcuffs around his wrists, using a set of zip ties to secure Striker, then bodily lifted Kash to his feet.

Kash mumbled something about not being dead, yet, but he didn't resist as Foster braced most of his weight before slowly limping back toward the chopper. Zain and Bodie had anyone still breathing hogtied at the edge of the clearing as Chase hovered over Mac.

Kash shoved him off, motioning toward Mackenzie. "Go. I'm good."

Foster shook his head, holding onto Kash until Saylor darted over and took his place. Then he was racing toward Chase and dropping to his knees beside him. Praying he wasn't too late.

Mac blinked a few times, grinning weakly at him as she touched his hand. "Not fair. I didn't get to shoot Striker in the ass."

He laughed, lifting her hand then kissing the back of it. "That can still be arranged."

She scoffed, inhaling when Chase jabbed

something in her arm. "Not as much fun when he's unconscious."

"Then, we'll wait until he wakes up." He leaned in close. "Pretty sure I told you not to get shot."

"No, you said to be…"

Foster squeezed her hand when she started to fade. "Safe. Which is the exact opposite of getting shot."

She barely responded, her eyes drifting closed.

Foster swallowed the bitter fear cresting his throat, turning to stare at his best friend. "Chase. Brother you need to keep her breathing."

Chase grunted, hanging a second saline bag on his makeshift hook. "She's lost at least a liter of blood. I'm doing all I can."

"Can't you do some kind of direct transfusion?"

"I could, if I had someone to match her blood type. She said she's O negative. Which would be ideal if anyone else needed blood. But it means I need another O negative donor for her, and the last time I checked, none of us fit the bill. And Bodie and Saylor aren't a match, either." He pushed another shot of something into the IV. "She needs to get to a hospital, Foster. Now."

Foster clenched his jaw then looked at the helicopter. There were bullet holes in the fuselage and part of the bubble was cracked, but he didn't see any obvious damage that would warrant not at least trying to start her up.

He nodded, gave Mac a kiss on her forehead then

stood. "Bodie? Is that state trooper buddy of yours on his way?"

Bodie nodded, kicking one of the men when he looked as if he was rousing. "He and a few of his colleagues just started hiking the trail. They should be here in about twenty. I'm sure we could head out and grab some keys — use one of their cruisers to get Mac to a hospital. Or procure whatever Striker and Thompson have."

Chase grunted. "Beckett."

Foster merely sighed. "I know. She doesn't have that kind of time. And since the boat's not an option..."

He darted over to the machine, doing a quick walk around before opening the rear doors. "Bodie? Are you okay holding down the fort until your friend gets here?"

"I'll stay with him." Saylor shifted in beside him. "I haven't gotten a chance to shoot anyone in the ass, either."

Bodie nodded, again. "We're good."

Foster walked back over to Mac and gathered her in his arms as Chase moved all the lines and meds he'd set up. "Then, get anyone else who needs medical support onboard."

Saylor frowned. "But how is Mac gonna fly when she's not even conscious?"

Foster stopped at the rear doors, looking at Saylor over his shoulder. "She's not. So, saddle up, folks. This is going to be one hell of a ride."

CHAPTER EIGHTEEN

Foster placed Mackenzie on the stretcher Zain had arranged on the floor, palming her cheek before taking a breath then shuffling into the cockpit and sliding onto the seat. Rain battered the bubble, a light spray misting through the bullet hole on the other side.

Mac's blood stained his hands, the sticky feeling a reminder of all he had to lose. That she was counting on him to push past his fears.

To fucking grow a set.

He rolled his shoulder, clenching his hand a few times before gripping the controls as he pressed in circuit breakers and got everything rocking. The nav system sprang to life, confirming every fear that this weather system was worse than anything he'd ever flown in. That maybe this time, he really was pushing his limits too far.

Foster glanced over at the empty co-pilot's seat, then back at the darkened horizon. Thunder rumbled in the distance, the gale force winds already buffeting the chopper.

A hand landed on his shoulder, and he looked up at Zain. His buddy arched a brow as he stared out at the horizon, wincing when the next boom of thunder rattled the aircraft.

Zain sighed. "I know we don't have many options, Beckett, but even I can tell that nav screen isn't looking very favorable."

"It rarely does. You'd better buckle up. This isn't going to be a fun ride."

Foster turned, took a breath, then lifted off, battling the gusting winds as they pounded the machine, nearly spinning it when they abruptly shifted. He adapted, nosing the bird forward as he picked up speed, keeping the aircraft parallel to the shoreline. The clouds thickened around him, blocking out any hint of light until he wasn't sure if it was day or night, the eerie gray blending in with the raging ocean.

He gained a bit of altitude, cursing when the aircraft started to buffet, the strong vibrations shaking through his controls. He just wasn't sure if it was the damage to the fuselage, some nicks in the rotors, or if one of the rounds had compromised the hydraulic line. Either way, it meant the situation was only going to get worse.

You're doing it, again, Beckett.

Foster jumped as the ghostly voice sounded around him, the wavering tone sending shivers down his spine. He glanced at co-pilot's seat, again, ensuring it was still empty before shaking it off.

It wasn't real.

It was just his nerves getting the best of him.

He could do this.

You never should have been out that night.

All he needed to do was focus. Everything was fine.

You're the reason I'm dead.

Foster huffed out a series of rough pants, his chest squeezing so tight he could barely breathe. He tugged at his collar, Mac's blood glaring up at him as he eased back on the controls, that voice taking on a life of its own.

An alarm sounded in the cockpit, some of the instruments edging into the yellow.

His comms buzzed as Chase clicked his mic. "Foster? Everything okay?"

He tried to answer, but he couldn't form any words. A gurgled rasp sounded behind him, the familiar sound only ratcheting up the tension.

Sean was right. It was too risky. Too severe.

Another buzz followed by Zain's hand on his shoulder, again, as he stood beside Foster.

"Beckett?" Zain motioned to the airspeed. "Buddy we're slowing down and losing altitude."

Foster blinked, scanning the instruments before shaking his head. "He's right. I'm doing it again. Pushing too hard. Playing with your lives…"

"Whoa, slow down. Who's right?"

Foster shook his head, banging on it with his other hand. "I never should have flown that night. I'm the reason he's dead. Why you all nearly died. I… I can't…"

Zain tightened his hold. "Easy, brother. Just breathe. Okay? Chase! I need you."

Foster swallowed as a flash of lightning lit up the darkness somewhere out on the horizon, the accompanying thunder sounding louder. Closer.

The cockpit started closing in, all that blood and noise swirling in on him. He gripped the cyclic, looking for some sort of anchor when his comms chirped.

"Foster."

He whipped his head around, his gaze clashing with Mac's as her voice sounded softly in his ear.

She reached her hand toward him, giving him a slight nod. "It's… okay." She paused to lick her lips, every breath sounding as if it might be her last. "Everything's going… to be okay. I'm right… I'm right here…"

Her hand dropped as she passed out, Chase cushioning her head when she went limp on the stretcher. The echo of her words hanging in the air.

He stared at her pale skin, all the fear and doubt

burning into untamed rage. He wasn't losing her. Not like this, and not because he was too damn broken to be the man she needed him to be. She'd already saved his soul. The least he could do was save hers.

He rolled his shoulder one more time, focusing on the map before shoving the cyclic forward, and picking up speed.

The aircraft shook, then it was screaming through the air, the rain streaking off the bubble. He adjusted the controls, scrolling through the nav as he looked for any slight change in course that would save him even a second of time. What could be the difference between Mackenzie coming back to him or fading for good. He found a small pocket of less turbulent air and banked the chopper over, skimming past trees and towers as he dropped the bird even lower, avoiding the worst of the clouds.

Chase muttered in the back, a few of the words spurring Foster on. Another alarm sprung to life, the chilling sound cutting off the din behind him. He scoured the instruments, tapping the fuel gauge as the needle slowly inched down.

He punched in the hospital's location, mentally gauging how far they could fly if their gas tank had been compromised as badly as he feared, and the answer wasn't encouraging.

Chase buzzed the comms, glancing at Foster when he chanced a quick peek over his shoulder. "Buddy? While I'm thrilled you're in the zone, should we be worried about that siren?"

Foster shrugged. "What do you always tell me? You worry about the patient, and I'll worry about the aircraft?"

"Shit, it's that bad?"

Foster cocked his head, lifting the bird up and over the rising landscape before dropping her back to tree height. "It looks like a couple of those bullets punctured the gas tank."

"Which means…"

"We're pissing out fuel at a… concerning rate."

"How concerning, Foster?"

Foster sighed. "We'll make it. You just make sure she does, too."

Chase didn't answer, and that heavy silence spoke volumes.

All the more reason to squeeze even more out of the chopper. Push it just a bit harder. Until a loud thud echoed through the cabin, the controls getting infinitely heavier.

Zain moved in beside him, sliding onto the other seat. "What the hell was that?"

Foster scanned the instruments, again. "Hopefully, just the hydraulics."

"Hopefully?"

"There were bullet holes all over the fuselage. I have no way of knowing what damage they caused, so yeah. Hopefully."

Zain muttered something under his breath. "Do you have any hydraulics left?"

"Nope."

"Well, shit. Can you ease up at all?"

"That depends. Would you rather I baby her, and we run out of gas, or push it, and chance doing more damage?"

Zain coughed. "Is there a third choice?"

"Not one that I can live with."

Zain nodded, then buckled up. "Then, give her hell, brother."

Foster battled the controls, screaming over the Raven's Watch hanger going some insane speed. Twin vortices trailed out behind him as the rain swirled then blew away. He followed the main road, dropping lower until he was damn near even with the semis kicking down the highway. He kept glancing at the fuel gauge, hoping Atticus had calibrated it because if it was off even a fraction, they wouldn't make it.

Knowing he needed to perform a running landing didn't help any. Not when he wasn't sure if there was even a suitable place to line up the aircraft, let alone drive it on. But he'd worry about that once he reached the hospital. Hell, he'd use the road if needed.

A string of power lines appeared in the bubble, and he barely got the machine up and over them before they'd scraped along the bottom of the skid gear.

Zain shook his head, looking as if he regretted claiming the seat. "I don't know if you're more intense than I remember or if I've just gotten soft."

"It's not you, buddy. And I promise our next flight won't be like this, but…"

Zain reached over and gave his arm a squeeze. "I know. You do whatever you need to. We've got your six."

"Then, scroll through that nav, and find me a place to run this baby on. Ideally, it'd be long and flat, but I'll take whatever I can get."

Zain didn't even flinch, just started advancing the map, looking at anything remotely viable. "Looks like you've got two options. You can chance the driveway or there's a set of ball fields just south of the hospital. And I doubt anyone's using them in this weather."

Foster looked over at the enlarged view of the map Zain had displayed on the screen. "The road's downwind, and I don't want to waste time going around. We'll head for the fields and see if I can make the parking lot work."

He didn't add that it was a race to which would ground them first — the machine or the fuel. But Zain knew.

The storm raged around them, the wind and rain trying to blast the chopper out of the sky. Foster held firm, alternating his attention between the map, the fuel gauge and the landscape. Constantly adjusting the controls in an effort to get one more mile in before it all fell apart.

Chase was telling Mac to hold on in the background as that dot on the map seemed to stall.

Foster went against that voice in his head and coaxed a bit more speed out of the bird, fully aware he might eat up the remaining gas too fast. But he'd risk it if it meant he gained that extra minute. Got her to the doctors just a bit quicker.

The machine shook, the engine chugging a couple times as the aircraft dropped a few feet. Foster held on, working the throttle. Using the wind and the drafts to give him a boost when the fields appeared in front of him. Trees surrounded the open space, an empty parking lot running down the left side.

He lined up the pavement, chancing it would be a safer bet than risking the grass. Possibly having the skid gear catch on a gopher hole or snag a fallen branch.

The aircraft chugged, again, the fuel gauge hugging the bottom, as he barely cleared the thrashing branches, allowing the chopper to virtually drop out of the sky. He flared off the speed at the last moment, then drove the helicopter onto the asphalt. The machine shook, rocking across the lot until it finally rolled to a stop, the engine cutting off a second later.

That ghostly voice whispered, "Hooyah," in his ear, then faded, leaving a sense of lightness in its place.

Foster bowed his head, uttering a prayer of thanks when Zain clapped him on the back.

His buddy grinned as he shook his head, staring

out at the pouring rain. "Now *that's* how you come out of retirement. Welcome back, Beckett."

Having Chase bark out orders killed any sense of accomplishment, and Foster was out of his seat and grabbing one end of the stretcher a moment later. Chase had the other, despite his shoulder not being close to healed, and they ran down the short stretch of road then turned onto the parking lot, still running.

The chopper must have made one hell of a racket — or maybe Atticus had heard them fly over and hedged his bet as to where they were headed — because there was a full medical team waiting next to the helipad. They converged on him and Chase, taking Mac then rushing her into the emergency room as more staff brought out wheelchairs for the other wounded.

Someone grabbed Foster's arm, asking him if he was okay, but he brushed them off, sticking on Mac's six as they wheeled her down the hallway then into a room. He stopped at the door, trying to keep his focus on her as the lead physician called out stats, none of which were encouraging.

A nurse blocked his way, muttering that they needed to work on her, but he simply pushed on through. He couldn't leave her. Not when he hadn't gotten the chance to tell her how he felt. That she was his anchor. His sanity.

His damn soul.

The scenery swam a bit, and he took a staggering

step back when Chase and Zain grabbed him, steering him into another room — tsking when he tried to resist.

Chase moved in front, arms mostly crossed, his death glare in full effect. "You can either sit your ass down and let them treat all those wounds, or I'll sedate you, myself. Your choice, brother."

"I'm fine. Mac..." He couldn't say it. Couldn't jinx it.

Chase didn't falter. "You're not fine. You've got a bullet lodged in your arm, some kind of graze across your thigh, and what I think is a knife wound on your ribs. So, sit down and stay there until they're done with you. Mac's in good hands, but they can't help her if you're in there, looking as if you might fall on top of her from simply breathing."

"If I did that, at least she'd know I was in the room."

"Foster..."

"I need her to know I'm there. That I'll have her back like she had mine." He paused to take a breath, aware the next few words would change everything. Make it acutely real. "That I fucking love her."

Chase grinned, then nudged Zain's arm. "Told ya. And she does know. Christ, you flew through a damn cyclone to get her to the hospital. She knows what it took for you to get behind the controls."

Foster swayed, again, tripping onto the exam table before fisting his best friend's shirt and dragging him in close. "Don't let them give up on her."

"I won't. Promise. Now, stay. I'll drag Kash's ass in here, too, and you can both sit there brooding while you wait for a doctor to treat you."

Chase disappeared out the door, yelling Kash's name. Foster thought about stumbling back to the other trauma room, but Zain stepped in front of him, shaking his head as he glared at Foster.

Foster groaned, nearly toppling off the table when everything shifted, again. "You don't have to glare at me, Zain."

"Oh, I do, or you'll think you've got a chance at besting me. You don't, by the way, even with my shoulder screwed. So, don't make me dump you on your ass."

Foster huffed, but didn't challenge Zain, looking up when Chase helped Kash stagger through the door.

Chase plunked Kash onto a chair, shaking his head as he took them all in. "Just once, I'd love for you jackasses to follow my orders without being dicks about it."

Foster shrugged. "Then, stop telling us shit we don't want to hear."

"Then, stop getting shot."

"I tried that. But you all kept on badgering me."

Chase sighed. "Guess we really aren't cut out for the quiet life." He nodded at Foster. "Glad to have you back. Though, Atticus is going to tear you a new one when he sees what state you left his helicopter in."

Foster blinked, cursing when he realized he was lying on the table, now. "He can try..."

"Rest, buddy. We'll get you fixed up, then we'll all wait together."

* * *

Did being dead hurt?

Because that's all that registered. Pain. Through her head, her ribs, her chest. Deep. Burning. It bled through the darkness, drawing her up for a few moments as she struggled to open her eyes only to plunge her back down.

Burying her in that numbing haze.

Voices echoed in the distance as she drifted somewhere between consciousness and sleep until a loud bang jolted her awake. She bolted upright, looking for whoever had fired the gun, when more of that red-hot pain shot through her shoulder and into her lungs, stealing what little air she'd gulped in.

A man tsked, holding her steady as he leaned in close. "Somehow I knew you'd go from zero to raging war the moment you woke up."

Mackenzie inhaled, staring up at Foster as he held her close, bracing her weight against his side. Stubble shadowed his jaw, his long hair tousled all over his head. But it was those blue-green eyes that held her focus. Staring at her as if he'd been convinced he wouldn't see her again. What looked dangerously like the love she felt bubbling through her chest.

She relaxed, groaning when even that small movement shifted her shoulder. "Where…"

Her mouth went dry, her tongue feeling too big to form more words.

He sighed as he grabbed a cup and offered her a sip of water. He smiled when she drank a few gulps. "I know the feeling. Anesthesia's the worst. And you're in the hospital where you should be sleeping, but you're awake, now, because some idiot just tipped over a cart in the hallway."

"Kash?"

"He's fine. In fact, everyone's fine, so you focus on healing, okay?"

"What about Striker?"

"No longer a threat, especially if your father has anything to say about it. He's been calling in every favor he has to ensure the creep gets tossed in some deep, dark cell."

She nodded, fading a bit before a few snapshots of the harrowing chopper ride shuffled in her mind. She fisted Foster's shirt, doing her best to tug him closer. "You flew the chopper!"

"I told you not to count me out. That I just needed the right motivation." Foster chuckled. "No surprise it was you, sweetheart."

"But…" Mac motioned him closer with a tilt of her head. "Thank you."

"Pretty sure you saved me more, but I'm not above accepting your undying gratitude once you're able to do more than sleep." He dropped a soft kiss on her nose. "We've still got some big plans to cash in on."

"Let's go."

"Oh, no. Chase will have my ass if I bust you out of here. Sleep. We'll see how you are in the morning."

She tightened her grip. "Don't leave."

He scoffed. "Not a chance. In fact…"

He scooped his hands underneath her and gently shuffled her over, freeing up a quarter of the bed. Then he climbed on, wrapping his arm around her back as he helped her settle across his lap.

She burrowed against him, closing her eyes as everything clicked into place. "Much better."

"Then, sleep. I'll see if I can sweet talk Chase in the morning. Get him to be your proxy medic. But for now, I've got your six."

She hummed, fading into the darkness only to rouse sometime later. Light streamed in through the far window, Foster's arm still wrapped around her back.

He gave her a light squeeze, holding her steady until she stared up at him. "Morning, beautiful. How's the pain?"

Mac stilled, then cautiously shifted, biting her bottom lip at the deep ache that throbbed through her left side. Less red-hot than before, but still more intense than she wanted to admit.

Foster sighed. "That bad, huh."

She allowed him to help her up, only cursing once

when her shoulder twisted funny. "It's a lot better than before."

"Has anyone ever told you that you're a horrible liar. Like, worse than Kash, and he's terrible."

"Hey, I heard that."

Mac snapped her head around, grinning at the rest of Foster's team all huddled together on some kind of love seat. One they'd obviously dragged in from somewhere else in the hospital.

Foster made a show of rolling his eyes. "Not anything we haven't told you a hundred times before, buddy. Why do you think you lose so often at poker?"

Kash leaned back against the cushions. "Because you mess with my cards."

Foster laughed. "See? Horrible."

Mac palmed his jaw, loving how he nuzzled into her touch. "Are you okay?"

"Physically or mentally? Physically, I'll have a few new scars for you to trace. Mentally…" He shrugged. "More ghosts. Fewer demons."

"I knew you could do it."

"Thanks to you. If you hadn't talked me off that ledge—"

"My chopper might still be in one piece."

Mac sighed as her father's voice boomed through the room before he stopped at the end of the bed. Arms crossed. His usual scowl firmly in place. "Do you have any idea how many bullet holes there are?"

"Of course I do. I flew the damn thing." Foster

eased back, allowing Atticus to shuffle over and give her a hug. "And at least I didn't crash it."

"No, you just pushed the poor thing to its limits then left it rotting in the middle of a parking lot."

"I was a bit busy not dying."

Atticus rolled his eyes. "Pilots. They're so dramatic."

Mac arched a brow. "You do realize you just insulted me, too, right?"

"Like your boyfriend said. Nothing you haven't heard a hundred times before."

"Boyfriend?"

Her dad simply snorted as he turned to face Foster. "So, I believe I told Mac that you were only authorized to help out if you agreed to sign up."

Foster scoffed. "Are you seriously trying to blackmail me right now?"

"I don't have to try, son. I'll drop the appropriate papers off at your house later today. I assume Mac's going back there after you four bust her out. Make sure you've got beer, coffee and plenty of pizza. Oh, and I'm putting you in the rotation once Charlie fixes that mess you made. So, make peace with it."

Atticus headed for the door, stopping short. "I've got an order in for another bird. It should be here within the month. Send me a few names of pilots you'd trust with your team's life, and I'll give them a chance. Give you and Mac a shot at a real life."

Foster chuckled. "The only two pilots I trust to fly *my* team around are in this room. But I know a few guys who more than measure up for the *new* recruits you'll need to hire to man two choppers."

"And to think I wanted you to join." Atticus looked back at Foster over his shoulder. "Welcome to Raven's Watch, Beckett. Your dad would be very proud."

Foster shook his head as Atticus ambled out, humming to himself. "He's never going to let me forget he won."

"Did he? Because I'm feeling pretty damn victorious myself."

Kash groaned, tossing a tissue at them. "Christ, can you both just confess your love so we can bust out of here? I need coffee."

Foster closed his eyes, looking as if he was seeking biblical intervention. "Not an ounce of tact."

She drew him in close. "And yet, not lying that time."

Foster's eyes widened and he got impossibly closer, his kissable lips just a breath away. "Is that your subtle way of telling me you love me?"

"It wasn't subtle."

"And yet, not concrete."

She brushed her finger across his lips. "You're gonna make me say the words, aren't you?"

His gaze softened. "How about I say them first?"

Warmth spread through her chest, and she knew this was the reason she'd kept fighting. Kept hoping. "And have you gloat about it later? I don't think so."

"Are you always going to keep score?"

"Not as long as I'm winning. And this kind of win lasts a lifetime because I love you, Beckett. Demons and all."

That got her a soul-searing kiss.

"Damn straight you do. Almost as much as I love you. So, don't get too cocky and think you've got the championship in the bag. This battle's only just beginning."

"Bring it. Now, what was that about busting me out?"

CHAPTER NINETEEN

"It's official. It's the end of days."

Foster chuckled as Mac flopped down on the bed, staring up at the ceiling as if it held all the answer. It had been two weeks since she'd nearly died, and he'd barely left her side for more than an hour or two.

If only Keaton could see him now, his cousin would bust a gut laughing. Not that Foster would blame him. Love had never been part of Foster's long-term goals until Mackenzie had breezed into his life like a damn hurricane and blown away all his plans.

He shut the door then made his way to the bed, standing in front of her. "Something on your mind, sweetheart?"

She huffed, motioning to the door. "My dad just spent an entire night hanging out with you and your buddies, playing poker, eating pizza, and he didn't threaten to kill you once. And that includes when he caught us kissing in the kitchen."

"We're adults. We're allowed to kiss."

"Not in front of him."

Foster went to his knees so he was level with her. "Should I be worried you sound disappointed?"

She frowned. "Do you have any salt? Maybe some holy water? Iron? Because we need to make sure that's really my father and he hasn't been body snatched or something."

Foster grinned. God he loved her. From her tousled mass of brown hair and sexy blue eyes to her unwavering conviction and adorable bare feet. She was more than just his heart. She was his soul.

He leaned over, loving how her pupils dilated as she gave him a thorough once-over. "Have you stopped to consider he's happy for you?"

Mackenzie cocked her head to the side. "I did, but that would make him human, and I'm not sure I can venture that far outside the natural order of things."

He laughed. "Damn, I love you."

"You'd better, because I officially cancelled that rental cabin, today." She levered onto her elbows, a slight tightening in the corners of her mouth the only indication her shoulder was still healing. "You aren't regretting giving me that key, right?"

"Do I look like I'm having second thoughts?" He silenced her with a finger across her mouth. "The answer's no. Especially if you plan on waking me up, again, like you did this morning."

"You needed to know I'm not broken because you've been handling me with kid gloves since we left the hospital."

"That's because you were literally broken. Though, I get the feeling we can take things up a notch." He bent over her, eating at her mouth when someone rapped on the door, the eerie echo effectively shattering the sensual atmosphere.

Mac glanced at the door as she raked her hand through his hair. "Ten bucks that's my dad."

Foster laughed. "You're on."

He offered her his hand, then they headed for the door, cracking it open as the knocker sounded a second time.

Greer jumped, shaking her head as she placed a hand on her chest. "Sorry to just drop by, but…"

Foster waved off any concern. "Never a bad time to talk to the new sheriff. Come on in. Would you like a beer?"

Greer stopped just inside the doorway. "I'm pretty sure Atticus rigged that impromptu election."

Mac gave her a gentle shove. "He did not. He just made sure everyone knew you were the catalyst behind catching Thompson and his asshole drug smuggling ring. That you nearly died in order to put him behind bars."

"Except you and Foster's team did that."

Foster shook it off. "We just cleaned up the mess. So, beer?"

"Sadly, I'm on duty."

He checked his watch. "Haven't you been on duty for seventy-two hours straight?"

Greer raked her hand through her hair. "Something like that, but I'm a bit short staffed."

"No, shit. Any luck hiring replacements for Thompson's crew?"

"Still going through extensive background checks. Though, Bodie's agreed to lend a hand until I've got some reliable backup. I've forgotten what it's like to have people I trust guarding my back. Which is one of the reasons I'm here. I wanted to thank you, again, for saving my ass. I still can't believe you two pulled me out of my Bronco."

"You wouldn't have gotten hurt if I hadn't asked you to do that deep dive, so consider us even."

Greer looked at Mac. "Is he still going on about that?"

Mac gave his hand a squeeze. "He's a work in progress."

"Aren't all men?"

"Ouch." Foster palmed his chest. "Why do I suddenly feel as if I need backup?"

"Easy there, big guy. I'm just yanking on your chain." Greer shifted on her feet. "And for the record, it wasn't my deep dive that got me noticed. It was running a search on that truck Jordan saw driving past the café that day. When Thompson saw me trying to track down a white Tacoma with California plates, he thought I was on to him and his involvement with Vexarin and that asshole Voss. It was just ironic timing that Voss tried to eliminate me the night I was coming over to talk to you about Carrington."

Foster nodded. "I appreciate the sentiment, but we still should have had your back before Voss blew your SUV off the road."

"Men." Greer toed at the floor, looking oddly nervous, and Foster knew whatever else she had to say wasn't going to be pleasant.

"You might as well just spit out the real reason you came over before you tap a hole in the floor."

She grunted, glancing at Mac before reaching into the inside pocket of her jacket then handing Foster an envelope. "I found Thompson's secret stash of all the cases he'd covered up. I thought you might want to see the actual evidence from your parents' accident."

Foster took the folder, staring at it before opening the end and fishing out the papers.

Greer pointed toward the sheets. "I know there was some speculation on whether he planted an identical bomb on your dad's vehicle like the one you found on mine, but it looks like that was Striker. There was an eye-witness account in the report that Thompson buried. An older woman saw someone matching Striker's description standing on the edge of the cliff that night. But when she pulled over to ask if he was okay, he jumped in a white truck and took off. She didn't get the plate number, but she spotted the wreckage and called it in."

Greer sighed. "I don't know if that helps or hurts, but I thought you should know the truth."

Foster nodded as he held up the file. "I appreciate it. Thank you."

Greer shook his hand. "You can keep that, and I'm around if you have any questions. I don't know if there's anything else hidden in the office, but I'll let you know if I find additional intel." She smiled at Mac then stepped outside. "Anyway, I just wanted to give you that and say thanks for everything. Though, it was probably overkill insisting I crash here after you captured Voss."

"We don't believe in overkill. And we could have missed some of his crew. Striker mentioned something about additional forces to Mac, so it's always better to plan for the worse. Besides, Chase would have had a coronary if you'd camped out at your place, alone."

"He's definitely unique. So, with most of the renovations done, are you planning on opening this place up anytime soon?"

"Honestly, I was thinking I'd hold off for a while. Keep it in the family for a bit. See if we might need a few more of the rooms for ourselves."

Mac's jaw dropped, her gaze clashing with his as a red blush crept up her cheeks.

Greer laughed. "And that's my cue to get the hell out. Glad we all got to see which side of that coin your finally landed on. Oh, and I need a lift up the coast later in the week, Beckett, so don't be calling in sick because you want to stay home and do nasty things to Mac."

She gave them both a salute then headed for her truck, her headlights bouncing down the driveway a few minutes later.

Foster closed the door, watching Mac as she stared at him. Eyes wide. Her foot tapping on the floor. He locked up then joined her in the middle of the room, taking her hand in his. "Are you okay? Because you look as if you're not sure whether to jump me or get my Sig and shoot me in the ass."

"You thought you'd wait to see if we needed more of the rooms? Is that your subtle way of saying you might want kids?"

"It wasn't subtle."

"Foster..."

He smiled, then pulled her close, smoothing his hand down her back and onto the top of her ass. "I never thought I'd ever fall in love, let alone find someone like you. So, yeah. I'd be lying if I said I hadn't thought about it. Not that it's required, but if it's something you'd like, too—"

She kissed him. No warning or hesitation. Just her mouth crushing against his as she all but climbed into his arms.

Foster wrapped his hands around her, holding her close as he started walking toward the stairs. "I'll take that as a yes."

"There's only one condition."

"Is this where you try to get out of owing me ten bucks? Because that wasn't your dad."

She palmed his face, holding his gaze when he placed her on her feet at the side of his bed. "If we end up having a boy, we name him Sean Joshua Rhett Beckett."

Foster choked on his next breath, then kissed her, keeping her close once he'd eased back. "You know, if Rhett ever wakes his sorry ass up, his head won't fit through the door once he hears that."

"I'll chance it."

"I really don't deserve you."

"I know."

He arched a brow. "And if we ended up having a girl?"

She frowned. "I hadn't thought that through."

"How about we call her Parker Beckett?"

Her eyes teared over as she tiptoed up and kissed him, again. "Were you always this charming?"

"The guys would say no." He smiled. "I love you, Mac. And you're on."

"Love you more. Now, what do you say we get started? Because I've got big plans, and it's only a matter of time before the rest of your team barges in, and I'm not sure I'll be willing to stop."

RAVEN'S CLAW

RAVEN'S CLIFF BOOK #2

New York Times & *USA Today*
Bestselling Author

ELLE JAMES
&
KRIS NORRIS

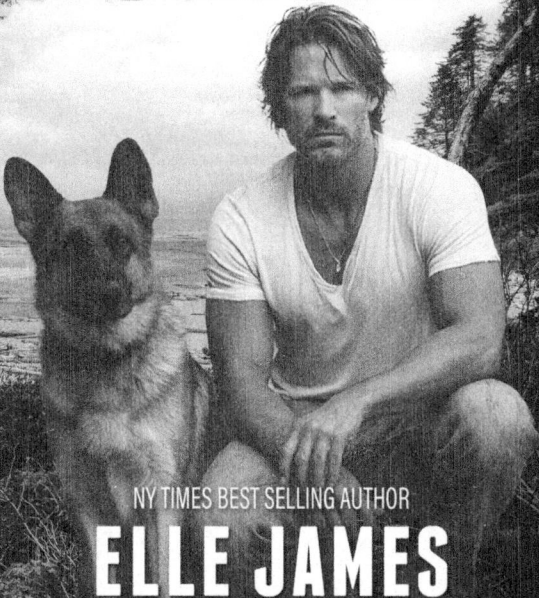

PROLOGUE

Operation Silent Veil
   Catskills Mountains — seven months ago

"Are you insane? We need to go!"

Ember glanced at the asset as he paced the room, eyes wide. Skin blanched white. A dead man walking if she was being honest. Because despite her skills, she had little confidence she'd be able to keep him breathing. Not with alarms already sounding inside the room — an increasing number of men converging on their location within the compound via a flickering camera feed.

She snagged his arm on his next pass, locking her gaze on his. "You need to calm down. You gave me the footage. You know the caliber of enemy we're about to make. If we're going to stab Scythe, and more importantly, Rook Donovan, in the back, we should be damn sure the intel's fully uploaded. Otherwise," she pointed at the dots on the security feed, "we might as well just wait for them to find us and save ourselves the gauntlet run out of here because we'll be dead either way."

She pushed down the riotous impulse to shoot the guy in the head and complete her mission as if she hadn't just discovered the past twenty years of her life had been a lie. That Rook was far from the man she'd thought he was.

That he was the real monster hiding in the shadows.

Former tier-one operator and current Scythe handler, Rook Donovan was Scythe's senior Shadow Asset Acquisitions Specialist and head of their Asset Operational Division. He believed in control through precision. He didn't send an army. He sent ghosts — the kind who slit throats, erased fingerprints, and vanished before sunrise. There were only two acceptable outcomes to every mission — success or death.

With his record thoroughly scrubbed, Rook operated with complete autonomy. He was the man Scythe sent in to clean up any of the agency's messes before they became visible. And she'd just risen to the top of his termination list.

Her asset, Bart Conrad, inhaled, his gaze darting to those dots on the screen. The wet squad slowly closing in on them. "Oh, god. You don't think we're gonna make it out, do you? This is insurance." He shoved his hand through his unruly ginger locks. "Where are you sending the intel? Some secure server that forwards it to a dozen newspapers if you don't put in some kind of code in the next twenty-four hours? Maybe to some of your other operatives? Are you even going to try to help me?"

Ember fisted her hands, pinning him to the far wall with nothing more than a stare. "If I was going to kill you, I would have put a bullet in your head instead of listening to you hyperventilate for the past ten minutes. But if we're going to have any chance at getting out of here in one piece, you'll need to do exactly *what* I say, *when* I say. So, stand there, shut up, and wait for my next set of instructions."

She turned when the computer pinged. "There. Now we can—"

The room went dark, the hum from the air exchanger in the far corner slowly winding down.

Bart gasped, the panicked sound excessively loud in the oppressive silence. "Shit! Did they cut the power?" He wheezed out a couple more raspy breaths, tapping on something in what she assumed was an effort to get the thing to pop back on. "How can they do that? I have backup generators. Batteries. An entire grid that's completely isolated."

Ember secured the decryption drive Conrad had made to decipher the intel, her comms unit nothing but dead weight in her ear. "They didn't cut the power. They hit it with an EM pulse."

"They have electromagnetic pulse weapons?"

356 | ELLE JAMES & KRIS NORRIS

"They have everything."

"That means they can breach the doors. Bypass all my magnetic seals and encrypted codes. Just waltz right in." More tapping, as if he thought hitting the damn unit harder would have a different outcome. "Christ, I never should have trusted you. I'm outta here."

Ember snapped her head toward him, his labored breathing the only means she had of tracking him in the utter darkness. "Don't move, and don't open that other door. It's likely rig—"

The explosion hit hard, lifting her off her feet and blasting her over a desk and into the far wall. Thick smoke curled through the room, distant shouts rising above the ringing in her ears. She blinked against the dust and debris, willing the room to stop spinning, when footsteps sounded off to her left.

Two scouts, searching the rubble. Laser sites mapping out their location as they scoured the room.

She pushed onto her hands and knees, staying below the top of the overturned desk beside her — judging their progression by the slight scuff of their boots. How the smoke swirled around them, making patterns in the air.

They stopped, those red beams skimming the top of the desk before she was up and over, kicking one in the chest as she caught the other in the throat. The first guy tumbled back, landing on something nasty because he started flailing — arms and legs shaking as if he was having a seizure — before stilling, blood dripping out of his mouth.

The other asshole managed to get his rifle braced in front, but she simply used it to smash his face, dumping him on his ass with a sweep of her feet. A boot to the head and neck, and he was out — head lolled to one side and foot twitching.

The rest of his squad must have heard the commotion because they fired a second later. Short controlled bursts punching through the smoke — cutting down everything in their path. Ember hit the ground, covering her head as wood splintered around her, raining down like bits of confetti. Sparks lit up the darkness, yellow muzzle fire flashing against the eerie gray.

More dots appeared amidst the smoke, fanning out across the room. The last man drew closer, AR-15 ghosting into view — laser site sweeping the far wall a good three feet above her. She counted it down then caught him in the knee, buckling his leg with a second kick to his ankle.

That got everyone moving.

Gathering together in the center to minimize any crossfire — keep her on the fringes.

She snagged a couple frags off the guy writhing on the ground then tossed one into the fray. She didn't know if it was smoke, incendiary or a light and sound show. Didn't care if it gave her a chance to make a break for the door.

The canister clicked along the floor, each tinny

strike bolstered by the thick vapor. Someone shouted — the dots scattered, but it exploded a heartbeat later, filling the room with light and sound. Damn near bringing down the roof as the entire bunker shook, more dust coming loose from the old wooden slats covering the ceiling.

The ear-piercing noise scattered what was left of her senses, tilting the room left and right as she stumbled toward the exit, climbing over what remained of the door. A few shots whizzed through the air next to her head, one of the men shouting her name.

Ember hit the tunnel half-running, half-tripping, the blast of cool air lifting some of the numbing haze. She took the second corridor on the right, then sprinted for the escape hatch at the far end — bouncing off the ladder when the signals didn't quite reach her limbs in time. She gave herself a shake, climbing the metal rungs before twisting the oversized wheel above her head.

It groaned in protest, finally releasing the thick lid with a rush of air. A foggy mist veiled the surrounding forest, a hint of moonlight shining from above.

She heaved herself up and out, crawling onto the wet grass as boots pounded the hallway beneath her. But she was already pulling that second pin — tossing the grenade through the opening. Covering her head, again, as it rattled down the rungs, clattering to the floor below.

Voices rose then retreated, a moment of uneasy silence settling over the area before the canister exploded, flames shooting out the hatch.

She waited for the shaking to stop then pushed to her feet and took off. Not nearly as fast as before, but at least she was moving. Limping and falling her way to the tree line then beyond. She took what looked like a deer trail, scrambling through the underbrush until she'd put at least a mile between her and the compound. Not enough to be safe. but she needed to catch her breath — stem some of the bleeding.

Ember leaned against a moss-covered tree, doing her best to take stock. Blood soaked through her clothes, a scattering of shrapnel poking through the fabric. Her head still rattled from the combined explosions, all her exposed skin caked in soot and dirt.

Pain teased her senses, but she was too numb to register anything but the cold bite of reality.

She was burned.

Every identity.

Every resource.

Every lifeline — gone.

All that remained was the bitter taste of regret, and a series of dead-drop sites scattered across the country. Her only chance of retrieving the intel, and her last hope in a lifetime of lies.

She closed her eyes, letting it all sink in, when her comms buzzed — Rook's voice sounding through her head.

"Bravo, Ember."

She inhaled, hating the stab of pride that warmed her chest. The part of her that still wanted his approval. To belong, even if it meant selling her soul. She scoured the forest, half-expecting the man to step out from the shadows. But nothing moved other than the odd flutter of wings.

She tapped her earpiece, all the pieces starting to fall into place. And she couldn't help but wonder if she'd really escaped, or if he'd simply lengthened her leash.

He chuckled, the sound hollow. Smug. "It's EMP proof, in case you were wondering."

She bowed her head, the truth cutting deep. "How long have you known?"

"That you had doubts?" He pushed out a long slow breath. "Since the day I saved you from that group home. Even at twelve years old, I always knew you were too smart, too unexpectedly moral, not to eventually question your place in the agency. I'd just hoped that after all this time — the years I put into beating every ounce of defiance out of you — it wouldn't come to this."

She grunted, blinking against the dots eating away her vision. "You didn't save me, Rook. You recruited me. I was just too young to see the difference. But I'm seeing everything clearly, now."

He sighed, as if her discovering his betrayal was inconvenient. "Are you sure? I've been five steps ahead of you this entire time. Why do you think I sent you here? It was a test." He let out a weary groan. "Congratulations. You failed."

"Did I? Because this feels like a victory."

"I suppose that depends on your perspective. Like your asset. How do you know Mr. Conrad wasn't part of the ploy?"

"Because I know you. And if that intel wasn't half as damming as I think it is, we wouldn't be having this conversation. Which means... You're scared."

He laughed. Louder. Deeper. "You're exceptional, Ember. The best I've ever trained. But there's no way you can ever win this war. No future without me and Scythe in it." Another slow breath, this one colder than before. Any hint of compassion gone. "You've had your fun. Proven you've still got those morals buried beneath the muscle memory. Ones I intend to finally bleed out of you. But we can talk about that later."

"There's no later, Rook. No *us*. There's just me."

"You know the score. No loose ends. If one ghost escapes, the whole house of cards collapses. Letting you go would set a precedent, and I can't afford to have anyone else think they can follow in your footsteps." He exhaled, the gruff sound bordering on a growl. "You're either with us, or you're dead."

"Then, you better hope the next group of men you send are better than the last."

"I won't just send a squad. I'll come for you, myself. Because you didn't just betray the program —

you betrayed me. And I can't let that go unanswered."

She straightened, pushing down the hurt and the pain. The absolute emptiness gathering in the pit of her stomach as she drew herself up. "Then, I guess this isn't goodbye."

A pause, as if he was still processing all the words. Coming to terms with the fact she'd defied him. Again._"Ember…"

"I'm the one giving the orders now. So, watch your back. I intend to stick a knife in it."

She tossed the earpiece on the ground, crushing it beneath her boot before striking off. There was a questionable diner not too far down the old state highway. She could hitch a ride. Regroup. Head west. Gather the intel.

One more target.

One last mission.

And she'd live by Rook's decree. She'd either burn him and Scythe to the ground or die trying.

Thank you for reading RAVEN'S WATCH. To read more of RAVEN'S CLAW, click HERE

ABOUT ELLE JAMES

ELLE JAMES also writing as MYLA JACKSON is a *New York Times* and *USA Today* Bestselling author of books including cowboys, intrigues and paranormal adventures that keep her readers on the edges of their seats. When she's not at her computer, she's traveling, snow skiing, boating, or riding her ATV, dreaming up new stories. Learn more about Elle James at www.ellejames.com

Website | Facebook | Twitter | GoodReads | Newsletter | BookBub | Amazon

Or visit her alter ego Myla Jackson at mylajackson.com
Website | Facebook | Twitter | Newsletter

Follow Me!
www.ellejames.com
ellejamesauthor@gmail.com

f X ⊙

ALSO BY ELLE JAMES

Deja Voodoo (#3)

Brotherhood Protectors

Montana SEAL (#1)

Bride Protector SEAL (#2)

Montana D-Force (#3)

Cowboy D-Force (#4)

Montana Ranger (#5)

Montana Dog Soldier (#6)

Montana SEAL Daddy (#7)

Montana Ranger's Wedding Vow (#8)

Montana SEAL Undercover Daddy (#9)

Cape Cod SEAL Rescue (#10)

Montana SEAL Friendly Fire (#11)

Montana SEAL's Mail-Order Bride (#12)

SEAL Justice (#13)

Ranger Creed (#14)

Delta Force Rescue (#15)

Dog Days of Christmas (#16)

Montana Rescue (#17)

Montana Ranger Returns (#18)

Brotherhood Protectors Boxed Set 1

Brotherhood Protectors Boxed Set 2

Brotherhood Protectors Boxed Set 3

Brotherhood Protectors Boxed Set 4

Brotherhood Protectors Boxed Set 5

Brotherhood Protectors Boxed Set 6

Mack's Witness (#2)

Ronin's Return (#3)

Sam's Surrender (#4)

Hellfire Series

Hellfire, Texas (#1)

Justice Burning (#2)

Smoldering Desire (#3)

Hellfire in High Heels (#4)

Playing With Fire (#5)

Up in Flames (#6)

Total Meltdown (#7)

Take No Prisoners Series

SEAL's Honor (#1)

SEAL'S Desire (#2)

SEAL's Embrace (#3)

SEAL's Obsession (#4)

SEAL's Proposal (#5)

SEAL's Seduction (#6)

SEAL'S Defiance (#7)

SEAL's Deception (#8)

SEAL's Deliverance (#9)

SEAL's Ultimate Challenge (#10)

Texas Billionaire Club

Blue Collar (#2)

Pirates (#3)

Stranded (#4)

First Responder (#5)

Cowboys (#6)

Silver Soldiers (#7)

Secret Identities (#8)

Warrior's Conquest

Enslaved by the Viking Short Story

Conquests

Smokin' Hot Firemen

Protecting the Colton Bride

Protecting the Colton Bride & Colton's Cowboy Code

Heir to Murder

Secret Service Rescue

High Octane Heroes

Haunted

Engaged with the Boss

Cowboy Brigade

An Unexpected Clue

Under Suspicion, With Child

Texas-Size Secrets

ABOUT KRIS NORRIS

I'm just a small town girl, living in a lonely world. I took the midnight train…oops, sorry. Got off-track.

Author, hobbit, and crazy lady running in the woods, I'm either madly creating masterpieces in my dungeon, or out chasing bears with my dogs.

I see myself as unapologetically Canadian, and I love all things maple syrup.

I loves connecting with fellow book enthusiasts. You can find me on these social media platforms…

krisnorris.ca
contactme@krisnorris.ca

facebook.com/kris.norris.731

instagram.com/girlnovelist

amazon.com/author/krisnorris

ALSO BY KRIS NORRIS

SINGLES

CENTERFOLD

KEEPING FAITH

IRON WILL

MY SOUL TO KEEP

RICOCHET

ROPE'S END

SERIES

RAVEN'S CLIFF SERIES with Elle James

RAVEN'S WATCH

RAVEN'S CLAW

RAVEN'S NEST

RAVEN'S CURSE

'TIL DEATH

1 - DEADLY VISION

2 - DEADLY OBSESSION

3 - DEADLY DECEPTION

BROTHERHOOD PROTECTORS ~ Elle James

1 - MIDNIGHT RANGER

1 - Sacred Talisman

2 - Twice Bitten

3 - Blood of the Wolf

ENCHANTED LOVERS

1 - Healing Hands

FROM GRACE

1 - Gabriel

2 – Michael

THRESHOLD

1 - Grave Measures

TOMBSTONE

1 - Marshal Law

2 - Forgotten

3 - Last Stand

WAYWARD SOULS

1 - Delta Force: Cannon

2 - Delta Force: Colt

3 - Delta Force: Six

4 - Delta Force: Crow

5 - Delta Force: Phoenix

6 - Delta Force: Priest

COLLECTIONS

Blue Collar Collection

Dark Prophecy: Vol 1

Into the Spirit, Boxed Set

COMING SOON

Raven's Claw

Raven's Nest

Raven's Curse

Delta Force: Fetch

Printed in Dunstable, United Kingdom